Honor and Integrity

*A collection of Pride and Prejudice-inspired
short stories*

by

**AIMÉE AVERY
JUNE WILLIAMS
ENID WILSON**

Aimée Avery, a California native, became a world traveller at the tender age of six. Moving from place to place, she spent a good deal of time dreaming up situations for her favorite characters from books and television. She put her imagination to work and earned a degree in graphic design, with a minor in journalism. Aimée is currently employed in the newspaper industry and is happily married and living along California's beautiful Central Coast. You can contact her via email at ThePemberleyCafe@gmail.com.

June Williams has always loved to write, although her first book – written at age eleven – had only one copy. In her checkered career path, she taught English as a Second Language, wrote for a U.S. Congressman and a business magazine, created technical manuals, ran a startup, and wrote advertising copy. She lives in Northern California.

Enid Wilson loves sexy romance. Her writing career began with a daily newspaper, writing educational advice for students. She then branched out into writing marketing materials and advertising copy. Enid lives in beautiful Sydney, Australia. She loves to hear from her readers. You can contact her at enid.wilson28@yahoo.com.au or www.enidwilson.com

Cover design by Aimée Avery
First published 2012
HONOR AND INTEGRITY © 2012 by Aimée Avery, June Williams and Enid Wilson

Dear Readers

Three authors of Jane Austen-inspired stories gathered together and came up with an idea to challenge each other. This collection includes nine short stories, in Regency, Fantasy and Modern genres.

The tagalong story is a fun creation, with Aimée starting it without letting June and Enid knowing her plot. Enid brought Jane Austen's favourite couple to the future which caused headaches for June. June concluded the tagalong by sending Darcy and Elizabeth to some wild places.

This book also includes two original stories from the authors.

The rule of the game was the authors must use the words "Honor" or "Integrity" in their creation.

We hope you like these short stories.

Aimée, June and Enid

Dedications

My many thanks go to Debra Watson for her tireless proofreading efforts; Sara Angelini and Casey Whitaker for giving me a place to share my stories; to June Williams and Enid Wilson for joining me in the fun; and to my loving husband for putting up with my obsession with Mr. Darcy.

~ Aimée Avery

I wish to thank Sue Forgue and Victoria Claughton for sharing their creativity, character insight, and knowledge of Regency history and language; they also caught plot holes. Debra Watson provided her eagle-eye proofreading. Lynne Robson provided Brit-picking and cheerleading. Linda Wells, Patrice Murphy Hamill, and Sonia Brande offered encouragement.

I wouldn't be here without Aimée Avery and Enid Wilson, published authors who let me play in their sandbox and shared their names with me on this book. Special thanks to Enid for being ringleader and queen of formatting.

~ June Williams

I'd like to give Debra Anne a big warm hug for her support throughout the years. Also, I send my love to Aimée and June, and thank them for coming along to this ride. The biggest thanks reserve to my online fans. You are my inspiration!

~ Enid Wilson

Table of Contents

Regency

Fantasy

Modern

REGENCY

Marry My Boy

By Enid Wilson

What if Mr. Darcy's mother was still alive?

"Which do you mean?" and turning round Mr. Darcy looked for a moment at Elizabeth, till catching her eye, he withdrew his own and coldly said: "She is tolerable, but not handsome enough to tempt me; I am in no humour at present to give consequence to young ladies who are slighted by other men. You had better return to your partner and enjoy her smiles, for you are wasting your time with me." – Pride and Prejudice, Chapter Three

Elizabeth overhead the comment and walked away from the arrogant gentleman and his friend with a shrug. She had no very cordial feelings toward Mr. Darcy and her spirit was not dampened. She intended to share the story with her close friend.

As she walked on, someone touched her elbow.

"I am so sorry about my son's behaviour, Miss Elizabeth," Lady Anne, Mr. Darcy's mother, said in a low voice.

"We cannot control the behaviour of our relations, Your Ladyship." Elizabeth looked at her two youngest sisters who were pushing around with some local boys and making a spectacle of themselves. She had been introduced to Her Ladyship earlier on, and had found her behavior to be similar as her son's. Lady Anne had conversed very little with the locals, so far, instead staying close to the Bingley sisters throughout the evening.

Following her gaze, Lady Anne remarked, "Your sisters are still young, but my son has had the benefit of a Cambridge education. I thought they would at least have taught him some manners and instructed him in how to be a gentleman. I am most displeased by their education!"

Elizabeth looked at Lady Anne afresh. Her Ladyship teased, no doubt. Perhaps the elegant lady looked on the follies of her son and the world with as much dry humour as Elizabeth's father. Warming to the lady, she jested, "I see that Your Ladyship is denying any responsibility for Mr. Darcy's present behaviour."

"Absolutely! My son has had a mind of his own since he first learned to walk, at the tender age of one. And he chose Cambridge against my advice. I prefer Oxford." Lady Anne smiled.

"Do you think Oxford would have made him a better man?"

"Are you saying he is a good man already? I am astonished by your generosity, given his earlier offending remarks."

"By appearance, indeed, he is a good man. He is tall and has a noble mien, with the most complicated knot in his cravat of the entire assembly, as well as ten thousands a year. Most of the women here and, I am certain, in London will find him very handsome indeed."

"His cravat. How very true! But I see you have a different opinion about my dear boy."

Elizabeth's mouth curled up. "I always try to return a gentleman's attentions in a similar manner."

"You find his character not handsome enough to tempt you. Oh dear! That is grave indeed but it serves him right. Still, this will not do. As his mother, I shall defend his honour. My boy avoids looking at women, in length, during a ball. I wager he did not see you properly, just then."

"How singular! Now you are telling me his ailment. Is he in need of glasses, like my sister Mary, but is too vain to wear them?"

"He is quite vain, but on this occasion, it is something else." Lady Anne smiled again. "Ever since his gaze followed Lady Alicia faithfully at a ball when he was fifteen, with the result that the lady's mother nearly locked them up together in a bedroom, he resolved not to pay attention to any woman at a ball thereafter."

Elizabeth gave a hearty laugh. She could not imagine the proud Mr. Darcy as a young lad of fifteen, nearly being compromised by a matron in Town. "Such a traumatic upbringing he has had! It does render him in a better light to my eyes. Poor Mr. Darcy. But I must tell Jane about his peculiar habit at a ball. He looked at my sister long enough to regard her as the only handsome girl in the room. That is quite an achievement for Jane."

"But he is not looking at Miss Bennet now. He is staring at you instead."

Elizabeth turned her eyes and met the gaze of the gentleman in question across the room. He frowned as he glanced back.

"Not with admiration, Your Ladyship. I wager he is trying to see whether I am planning to steal away any of your jewellry."

Lady Anne laughed aloud, which drew her son to walk toward them with decisive strides.

"I think he has not seen me this entertained for quite some time. He is afraid I may take you to my bosom and disown him instead."

Elizabeth chuckled. Mr. Darcy's eyes remained fixed on her cheerful face as he continued his approach.

Lady Anne's mouth curled up and she called out to her son, "Fitzwilliam, why are you not dancing?"

At that, Mr. Darcy withdrew his gaze from Elizabeth and scowled at his mother. "I have been asked that question already, Mother."

"Yes, and Miss Elizabeth and I both heard your *candid* answer." Her eyebrows rose, and the gentleman's face turned red.

"I...was not introduced to Miss Elizabeth."

"I can perform that honour."

"Thank you, Lady Anne." Elizabeth dropped a deep curtsey, licked her lips and dabbed exaggeratedly at her mouth with her handkerchief, as if she were drooling over a particularly fine piece of beef. "I am in *great humour* at present to give consequence to young men who are sought after by other women."

Mr. Darcy's mouth gaped open as he drew in a loud breath. This was not the behaviour of a composed gentleman.

His mother's loud merriment soon drew another person near them. "Your Ladyship, you seem to be enjoying the quaint entertainment here," the elegant lady said, stepping close to Mr. Darcy.

"Not really, Miss Bingley. Miss Elizabeth has just been telling me about some of the boorish behaviour of the gentlemen nowadays. But she told it in such an *elegant* way that I could not help but laugh at her *politeness*. Had I met with such manners, I would have smacked the gentleman in question on the head and knocked some sense into him." She gave her son a knowing look. He had finally closed his mouth but his face looked like a ripe tomato. "Let me perform the introduction. Fitzwilliam, this is Miss Elizabeth Bennet. Miss Elizabeth, this is my *lovely* son, Fitzwilliam Darcy, and this is his friend's sister, Miss Bingley."

Elizabeth felt strange about Lady Anne's choice of wording. From the way Lady Anne had spent her time, earlier in the evening with the Bingley sisters, Elizabeth had thought Her Ladyship would consider them her family friends instead. But then, she had originally thought Lady Anne to be as proud as her son. Apparently she had been mistaken in that estimation.

"I hear that you have four sisters," Miss Bingley said.

"Yes. Jane is currently dancing with your brother. And my other sisters are around, enjoying themselves."

"It seems, here in Hertfordshire, that young girls are allowed to be out while the eldest is still not married. You do not observe society rule as in London."

Lady Anne pivoted to regard her. "I dare say, Miss Bingley, that you sound like my sister, Lady Catherine de Bourgh."

Mr. Darcy turned his face to hide his smile at hearing his mother tease Miss Bingley. Elizabeth raised her eyebrows, and he curled up his mouth at her.

Miss Bingley's eyes lit up. "Thank you for the compliment, Your Ladyship. I have not had the honour of meeting Her Ladyship Lady Catherine yet."

"*Compliment* indeed. Catherine is most proper about the rules in society. Miss Elizabeth, what do you have to say about this? Why are you out this evening, when Miss Bennet has yet to marry? You should be confined to your nursery."

Elizabeth had not ever before had so much fun at an assembly. Apparently Lady Catherine was not a favourite of her sister or nephew. Did Miss Bingley not understand that Lady Anne was mocking her? She replied, "My parents are most anxious to get rid of all of us. They disregard any proper rules at all."

"That is not surprising, as I have heard that the Bennet estate is entailed away."

"You are a *wealth* of information, Miss Bingley," Lady Anne said.

Miss Bingley thrust out her chest and tilted her head. "I am very conscientious, especially concerning those whose acquaintance we might make. I take prodigious good care in guiding my younger brother, and I shall do the same for my future family." She then batted her eyes at Mr. Darcy.

"And I see that you love to share the information," Elizabeth said, trying to suppress her laughter.

"Especially with my son," Lady Anne commented, and smirked.

"Now that we are introduced," Mr. Darcy said, shifting his weight from one foot to another, "Miss Elizabeth, might I have the honour of this dance?"

Elizabeth raised her eyebrows. Did he want to escape the teasing? Why did he not ask the other eager lady to dance, instead? Surely, she herself was still not handsome enough to tempt him. Lady Anne smiled widely while Miss Bingley glared at them for a moment before snapping her fan shut with force.

Elizabeth could not discern his intention and did not care to make an enemy of Miss Bingley. "Mr. Darcy, I walk this way to get some refreshment, not in search of a dance partner."

"Indeed, Fitzwilliam, I can give testimony to that. Miss Elizabeth will not want to dance, due to a most unpleasant encounter with a certain gentleman earlier."

"Unpleasant?" Miss Bingley interrupted. "Pray, tell us the story, Miss Elizabeth. Perhaps Mr. Darcy can give this man a piece of his mind and teach him how to behave. Mr. Darcy is the *perfect* gentleman."

Lady Anne and Elizabeth burst out laughing. Mr. Darcy's face was so red that Elizabeth feared for his heart.

Miss Bingley's lips thinned. "What is so funny?"

Mr. Darcy interrupted. "I find this to be a lovely piece of music, Miss Elizabeth, much more tempting than the one I was hearing when Bingley spoke to me. Indeed, I feel strongly inclined to dance to this tune. Might I have the honour of a dance?"

"Mr. Darcy is all politeness." Elizabeth curtseyed. "But I think I have danced quite enough for one evening. I shall go and fetch my refreshment, as I stated earlier."

"May I be of service then?" He extended his arm to Elizabeth.

Miss Bingley was breathing heavily at his side. She seemed not at all happy that he insisted on keeping Elizabeth company. When Miss Bingley raised her hand as if to take his other arm, Lady Anne said, "Miss Bingley, could you take me to your sister? I wish to ask her where she bought the burgundy lace."

Miss Bingley's hand dropped like a broken stick, and her face twisted into a scowl. She bit her lips and looked to Mr. Darcy one last time before uttering, "Of course."

Elizabeth placed her hand on the gentleman's arm. Once they were out of earshot of the other two ladies, Mr. Darcy said, "I apologise."

"For?"

"For the unfounded view which I expressed to Mr. Bingley earlier. I really would like to dance with you, if you will allow me. I confess that I had not looked at you properly, until just now."

"Yes." Elizabeth's mouth curled up. "Your mother told me about Lady Alicia and the *ailment* relating to your eyes."

"Shocking! Mother seldom tells other women about the escapades of my younger days."

"Why is that, do you suppose?"

"She does not warm to anyone easily."

"Are you talking about your mother? Or yourself?"

"I am her son. I have inherited much of her temperament."

She giggled. "Do you deny responsibility for your own proud manner? Her Ladyship blamed it entirely on your Cambridge education."

He smiled. "Yes, she has not been shy about lamenting my decision to go to Cambridge rather than Oxford. But was I prideful? I thought I was only too hasty in my judgment in regard to your allurement."

Elizabeth's heart jumped. Could he really mean that? Did he find her alluring now? Did she want him to? She would not let him get away with flattery. "Well, you danced only once with Mrs. Hurst and once with Miss Bingley, declined being introduced to any other lady, and spent the evening in walking about the room, speaking occasionally to one of your own party. How should I describe your manner?"

"I did not know that you kept such a close watch on me."

"In a country setting such as this, every newcomer draws our attention."

"I certainly have not the talent which some people possess," said Darcy, "of conversing easily with those whom I have never seen before. I cannot catch their tone of conversation, or appear interested in their concerns, as I often see done."

"The deficiency of your Cambridge education again? Or does it arise from a lack of willingness to practice?"

"I stand corrected and look forward to practising the fine art of conversing with strangers, under your kind guidance." He poured her a glass of punch and brushed her fingers for a touch too long.

His smile and gaze urged her heart to gallop. She took a big gulp of the drink. Then she made use of the rest of the evening, introducing Meryton's neighbours, pleasant or obnoxious, to the proud gentleman. Much to the surprise of both the locals and Elizabeth, Mr. Darcy stayed by her side, bearing all the admiration and speculation with good grace. Miss Bingley's face turned green, while Lady Anne wore the smuggest of expressions.

~*~*~*~

"Fitzwilliam?"

Lady Anne opened the doors to the breakfast room at Netherfield and found her son with his face buried in Elizabeth's bosom. The younger woman was sitting on his lap, with her dress half pulled down. "Heaven forbid! The guests are about to arrive! Make yourselves presentable and come to the ballroom immediately," Lady Anne ordered, and slammed the doors shut. "And lock the doors, the next time!" her muffled voice could be heard exclaiming by the pair inside the room.

Elizabeth tried to drag her clothing back up to her shoulders and climb down from Mr. Darcy's lap. "I told you that this was not a good idea."

But Mr. Darcy's hands imprisoned her arms. "One more moment," he murmured, and suckled her nipple one last time. His talented tongue left Elizabeth at a loss for words or actions for a long moment. When he stopped his ministrations and rested his head on her breasts, drawing in deep breathes, he said, "Mother always knows where to find me and has the most inopportune timing."

"Fitzwilliam, we have to get ready."

"I know. The ball is about to begin."

"And we are the hosts."

"It is not good for us to be late, I know." He sighed.

"We do not want Alex's new parents to think we are slighting them."

Reluctantly, Mr. Darcy released Elizabeth and helped her button up the gown. "I cannot help it that my wife of five-and-twenty years is as handsome as she was when we first married."

She helped him tidy the cravat and swatted his arms. "Flatterer! My waist has doubled its size in the last decades, and our second son is getting married in three days' time. I permit you to say that I am not handsome enough to tempt you now."

"Never, my dearest and loveliest Mrs. Darcy. I love you, Lizzy. We have been through fire, drought, flooding, sadness and happiness. Thank you for loving me and giving me six wonderful children. My life would not have been nearly as happy, if you were not by my side." He lowered his head and kissed her deeply.

Outside, even at the grand old age of three-and-seventy, Lady Anne walked towards the grand ballroom with gay steps. Her son had six lovely children. He was still as passionate with his wife as in the days he first met her in Hertfordshire, some two-and-a-half decades ago. They loved and supported each other, Pemberley prospered, and the Darcys were upstanding people in society.

She was very proud of her own machinations. When she heard the rumour that Miss Bingley was about to ensnare Fitzwilliam during his stay at Netherfield Park decades ago, she had wangled an invitation for herself, even though it meant leaving behind Georgiana, her daughter, in London for some months.

She was determined then to find a worthy bride for Fitzwilliam herself. She thanked Providence that it had not taken her long to do so, for during the first assembly, Fitzwilliam's arrogant manner led him to slight Miss Elizabeth Bennet.

Once Lady Anne had ascertained the young woman's wit, unassuming manner and caring nature, she spent all her time during her stay at Netherfield working to throw

Fitzwilliam and Elizabeth together, and steering Miss Bingley away.

She was proud of her scheme, for her son had mended his prideful manner, disregarded the Bennet family's improper behaviour, and proposed marriage to Elizabeth roughly a month after they had made each other's acquaintance.

Some ten years ago, Lady Anne had made a lovely home in Netherfield. The weather in the south suited her more, as she grew older, and the now-more-sensible Mrs. Bennet had become her fast friend. Lady Anne, having purchased the property with the interest from some investments she made with Elizabeth's uncle Gardiner, had determined to leave Netherfield to Fitzwilliam's second son, Alex, as his older brother Ben would inherit Pemberley. Her grandson Alex looked even more like her husband George than Fitzwilliam did. She was happy to provide for him. And she would have other, smaller things to leave for the other grandchildren, both Fitzwilliam's and Georgiana's.

Life had become blissful. Lady Anne entered the grand ballroom to placate the anxious family members. She reckoned it would take Mrs. Darcy and her besotted husband another quarter of an hour to appear.

Shaking her head, she reflected that they had been quite a pair, for the past five-and-twenty years. Lady Anne smiled smugly. She would not complain, for she had hand-picked Elizabeth to marry her boy. And their marital bliss lightened her heart beyond measure.

Barriers To Love
By June Williams

What if Mary and Kitty Bennet had suitors who were unacceptable?

The strangeness of Mr. Collins's making two offers of marriage within three days, was nothing in comparison of his being now accepted. – Pride and Prejudice, Chapter 22

PART ONE: THE BRIDEGROOM SWITCH

August 1812 – Longbourn, Meryton

Elizabeth Bennet thought it had been a horrid few weeks for everyone in her family, although she knew her sixteen-year-old sister Lydia would disagree. In July, Lydia ran away with the scandalous Lieutenant Wickham. Miraculously, they had been apprehended in London by Uncle Gardiner, who wrote that he had made their wedding arrangements and was sending the newlyweds to Longbourn.

Mr. Darcy would not want to marry me now, Lizzy believed. *He would not want to be brother-in-law to Wickham.*

The newlyweds' carriage came and was seen driving up to Longbourn House. The Bennet family was assembled in the breakfast room to formally receive them. Mrs. Bennet smiled broadly as the carriage drove up to the door; her husband looked impenetrably grave; her daughters, alarmed, anxious, and uneasy.

Lydia's voice was heard in the vestibule; the door was thrown open, and she ran into the room. Her mother stepped forwards, embraced her, and welcomed her with rapture; gave her hand, with an affectionate smile, to...

"Who are you?" Mrs. Bennet stared at the handsome officer in an Army uniform. She looked beyond him to another man. "Mr. Darcy? What are you doing here? You are the last man I expected to see again. And where is your delightful friend, our dear Mr. Bingley?"

Lizzy was stunned. This was the first time she had seen Mr. Darcy since the inn at Lambton. *Why is he here,* she fretted. *I am ashamed that he knows my sister eloped with Mr. Wickham – after Mr. Darcy warned me so strongly against him.* Lizzy was also humiliated at her mother's rudeness, but she could do nothing – she was not the mistress of Longbourn. She could only give her father a despairing look.

"Come in, come in," Mr. Bennet said grudgingly as he led everyone to the drawing room. "Lydia, where is your husband, Mr. Wickham?"

"Who cares where Wickham is? I have got myself a more handsome husband," Lydia said proudly, forgetting the man she had so recently called the "one man in the world I love." Today she had switched her loyalties to a new bridegroom. "Isn't this a good joke? I had two offers of marriage within three days! You were expecting me to marry a mere lieutenant in the militia, and instead I have brought home a captain in the regulars, and he is going to be a major. Even Mr. Darcy supported the match."

The Bennets all stared at him, as Darcy could only look grave and stoic.

"Mr. Darcy is buying us everything we need, for we are going to join my husband's new regiment in Spain."

"Spain? My dear girl, you will have such adventure when you travel!" Mrs. Bennet was excited.

"But Spain is where the fighting is!" Lizzy felt faint and needed to sit.

"It will be so much fun!" Lydia babbled. "I am the first of my sisters to marry, and the first to go abroad. I may even dance with Wellington himself."

Lizzy gave her father another look, but Mr. Bennet was speechless.

"Might I introduce Captain David Carter," Mr. Darcy said, stepping nearer. "It seems he and your daughter made a love match, and Mr. Wickham found he was needed elsewhere."

"Carter? We had a Captain Carter here recently with the militia." Mrs. Bennet remembered all the handsome officers.

"That is my younger brother, Edmond, who introduced me to your daughter when I visited him in Brighton this summer. When I met her again in London, I was overcome by her charms and had to marry her," said the smiling Captain, as his bride and mother-in-law giggled.

"Isn't he taller and more handsome than any other officer?" Lydia cooed over her bridegroom.

Mr. Darcy is taller and more handsome, Lizzy thought. But she had to acknowledge that Lydia's husband was more strongly built than any of the militia officers and had a charming demeanor. Still, Lizzy was careful to not trust men on the basis of looks and charm, having learned her lesson from the unlamented Mr. Wickham.

As the Captain continued to entertain his new female relatives, Lizzy signaled to the housekeeper to bring in refreshments, but she noticed Mr. Darcy take her father aside. She knew it was rude, but she had no interest in listening to this Captain Carter flirt with her mother and sisters – and she was desperate to know why Mr. Darcy accompanied them here. Lizzy quietly went outside and hid behind the bushes outside her father's library window, where she could overhear what her father and Mr. Darcy were saying.

"Mr. Bennet, I am fully aware of how this must look to you." To Lizzy's ears, Mr. Darcy sounded uncomfortable but determined.

"A strange man has married my daughter, and I cannot guess how you are involved or why you are here." *Father seems annoyed by Mr. Darcy's manner*, Lizzy thought, wishing he would be more polite to the man who had saved them.

"Your daughter, Miss Elizabeth, and the Gardiners were visiting in Lambton when Miss Bennet's letter arrived. I became aware of your youngest daughter's elopement. As I was already acquainted with Mr. Wickham's habits and his father was my father's steward, I felt a responsibility to help locate him so I traveled to London. Your new son-in-law, David, told me that Colonel Forster had brought two militia officers – Lieutenant Denny and Captain Edmond Carter – to assist in the search. Before the men returned to Brighton, Edmond Carter contacted his brother David in the regulars; it was the elder brother – David – who found the couple in Town and left a message for me at the Gardiners' home."

"So why did my brother Gardiner tell me that Wickham was going to marry her?"

Mr. Darcy looked uncomfortable. "It was apparent that your daughter enjoyed having two suitors competing for her hand. Captain David Carter won her favor, and Mr. Wickham left the country. I wish she would have waited to marry until she is older, but of the two men, I believe Captain Carter is the better match; he has an established career, and he is a younger son of a gentleman whose estate is the size of Longbourn."

"He is taking my youngest daughter to Spain. There is a war there."

"He insists on going to Spain to advance his career. She insists on going with him. She said something about a campful of soldiers and only a handful of women."

Both Mr. Bennet and Lizzy rolled their eyes at this, although they could not see each other.

"What if she becomes with child while in Spain?" Mr. Bennet asked Darcy.

"Captain Carter said his mother's tea is something that prevents such an occurrence."

Mr. Bennet was still not satisfied. "A battlefield is no safe place for a gentlewoman!"

"I tried my best to persuade your daughter to let the Gardiners advise her, but she would not listen. She insisted on marrying Carter and no one else; the Gardiners had no choice but to support the marriage, and I chose to support the Gardiners. Truly, the Gardiners and I had no part in your daughter's decision. While Miss Lydia – Mrs. Carter – is here, perhaps you and Mrs. Bennet could convince her to stay where it is safe."

"Do you really think we could change that headstrong girl?"

Mr. Darcy was silent. Outside, Lizzy shook her head at the idea that Lydia could ever change.

"I thought not. Now, Mr. Darcy, where will you be staying in the neighborhood?"

"I have urgent business in London, so I must leave as soon as my horses have rested sufficiently." *He must want to get away from us,* Lizzy suspected. *Will I ever see him again?*

The men rejoined the others in the drawing room. Lizzy walked in and sat quietly in the back of the room with her sewing, as if she had just returned from fetching another floss of embroidery thread.

Captain Carter smiled, looked handsome, and said many pretty things. He knew how to make love to an audience of women while still paying attention to Lydia. Even Mary Bennet was silent, not one word of criticism on her lips. Lizzy held fast to her opinion of the superiority of Darcy's person, but she said nothing.

Oddly enough, Lizzy observed the Captain glancing at her father and Mr. Darcy as if expecting them to say something. Every few minutes, he would make a flattering statement about Mr. Darcy – "Mr. Darcy graciously brought us here in his carriage," "Mr. Darcy kindly arranged for me to have leave from my regiment," "Mr. Darcy honored us by attending our wedding, where he stood up for me," and "I am the envy of all my friends for having Mr. Darcy as my sponsor." He aimed his remarks to Mr. Bennet, who would glance briefly at the uncomfortable Mr. Darcy.

When Mr. Darcy's driver was seen through the window, leading the large carriage to the drive, all the men stood.

"I do not wish to embarrass Mr. Darcy, but Lydia and I are grateful that he will return for us shortly, and will see us off to our grand adventure on the Continent. Thank you, Mr. Darcy."

Lydia sulked at having to share any of the attention, but Mrs. Bennet smiled at him. "Any friend of Captain Carter's is welcome here."

Mr. Darcy bowed and then left, after a brief glance at Elizabeth who quickly looked away. *She hates me*, he thought; *she has not said a word to me.*

He hates me, she thought; *he has not said a word to me.* Still, she looked out the window and stared until the carriage was gone from sight.

That night, Lizzy wrote a short letter to her Aunt Gardiner, to request an explanation of what she had overheard between her father and Mr. Darcy.

"I know Mr. Darcy would not lie to us, but there is something suspicious about Captain Carter's convenient presence in Town and his magical ability to find Mr. Wickham. Why would an officer and younger son want to marry a penniless girl as silly as Lydia? And why does Lydia say that Mr. Darcy supported the match to Captain Carter?"

If I were a matchmaker, I would not match Lydia with anyone – not until she has matured, Lizzy thought.

~*~*~*~

Elizabeth had the satisfaction of receiving an answer to her letter as soon as she possibly could. She was no sooner in possession of it than, hurrying into the little copse, where she was least likely to be interrupted, she sat down on one of the benches and prepared to be shocked.

"Gracechurch-street.

MY DEAR NIECE,

I have just received your letter, and shall devote this whole morning to answering it. Knowing your sharp mind, I have been expecting your questions.

You are correct in wondering about the convenient presence of Captain David Carter. He is one of five sons of a gentleman, and his elder brothers already have sons, so he has no expectation of inheriting. While visiting his younger brother in Brighton, he first met Lydia who told him about Mr. Wickham's connections to the Darcys of Pemberley and the loss of a promised living. Here in Town, David Carter learned from his brother that Mr. Darcy was looking for Mr. Wickham and Lydia, and he contacted Mr. Darcy to say he knew their address. We expected that a small reward would suffice.

But when David Carter met in our home with your uncle and Mr. Darcy, it was apparent he is sort of a fortune-hunter. Of course Lydia has no money, but she has something just as valuable: the possibility of a connection to the Darcys. The Captain has family near Kympton, so his own network of friends had told him that you had been seen with us on visits to Pemberley, that he was seen visiting the inn at Lambton, and that Mr. Darcy was expected to marry you.

Lydia needed to marry to repair your family's reputation, and the Captain convinced her that he was the superior match. So instead of having Mr. Wickham for your brother, you have the Captain, and I do not know which man is better. Mr. Wickham had demanded payment of all his debts, a commission in the regulars, and one thousand pounds dowry for Lydia. Captain Carter demanded a major's commission in a regiment assigned to Spain, and everything an officer needs for war. You know what that entails – horses, donkeys, swords, pistols, uniforms, shirts, boots. In addition, Lydia needs servants sent with her; their travel to Spain will be paid by Mr. Darcy, as the army provides transport only for officers and soldiers.

Even now, Mr. Darcy is purchasing the major's commission for your new brother and arranging for everything he needs to purchase for war. His cousin, Colonel Fitzwilliam, is using his own connections to get the Captain into a better regiment. Perhaps this is why Lydia says that Mr. Darcy supported the match, but you know Lydia – she only follows her own opinion.

Mr. Darcy did not wish you or your family to know of any of his assistance, but Captain Carter begged him to accompany them to Longbourn. Mr. Darcy agreed after much consideration because he is a man of honour and integrity, and he felt he owed your father an explanation. I have no hesitation about telling you this, as I know

Captain Carter is already boasting of his new Darcy connection – and it cannot hurt his career that his new regimental assignment is being arranged through a son of the Earl of Matlock.

Yes, I am angry with Lydia for what trouble her actions have caused us, but I will be consoled when you invite us to visit you at Pemberley. Mr. Darcy hardly mentions your name, but when he does, it is clear that he loves you with the deepest kind of love, and that everything he did for Lydia was to spare you the pain of having a ruined sister. Whenever Mr. Darcy comes to dinner, his countenance always lights up when we talk of our dearest Lizzy. You know a man loves you when he stays true in time of trouble – 'for better, for worse,' as the marriage vows say.

Yours, very sincerely,

M. GARDINER."

Lizzy was stunned and horrified at the revelations. Was Lydia's husband a better choice than Mr. Wickham? Perhaps, if he had never tried to seduce a young girl such as Mary King or Miss Darcy. Such a poor selection! Both men had wanted Lydia only for Mr. Darcy's money.

She again read the letter's last paragraph. The deepest kind of love?

"Could Mr. Darcy truly love me, after all I said to him at Hunsford?" Lizzy whispered to herself. "Do I dare ask him and risk losing his respect, or should I stay silent and risk losing him forever?" The choice was clear, but how could she find a few minutes with him alone. The next time he was expected at Longbourn was when Lydia and her husband were leaving, and her sister would likely make a spectacle of herself and demand everyone's attention.

~*~*~*~

Lizzy walked a great deal each day, to avoid seeing Lydia flaunt her wedding ring and handsome husband throughout Meryton, led by the doting Mrs. Bennet.

Had Lizzy accompanied their circus, she would have seen Captain Carter frown at his bride's silliest remarks. Lydia spoke gaily as if she would be dancing on every battlefield in Spain, as her husband smiled and held his tongue.

Neither did Lizzy notice Mary burying her loneliness at her piano, or Kitty sighing enviously at Lydia's good fortune. Lizzy did notice Jane's continued serenity, and had no doubt that her eldest sister was genuinely happy for Lydia's marriage.

"They must have true affection for each other," Jane insisted, "for our sister has no money."

But Mr. Darcy has money, and Captain Carter is in love with it, thought Lizzy. *If only I had recognized Mr. Darcy's true character before I rejected him so callously at Hunsford. Then Lydia would have had to stay home for my wedding, instead of going to Brighton.*

At breakfast on the day the Carters were to leave, Lydia's husband bragged Mr. Darcy would personally arrive to escort their carriages to Plymouth. Lizzy barely stopped herself from saying that Mr. Darcy was not their servant or a trained monkey from Astley's Amphitheater, so she avoided the hubbub by taking a long morning walk on one of her favourite paths near Longbourn.

What should I say to him, she wondered. *I am nervous about seeing Mr. Darcy, if he truly is coming, but I still do not know how I can get him away from everyone. I may never see him again.*

About an hour into her walk, she unexpectedly heard the voices of two men and was about to turn back when she recognized one voice as Captain Carter's – and he was discussing Mr. Wickham. She stayed quietly hidden in the bushes. *I am reduced to tricks and stratagems to find out more,* she thought ruefully.

"No problems in getting away from your camp in Brighton, Edmond?"

"No. Colonel Forster was relieved that Lydia was found and married off to you, since he and his wife were supposed to watch the wild girl. Since then, he lets me make all his deliveries to London instead of Denny, since I am so trustworthy."

Both men snickered. Lizzy peeked and recognized the other man as Captain Carter of the militia – the man that Lydia had unsuccessfully chased for months while the militia was in Meryton.

"Did Denny remember anything from that night?" Lydia's husband asked his brother, Edmond.

"Denny remembers being drunk, but does not remember that he told me where to find Wickham. If only his fellows knew that Denny was hiding his old friend Wickham, who owes money to practically every junior officer in Brighton."

"Wickham has one thing he wanted – a commission in the regulars. It was easy to get him a free first commission in the infantry, the cheapest branch. If only I could have seen his face when he woke up on the transport... to Spain."

The brothers laughed at this.

"Is that why you rarely drink, David?"

"Yes. You remember how I got my captain's commission – I got the man drunk and then beat him at cards. Now nobody in my regiment will play or drink with me. I am indebted for my lieutenant's commission to an officer who slept with his colonel's wife; I saw them and he paid me for my silence."

"All new pigeons await you in Spain. Do you think you can fleece Darcy into buying a second horse, for Lydia?"

"I think so. But the reason I asked you here was for you to look at Miss Kitty again. You know the militia will be disbanded as soon as Napoleon is defeated, and then you will have no career. Darcy is buying my major's commission for marrying Lydia; perhaps he will buy you a commission in the regulars if you marry Miss Kitty."

"No, David. Wickham once told me that with his good looks, he hoped to marry an heiress. His plan sounds good. I understand Darcy has a rich sister..."

"No!" Elizabeth shouted as she stormed up to them. "My sister was foolish enough to fall for your charms, but I will not permit you continue to abuse Mr. Darcy's charity. He is the best man I have ever known, far too good for the likes of you."

The men were startled by her presence, then Lydia's husband smiled weakly. "Come, Miss Elizabeth, we are brother and sister, you know. Do not let us quarrel about the past. Think instead of your sister's good fortune in having an officer for her husband and the adventure she always wanted."

"Stay away from Mr. Darcy," Lizzy said angrily. "I will warn you only this once. No scheming for more money or connections from him, ever again."

"Your support for Mr. Darcy is admirable, sister. When shall I congratulate you on your engagement? I wondered why your father did not announce it after Mr. Darcy met with him. I certainly give your match my full support."

She could feel her face turning red with fury. "Do not call me your sister."

"But Miss Elizabeth..."

"That is enough, gentlemen." Mr. Darcy appeared. He looked proud, with a forbidding, disagreeable countenance.

Lizzy's heart raced when she saw him. She was not completely surprised at his arrival – this was the man who mysteriously showed up on her walks at Rosings, somehow able to find her. She had no fear of him, as she had seen him as the kind Master when she visited Pemberley. But at the moment, she was grateful for every bit of arrogance he displayed to the greedy Carter brothers.

"I will fulfill every part of our agreement, Major Carter, and no further," he said coldly after he dismounted his horse. "Your new commission has come through, and your carriages have arrived. It is time for you to take your leave and go to Portsmouth."

"Will you still escort us there?"

"No, he will not," Lizzy snapped. "Mr. Darcy has given you far too much already. He will not allow himself to be paraded at Portsmouth solely for your conceit and vanity." It was rather brave of her to speak to the men in this way, but she was confident Mr. Darcy would support her.

The Carter men looked at her and Mr. Darcy, who both looked fierce and superior. It would be easier to argue with a stone wall.

"Thank you, Mr. Darcy," Major Carter said. He and his brother turned quickly for Longbourn. Unlike Mr. Wickham at the card table, the Carters knew when to quit when they were ahead.

Darcy waited until the men were completely gone from sight. "Miss Elizabeth, I must apologize for matching your youngest sister to –"

"No, Mr. Darcy, you will not apologize. All of this was Lydia's own choice; she chose to elope, and she chose her own match."

"It was unexpected. I did not know she would have a second suitor."

"I know, sir – such a greedy man, matched with my greedy sister. All we can do is pray for their safety."

He was afraid to look at her face and see that she was angry with him – but he looked anyway. "You remind me of Boudica."

"The Celtic queen who led a revolt against the Romans? How so?"

"You were fierce."

"I knew I was right. I am right."

"Nero almost abandoned Britain because of Boudica."

"Perhaps if her husband had lived and fought beside her, with their combined strength they might have succeeded."

He hesitated. "Miss Bennet, if your opinion of me has truly improved, if you would agree to marry me, I swear I would stay by your side and always share your battles, your defeats, your victories – in all things."

She thought of her Aunt Gardiner's words to her: *You know a man loves you when he stays true in time of trouble.* Mr. Darcy had not stopped loving her despite her strongly-worded rejection of him at Hunsford, despite Lydia's elopement with Wickham, and despite Major Carter using him as a personal banker. Lizzy was grateful that he still loved her faithfully, but more than that, she loved him and could not imagine finding anyone better. "You would marry me for better, for worse?"

"For richer, for poorer."

"In sickness and in health."

"To love and to cherish."

"Until death us do part," they finished together.

She held out her hands, which he took and kissed. They gazed at each other, savoring this new understanding between them. Without speaking, they knew they had already demonstrated their love for each other – their love had endured Wickham's lies, a misunderstanding at Hunsford, the crisis of Lydia's elopement, and now the mortification of being related to a fortune-hunting officer. Nothing could separate them now.

They began walking back to Longbourn, knowing they were expected to see the Carters off. "How did you find me, Mr. Darcy?"

"At Rosings, you told me of your favourite haunt there and how it compared to Meryton. This morning, I hoped for a few moments with you in private, so I rode ahead of the Carters' carriages and searched for a walk that fit your description. Fortunately, I heard your melodious voice shouting at someone."

"The Major."

"You said I was too good for the likes of them. It gave me hope that your feelings for me had changed."

"It is true, but must I flatter you now?" She gave him a saucy look.

"Miss Bingley would flatter me."

"I am less accomplished at flattery than she is."

"LIZZY!" Mrs. Bennet called as they approached the house. "Come see your brother's new sword!"

They both sighed. "Shall we tell them our good news, my dearest, loveliest Elizabeth?"

She shook her head. "I wish to wait until the Carters are gone. I do not want to share this moment with them, or with anyone. Shall we elope, Mr. Darcy?"

He looked stunned until she laughed at him. "Teasing woman!" he exclaimed. "I shall have to speak to your father about you."

She pinched him on the arm, but they were both smiling at each other.

At Longbourn, they were in time to say farewell to the Carters and to see the heavily-laden carriages. Edmond Carter did not attempt to flirt with Miss Kitty, despite Lydia's obvious attempts to matchmake them. The newlywed Carters eagerly showed off all their new items until Mr. Darcy reminded them that their transport would be sailing at the next high tide.

"Heartless brute," Mrs. Bennet muttered, loud enough to be heard by all but low enough to give the impression she had not wanted Mr. Darcy to hear it.

Major Carter caught Darcy's eye and began to say something, but Darcy motioned to him to keep silent. The officer approached them and bowed his head to Darcy and Lizzy. "I do not understand why she is not more appreciative of all you have done for her family," he whispered.

"I did not do it for praise or recognition," Darcy said firmly.

The Major looked back and forth between Darcy and Lizzy. He did not see any sign of their engagement, but he knew they must have walked here together. He smiled and offered his handshake to them. "My congratulations to you both," he said quietly so that Mrs. Bennet did not hear it.

Darcy accepted the handshake but said nothing.

Lizzy said nothing except, "Please take care of my sister and yourself, sir."

The Major did not expect them to confirm or deny their engagement, but he was almost certain of it. *Even if Darcy gives me no additional funds, he will still be my brother by marriage – an excellent connection*, he thought as he walked back to his bride.

The farewell between Lydia and her family was more boisterous than sad, despite the fact she was going to an army camp in the middle of a war, in which women could be killed as easily as men.

Mrs. Bennet embraced Lydia tightly. "Come home safely, my darling daughter. Do not miss the opportunity of enjoying yourself as much as possible. Dance with all the officers and generals."

She waved at the carriages until the Carters were completely gone from sight. Mr. Bennet quickly retreated to his library, not wanting to hear his wife's loud complaints about the loss of Lydia. But before she could start her complaints, Mr. Bingley's carriage suddenly appeared from the direction of Netherfield.

"Mr. Bingley! Mr. Bingley is here! Jane, go put on your new dress. Into the house, girls – quickly!" Mrs. Bennet was so excited that she forgot all her previous irritation at Bingley for not returning sooner. In her haste to go make Jane look even more beautiful, she lost track of Lizzy and Mr. Darcy, who stayed outside.

Lizzy looked at her new fiancé, who had a smug look on his face.

"Is this part of your 'urgent business' in London?" she asked archly, sure of his answer.

Darcy only nodded his head. "I did not want Bingley to meet Major Carter," he said softly to her. "Bingley's good heart is so easy and generous, that Carter could have taken him for half his fortune."

She laughed, then stopped when she realized something. "You proposed to me before Bingley could arrive."

"I did not want to purchase your affection. Now it is up to your sister and Bingley to decide their own happiness."

Lizzy glanced at the house to see if anyone was watching from the windows, then sneaked a sweet kiss with him. But she would not be Lizzy if she did not tease him. "I suppose you are handsomer than Mr. Collins," she said with a reluctant pout.

He laughed, as they turned to greet Mr. Bingley's carriage.

"I saw you kiss," Bingley said happily as he joined them. "Is this a good omen for me?"

"I do not know what you mean," said Mr. Darcy. He and Lizzy tried to look proper and serious, but he saw the laughter in her eyes. Soon, all three were laughing as they walked into Longbourn.

The butler greeted them at the door and took their outerwear. "If you are looking for my mistress, ma'am, she is upstairs with your sisters," he said to Elizabeth. His explanation was proper but unnecessary.

From the entryway, Bingley, Darcy, and Lizzy could hear Mrs. Bennet shrieking at Kitty – "no, you may not borrow any jewelry! Bingley is not here for you." The poor maid received conflicting instructions – "put her hair up in curls. No, in the eastern style. No, the antique Roman style would be more elegant. No, put the pearls in her hair. No. put the pearls on her neck. Oh, you wretched girl!"

Lizzy was ashamed of her mother's behaviour, but Darcy was quick to reassure her. "I know what your mother is like."

"And yet you would still love me?" she had to ask.

"'For better, for worse' as the marriage vows say."

She smiled as she gazed at him lovingly.

"Kiss him again, Lizzy," Bingley urged her.

Darcy turned to his friend and glared at the little devil.

Bingley laughed and tried to whisper to Darcy, who avoided his friend – guessing correctly that Bingley wanted to ask if he was engaged to Jane's sister.

They sat in the drawing room. Mary wandered in, her nose in a book, oblivious to Kitty's chattering.

"Who is going to talk to me now that Lydia is gone?" Kitty whined petulantly as she slumped into a chair. Then she realized Mr. Bingley and Mr. Darcy were in the room, so she sat up straight and picked up her sewing project, trying to look good.

The men smiled knowingly; they both had sisters. Kitty peeked at Mr. Darcy, having never seen him smile.

Mrs. Bennet finally entered with Jane, who truly looked beautiful as she saw Mr. Bingley for the first time since the Netherfield Ball. Darcy finally saw emotion on Jane's face, evidence she was not indifferent to his friend.

It was quick work for Mrs. Bennet to invite the gentlemen to dinner, and to arrange for Bingley to walk with Jane, Lizzy, Mr. Darcy, and Kitty.

After one week of being invited to Longbourn for dinners, tea, and walks, Mr. Bingley proposed to Jane. Neither of them had switched from their affections for each other; their love had survived months of separation.

They would even survive Mrs. Bennet's plans for the grandest double wedding ever. "Three daughters married!" she exclaimed when Lizzy told her of her engagement to Mr. Darcy. She switched her opinion of him from "that disagreeable Mr. Darcy" to "such a charming man, so handsome, so tall!"

Why did not you all learn? – You ought all to have learned. – Pride and Prejudice, Chapter 29

PART TWO: LEARNING

August 1812 – Longbourn, Meryton

The Bingleys planned to go north to visit his family in Scarborough after their September wedding, and the Darcys would travel to his home of Pemberley with his sister, Georgiana, who had arrived for the wedding. The only question was whether to take the bride's two younger sisters. Jane and Elizabeth thought that Kitty and Mary should decide for themselves.

"Mr. Darcy, you should take Kitty and throw her in the way of other rich men," Mrs. Bennet declared. "Mary would not appreciate it; she can stay here and care for my poor nerves."

Mr. Darcy noticed Mary's shuttered expression, which Elizabeth noticed only because her new husband was looking. She looked at her sister Jane, who instinctively began distracting Mrs. Bennet – "Mama, should there be more lace on my gown?" – so that Mr. Darcy could speak quietly with their sisters. Jane always knew how to turn her mother's thoughts to more positive subjects.

"It does not matter what I want," Mary said sullenly, looking at the floor. It reminded Mr. Darcy of his own sister, who was afraid to voice her own wants. "As long as I have a piano and books, I will be well."

"I have never been anywhere. I would enjoy anything new," Kitty admitted.

Darcy thought of Lambton, the town nearest to Pemberley. It was larger than Meryton, but he wondered if it would be exciting enough for a girl who longed for the pleasures of London, even if no one was in Town in September except for those with business. From his visit to Netherfield last year, he doubted Kitty would enjoy Pemberley's hunting season or the beginning of the harvest. He knew he was not good at making conversation, but he did have experience in speaking with a younger sister.

"Perhaps you would like to attend a ladies' seminary in Town, where you would study dancing, music, singing, and drawing," he offered. "There would be other girls there who could become friends, and you could prepare for the Season in February."

"Oh, that sounds wonderful!" she exclaimed, and Kitty's future was resolved. Mr. Darcy would pay for the school, and let Elizabeth ask her father to pay for new clothes for Kitty. Jane would ask Bingley if he would help Kitty, but Lizzy suspected that the Bingleys would be working to find a husband for Caroline next Season, whereas Kitty and Mary were still too young for the marriage market. Wisely, Darcy sensed that Kitty was not interested in learning the modern languages, history, geography, or arithmetic; he would find her a school that focused more on manners, decorum, and deportment.

Mary had already resolved that she would be stuck in Meryton forever, so she barely glanced at Mr. Darcy.

"Miss Mary, would you like to come with us to Pemberley? You and my sister could help my bride with the tenants. Also, Georgiana is a great student of music; I suspect the two of you would enjoy playing together. We have a large library at Pemberley; I have heard it said that it is delightful."

He winked at Lizzy, who remembered exactly when Caroline Bingley had said it.

"The Pemberley library ought to be good. It has been the work of many generations," Lizzy said pertly, quoting his remarks to Bingley's sister.

Mary had no understanding of their innuendo, but she was intrigued by a new library.

"May we stay in Town, brother?" Georgiana asked shyly. She hoped to give the newlyweds privacy, but she was also eager for an excuse to stay in Town, near her masters. "Perhaps Miss Mary would enjoy studying with my music masters. I am sure they would be pleased to have her as a new student."

"M-m-music masters? Me?"

"You may also study with my sister's history and drawing masters, and any other masters you wish for."

At Rosings, Lizzy had once told her fiancé's Aunt Catherine that the Bennet girls had had all the masters that were necessary for their education, but she realized that was not true: she and Jane had all the masters they wanted. When Jane and Lizzy no longer needed lessons, Mr. Bennet told Mary to read and study on her own, and Kitty and Lydia were only too happy to be free of a classroom. Now, Lizzy could see how much Mary had wanted to have an education with real teachers – not just sheet music and whatever books their father was willing to part with. She was touched by how perceptive Mr. Darcy had become, and knew Mary would have new opportunities soon.

"I do not know how to dance. I always play the piano so my sisters and their friends may dance."

"I will hire you a dancing master. I would offer to dance with you myself, but I have been refused by your sister on two occasions, so there must be something flawed in my performance."

Two pairs of eyes looked at Lizzy – Mary's filled with curiosity, Mr. Darcy's with impishness.

"You wicked man," Lizzy said laughingly. "For your impertinence, I should punish you by making you dance with my cousin, Mr. Collins."

Her fiancé struggled to hide his laughter with coughing. He had witnessed the man's poor dancing skills at the Netherfield ball, where Mr. Collins kept moving the wrong way, oblivious to all the dancers around him.

"Mr. Collins? What about him, Lizzy? What are you saying there?"

"Nothing, Mama." Lizzy smiled as Mr. Darcy excused himself and left the room, still coughing.

September 1812 – Longbourn, Meryton

The Darcy and Bingley weddings took place smoothly. The Gardiners and Collinses attended; the Gardiners were happy to be invited to Pemberley for Christmas, and Mr. Collins occupied the entire time in uselessly glaring at Lizzy for having seduced the fiancé of Miss Anne de Bourgh. Charlotte Collins and Colonel Fitzwilliam had sat on each side of Mr. Collins to ensure he did not object during the ceremony, conducted by the same Meryton rector who had baptized each Bennet girl.

At the wedding breakfast, Charlotte apologized to Lizzy. "I had planned to attend your wedding alone, but Mr. Collins insisted on escorting me to visit my parents. He thought this was only Jane's wedding; he did not know you were marrying Mr. Darcy until we were inside the church. I told him that he needed to behave with decorum, as befits Lady Catherine's rector."

The bride laughed. "Mr. Darcy wrote of his engagement to his aunt. Perhaps she did not believe him, but Mr. Collins' report may convince her it is true."

After the breakfast, both newlywed couples traveled north in their carriages.

Miss Bingley had failed to win the attentions of Mr. Darcy's unmarried friends who had attended, and left for London with the Hursts.

Mr. Collins told Mr. Bennet repeatedly that Lizzy's marriage would upset his patroness, the very noble Lady Catherine, until Mr. Bennet reminded him that Mr. Darcy was now his cousin – who might have a valuable living available up north. From that point on, the rector was hard at work planning all the little elegant platitudes he would offer to Lady Catherine to soothe her feelings; he told himself he was honored to carry an olive branch between Pemberley and Rosings.

The Colonel spoke politely with Mrs. Collins, who promised to deliver his regards to his aunt, Lady Catherine. He escorted the carriage south to London to deliver Kitty to her school, and Georgiana and Mary to Darcy House to stay with Mrs. Annesley. At Christmas, he would escort the girls to Pemberley. The Colonel had no complaints about this escort duty; anything was better than the Battle of Corunna in 1809, where he had fought and seen hundreds of British soldiers die, and even more died on the retreat. Every survivor of Corunna was lucky to escape and return to Britain, and Colonel Fitzwilliam was thankful his father's connections had been able to keep him in Town. That was his last time in battle; since then, every nightmare – every news report of the war – every wounded soldier he met – reminded him that he needed to marry an heiress, or else he might have to return to the Peninsula.

Mrs. Bennet finally had no daughters at home, and Mr. Bennet barricaded himself in his library. All she could do was visit the neighbors in hopes of conversation.

~*~*~*~

September 1812 – Library at Pemberley, Derbyshire

"Should you have sent me to Kitty's school, where I too could have learned manners, decorum, and deportment?" Lizzy said teasingly to her new husband.

"There is no hope for you, Mrs. Darcy. I suspect that not even my Aunt Catherine could reform you or make you bend to her will."

"I would have told her that I am only resolved to act in that manner, which will, in my own opinion, constitute my happiness, without reference to her, or to any person so wholly unconnected with me."

"I am connected with you, am I not?"

"Yes, and thus your happiness is my happiness, dearest William."

They were distracted for a while by kissing and other physical activities, but eventually he remembered he wanted to raise a topic of discussion.

"I must confess that I am relieved your sisters are in London, where Kitty's teachers and Mrs. Annesley are looking after their education. I still regret Lydia's match..."

"We could not have expected or prevented that match," she reminded him gently.

"I barely prevented Georgiana from a match with Wickham," Darcy said, still anxious at the memory. "Do you think we should attempt to introduce your sisters to potential suitors? Georgiana is not at that age yet, but your sisters are older. I am not a matchmaker, but I wish to prevent a similar situation. If your sisters knew there were good men available to them, men of honour and integrity, they might not be tempted by men of weak character."

She thought about her two unwed sisters. "Mary would want a man of godly character, but she might accept the first man who proposed – as my friend Charlotte did – for fear that he is her only opportunity. Kitty would not want a churchman; she would want a good dancer who is handsome, perhaps an officer who could promise excitement."

"No more officers, I beg of you."

"Then a gentleman of good character. But both sisters need men who are not frightened by their small dowries."

"I can help make up for that. If Mary finds a rector or curate, I might be able to offer him the living in Kympton in a few years. If Catherine finds a barrister, my family has connections through my great-uncle, the judge. Perhaps Bingley can send us any suitors rejected by his sister."

Lizzy had to laugh. "William, are you certain you are not a matchmaker?"

"No men like Wickham or Carter, please. I could not bear it."

"I agree." She was grieved that he seemed unable to forgive himself for Lydia's match, but that was his nature, to be conscientious and responsible for his family – and she loved him for who he was.

They were each lost in thought for a while. "William, my sisters are happy with their studies. They are not old enough to be on the shelf. Perhaps this can wait for one more year."

"Very well," he said reluctantly. "No matchmaking and no introductions, but in Town or at Pemberley, no man may cross your sisters' path unless he is known to me or your Uncle Gardiner."

They did not mention Mr. Bennet, who had not tried to find a suitor for any of his five daughters. His one contribution to their happiness was to make a brief introductory visit to Bingley when he first arrived at Netherfield.

"Is my opinion not important?" she asked, looking not quite serious but not fully teasing.

"Of course your opinion matters. You and I are both excellent judges of character. However," he said, then hesitated, "we are both deficient in reading others' feelings."

Lizzy paused to think. "Yes, we both misread each others' feelings before Hunsford, and you misread Jane's feelings for Bingley – although he too misread her. Do you think we have both grown in our ability to understand the other sex?"

He gave her a look she did not understand.

"Oh," she said, realizing she was not fully expert in reading a man's face. Then she gave him a look that he did understand, and they spent the next hour in deepening their marital bliss.

~*~*~*~

September 1812 – Bloomsbury and Cheapside, London

Kitty's school in Bloomsbury was everything Mr. Darcy had promised, although she felt disadvantaged by her limited experiences. Many of the other girls had gone to London museums, concerts, shops on Bond Street or Oxford Street in the fashionable West End, or to Gunter's Tea Shop for ices. Kitty felt more comfortable with the girls who had also been kept at home. But all the girls enjoyed hearing stories from those with older sisters or cousins, and they ooh-ed and ahh-ed over many.

"My cousin went to Almack's and danced with Beau Brummell himself."

"My sister witnessed an argument between Lord Byron and Lady Caroline Lamb. She is still married to Lord Lamb, a member of Parliament!"

"My brother bought a horse from Lady Letitia Lade. Before she married Sir John Lade, she was married to that highwayman, Sixteen String Jack, who was hanged. Weren't they married? You think she was his mistress?"

"My brother's friend, Viscount Petersham, has 365 snuff boxes, one for each day of the year. Petersham is a special friend to the Prince Regent."

"In May, my father was in the lobby of the House of Commons when Prime Minister Perceval was killed. He also watched the man hang for murder. Have you ever seen a hanging? I don't know if I could watch. They even hang ladies."

It was a long way from Longbourn, and Kitty felt very adventurous. Lydia wasn't the only Bennet with an exciting life.

The school also aimed to correct Kitty's deficiencies in French and art, which were barriers to her success in the marriage market. Kitty was hopeful that one day, perhaps she too could marry a rich man, just as Jane and Lizzy had.

But on Sundays, Kitty spent the day in Cheapside with the Gardiners, attending church services and playing with her young cousins. It kept her from becoming too silly with schoolgirl talk, as her aunt taught her practical lessons such as how to make medicines and remedies.

Often, the Gardiners had Sunday dinner guests, including Mary, Kitty, and Georgiana. Sometimes their parish's curate, Mr. Luke Goodman, attended; he was a good conversationalist, paying attention to all the guests. Like all curates, he had little money, so Mrs. Gardiner sent him home with extra rolls, biscuits, cheese, and fruit. He had a pleasant appearance and a ready smile, but he paid as much attention to the unmarried ladies as he paid to the Gardiners' small children.

The first time he met Kitty and Mary was memorable.

"Mr. Goodman looks like a very boring man, as all clergymen are," Kitty whispered to Mary.

Unfortunately, this was heard by the Gardiners' four-year-old son. "What is boring, Kitty? Why is Mr. Goodman boring?"

Mary shut her eyes and acted invisible, until she was able to take their little cousin and slink away.

Kitty frantically imagined how Lydia would have handled this. She then smiled and tried to look coquettish. "We need some dancing so that it will be more lively here."

Mr. Goodman looked impassively at her. "Is that your idea of liveliness – to dance?"

"Yes. Dancing is an excellent form of exercise." Kitty stumbled to say anything coherent. "Exercise is good; it puts color in ladies' faces even without cosmetics."

He started to grin at her.

"And dancing is not boring. Dancing is how gentlemen and ladies become acquainted."

"Would you not learn more about me from my conversation?"

Increasingly nervous, Kitty found herself babbling. "Oh. Oh, yes. Conversation while dancing. We could discuss the dance. We could discuss – discuss the next dance, and the ladies' dresses. And we could discuss the other dancers."

He chuckled. "I see that my life as a curate is indeed very boring. Perhaps I should tell you about my visits to prisoners – those in Fleet Prison, Marshalsea, King's Bench – does that sound boring to you?"

Kitty turned red with embarrassment. "No, sir," she whispered.

"I do not mean to chasten you," he said quickly. "I was only teasing. I enjoy talking with you and the other guests of the Gardiners. A minister should be aware of the needs of others – members of the parish, and those living in the area. When I visit the prison, I am not being paid to visit; it is just something I feel is right. I am sorry if you felt I was lecturing you."

"I do not mind," she said, as she looked at the floor. "My father says my sister Lydia and I must be two of the silliest girls in the country. Although Lydia is now in Spain with her husband, an officer, so I suppose that means I alone am the silliest girl in the country."

His heart sank with sympathy. "Please forgive me. I would never call you silly."

"I am trying to improve myself," she said, looking up at him. "My brother Darcy is sending me to school so I can learn."

The curate knew what subjects were taught in ladies' seminaries, but there was no better alternative for women. "I am sure you are an excellent student," he assured her. Privately, he thought it was good that she was away from her father's hurtful words, and he admired her for her spirit and strength.

The rest of their conversation was pleasant, as he made amends for his initial remarks. He complimented her on her rose-pink shawl – "a very nice colour with your hair," asked about the dances she was learning, and listened to her fears for Lydia's safety in Spain.

Unknown to him, Kitty believed he despised her for being stupid. *From now on*, she thought, *whenever I see him, I will be polite – but no more.*

The second time he met the Bennet sisters was an improvement, Mr. Goodman thought. He said nothing hurtful, and Miss Kitty was polite. He asked Miss Mary Bennet to play the piano so there could be dancing, but Miss Kitty unfortunately had a headache that day and could not dance. He and Miss Darcy played with the Gardiner children as Miss Kitty sewed something that resembled a flower for a hat. He peeked at her every so often and she peeked at him, but never at the same time.

~*~*~*~

September 1812 – Mayfair, London

At Darcy House, Georgiana had her own separate establishment – a suite befitting an adult with bedroom, dressing room, and sitting room. Mary was content with just a bedroom, as Georgiana's sitting room was large enough for them to share. With her companion, Mrs. Annesley, and Mary for company, Georgiana was no longer lonely. She finally had a friend who loved music as much as she did.

Signor Peppino had taught Georgiana for four years and worked for many good families in Town. Mary watched the lesson, impressed by the man's patience and talent, but intimidated by her friend's advanced music skills.

"Come, Miss Bennet, it is your turn," the music master said. "Do not be nervous. I do not expect you to be perfect on your first lesson."

He had her play a movement from her favorite piece and then sing. She soldiered on, experienced in being mocked by her younger sisters. But Georgiana only smiled encouragingly at her. Mary finished and stoically looked at Signor Peppino.

"Young lady, you cannot sing, not even with many music masters. But you can play the piano, and you can accompany those who sing. No shame in that. Handel did not sing, Mozart did not sing, Beethoven does not sing – I have friends in Vienna who know him and they say he has lost his hearing. But these composers all created beautiful music, and so will you. I will teach you to sing with your fingers."

It was the nicest thing anyone had ever said to Mary about her playing, and Mrs. Annesley wrote to the Darcys about it. "Your sister improves daily. She and Miss Darcy play duets, or Miss Bennet accompanies Miss Darcy as she sings. I have never seen Miss Darcy smile so much, now that she has a friend."

As for Signor Peppino, he was used to teaching lazy students and withholding his criticism for fear of losing wealthy clients. But these two girls worked hard, and he enjoyed seeing their progress.

~*~*~*~

September 1812 – Rosings, Kent

Lady Catherine summoned her younger brother to her home. Other sisters might invite a brother, but she was arrogant enough to summon him, despite his being the Earl of Matlock, a respected member of the House of Lords. To her, he would always be an insolent spoiled child. He knew this, which is why he never saw his sister unless it was urgent, as he suspected this was.

"Brother, your nephew Darcy has left my Anne in an intolerable situation. She is the heiress of Rosings, descended from a respectable, honourable, and ancient – though untitled – family. Yet I have learned of no decent gentlemen in Town who are worthy to marry her."

"You mean you have found no gentleman willing to let you reign over Rosings while he takes your daughter far away to his own family home," the Earl said drily. Unlike his sister, he'd always seen Anne for what she was – a fragile and quiet woman whose entire life, from cradle to now, had been dominated by an overbearing mother. The Earl guessed that Sir Lewis de Bourgh – a spendthrift baronet – had married Catherine only for her dowry of 30,000 pounds, which is what Anne would inherit if her mother's claws could ever be pried from it.

"I am only looking out for my only child. I could never trust a man to care for her inheritance as diligently as I would."

"Not even Darcy?"

Lady Catherine glared at him. "You know the girl Darcy married is the cousin of my own rector, Mr. Collins. She has no dowry. So unsuitable a match I have never seen in this family."

"Is this the urgent reason you called me here? To complain about our nephew's wife?"

-

"I need to find my daughter a husband who meets my expectations. Your son will do."

The Earl choked.

"Not the Viscount, of course; a pity that his wife's dowry was so small."

"Her dowry was 10,000 pounds and an estate the size of Rosings."

"Exactly! My Anne has 20,000 pounds more than the Viscountess." Lady Catherine looked smug.

"But could Anne have borne two healthy sons? She cannot even sit at a piano."

His sister could only look away. "Your son Richard is not the nephew I had wanted for Anne, but he is available. Bring him here."

"He is not a horse, Catherine! He is a colonel who has served his country well."

"Does he have another heiress waiting to marry him, or does he wish to return to the war?"

Now it was the Earl's turn to look away. "I will have him here tomorrow," he muttered.

~*~*~*~

Hunsford Parsonage, near Rosings, Kent

Mrs. Collins was surprised to see Anne de Bourgh and her driver stopping in her low phaeton outside the parsonage. She hurried to meet her.

"Miss de Bourgh, it is a pleasure to see you. Mr. Collins is out visiting tenants..."

"I came to visit with you, Mrs. Collins, if that would be welcome."

"Of course! Please come in." Charlotte helped the thin, small woman into the cottage, where she set out biscuits and began making tea. It was rare that Miss de Bourgh entered the Parsonage, but she did on occasion.

There were a few minutes of awkward silence as both ladies wondered who should speak first – the hostess, or the daughter of Mr. Collins' patroness. Had Mr. Collins been there, he would have filled the void with endless words of great bombast and little sense.

"I hope I am not being inquisitive," Anne said hesitantly, "But I am curious as to how you and Mrs. Darcy first became friends."

"I was seven years old when she was born, but she was always a bright and lively child," Charlotte reminisced. "Even at an early age, she could discuss literature and history with me, and I enjoyed hearing her sing. A true friend is good to find regardless of any difference in age. Our parents were neighbors and friends, so it was natural that my sisters and I became friends with the Bennet girls."

"That sounds delightful." There was another awkward pause. "Am I presuming too much in asking if you and I might be neighbors who become friends, Mrs. Collins?"

If Mr. Collins were present, he would have been in raptures about the great honour. Still, Charlotte's compassion saw that Miss de Bourgh had no friends; with no siblings and only rare visits from her cousins, the heiress of Rosings must have a lonely life.

"I would be delighted to be your friend. Please, call me Charlotte."

"Then you may call me Anne, but only when we are alone – especially if my mother or Mr. Collins may hear us."

They both smiled.

"You and I are both gentlewomen; so far we are equal. May I tell you a secret, Charlotte?"

"Yes, and I will never tell anyone without your permission." Charlotte hesitated, then held out her little finger. Anne looked puzzled, so Charlotte took her hand and hooked their little fingers together. "Make friends, make friends, never ever break friends; if you do you'll catch the flu and that will be the end of you."

Anne was stunned, and then she began laughing. "Is this something that children do when they make promises?"

"It is something that friends do. Mrs. Darcy and I did this often as children, especially if it was something we did not want our mothers or siblings to know."

"Then I will tell you a secret, my friend. I admire Mrs. Darcy, and I would like to be a little more independent, as she is. I know she walked alone at Rosings, so today, I went for a ride without Mrs. Jenkinson. I am twenty-eight years of age; it is time that I do things by myself."

"Well done, Anne!"

"And today, I am learning to make friends."

Another friend Mrs. Collins gained was Colonel Fitzwilliam, who seemed lost at Rosings without his cousin Darcy.

"I am curious how Darcy will change now that he is a married man," the Colonel said the next day, when he escorted Anne to the Parsonage. "Mrs. Collins, have you heard from Mrs. Darcy? What are the newlyweds doing at Pemberley?"

Charlotte related a story from her last letter. "It seems Mr. Darcy wanted to see her ride a horse, so she said she would take the horse for a walk – by herself. He could not resist checking on her, but he found Eliza walking beside the horse instead of on the horse."

The Colonel and Anne laughed.

"Yes, Mr. Darcy laughed as well," Charlotte said. "He tried to be stern with her but you know Eliza – she gave him an impertinent look that made him laugh even more. Her father could never discipline her because of those eyes."

"Such teasing looks would not work in the army, nor with Lady Catherine," said the Colonel. He turned to Anne. "Perhaps Mrs. Darcy can teach you other tricks to turn your mother up sweet."

"It helps that Eliza defends her opinions with great conviction. I remember when she first met Lady Catherine, who said that Eliza gives her opinion 'very decidedly for so young a person.' When Mr. Collins..." Charlotte hesitated, then continued. "When Mr. Collins proposed marriage to Eliza, she refused despite her mother's insistence and threats. Fortunately for me, he turned his attentions quickly and proposed to me three days later."

Anne and the Colonel were amazed.

"Well done, Mrs. Darcy! I am impressed with her courage," said the Colonel. He turned to Anne. "Can you imagine doing that?"

Anne wanted him to admire her. *Could I be that brave with my own mother*, she wondered. "Yes, I can imagine that."

Both ladies saw clearly that Colonel Fitzwilliam admired Elizabeth Darcy, but Charlotte had no idea this would plant seeds of rebellion, courage, and independence in Anne.

As they played cards and ate tea cakes, the Colonel continued to ask Mrs. Collins for stories, including childhood tales of Mrs. Darcy and Mrs. Collins as mischievous scamps – "oh, no, it was Eliza who corrupted me."

Anne enjoyed the stories too, and asked the Colonel to escort her to the Parsonage the next several days until he had to return to his army duties in Town. Charlotte demonstrated her skills in secret-keeping by sending Mr. Collins on errands, so he never knew his humble cottage had been frequently visited by Miss de Bourgh herself.

~*~*~*~

Rosings House, Kent

Colonel Richard Fitzwilliam was not handsome, but he was a well-bred man who was confident, sociable, and able to bring others easily into conversations. He was always patient with his Aunt Catherine, and kind to his cousin.

"Anne, my father told me nothing. Do you know why your mother wanted me here?" he asked when they were alone in the library, while his father and aunt argued about something. "I was just here at Easter, and she has never before wished to see me more than once a year."

"Mother wants you to marry me, now that Darcy has wed Miss Bennet. He made the right choice; she is spirited enough for him."

He said nothing. He never offered her meaningless statements, lies, promises of false hopes, or compliments about talents she did not have; it was one of many reasons Anne loved him. But she knew he was a man with physical needs, and she was aware that she could never withstand the rigors of childbirth, even if her mother was in denial.

"I want you to tell my mother that you and I will have a long engagement of a peculiar kind, because I do not want her to look for another husband for me. I do not ever want to marry."

"But how long could we put off our wedding?"

"Darcy is now twenty-eight; he put off marrying me for six years. We can learn from his example." This was as bold as Anne could be for now; this did not require her to confront her fearsome mother – the Colonel would do all the talking. But she hoped he would admire her as he admired Eliza Darcy.

It seemed to work. His father and her mother were pleased at the supposed engagement, and they agreed that the announcement and wedding could wait until the

Season, when Darcy could attend. Richard knew he would have to visit Pemberley at Christmas to beg Darcy to not travel to Town for the Season.

Meanwhile, as long as he and his father were at Rosings during hunting season, they hunted for birds, deer, and hares; it was how the Earl had lured his son into coming to the hag's house.

"How did you like last night's entertainment, Father? I asked my aunt to invite the Collinses for dinner, so that you could see Mr. Collins grovel."

"I do not tolerate toad-eaters, but this Collins is amazingly quick with his compliments, never repeating himself despite hours of endless flattery. I can see why my sister chose him."

"His fawning is somewhat understandable, as there are far more churchmen than livings and the man had no connections. Now he is cousin to Darcy."

"I still cannot believe he is Mr. Bennet's cousin, and that he wanted to marry Elizabeth. She would have eaten him alive for breakfast."

They laughed loudly.

"What if he applies to my nephew for the living at Kympton?"

"I think Darcy will find a more suitable candidate. Father, did you observe how Mrs. Collins skillfully maneuvered her husband? She spends little time with him, sending him to work on his sermons or in his garden, encouraging him to visit tenants, or telling him to visit Aunt Catherine to see if she has need of his encouragement."

The Earl chuckled. "His poor wife must tolerate him long enough to produce the Longbourn heir, but there may be no spare. Still, I admire her practicality in marrying him, and I am glad you are practical enough to accept your own match with Anne. It is best for you both, as now we have no worries about her marrying a fortune-hunter."

The Colonel was silent about the match; it was a tactic he had often observed Darcy use. Every Easter, they visited Rosings. Darcy would say nothing and let Aunt Catherine assume what she wished, then leave.

As for Mrs. Collins, the Colonel was not a good judge of women's emotions, but he knew good character – and he recognized Mrs. Collins as a strong woman, trustworthy and practical.

I do not know when I have been more shocked. It is almost past belief.– Pride and Prejudice, Chapter 40

PART THREE: BROKEN ILLUSIONS

October 1812 – Darcy House, Mayfair, London

Mary and Georgiana had both been lonely girls with no friends their age, and their shared fondness for music gave them common ground with each other. The new friends also loved reading from the Darcy House library, although Georgiana assured Mary that the Pemberley library was even larger.

At Longbourn, Mary had access to her father's library, but she was the middle child. Her older sisters had grabbed the poetry, Shakespeare, and Milton collections; her younger sisters hogged the novels. This had left Mary with books on conduct, philosophy, and religion. Mr. Bennet was not interested in buying new books on religion or conduct, so those tomes in his library had been obtained by previous masters of Longbourn. For example, *Fordyce's Sermons to Young Women* were published in 1766, when Mr. Bennet was a child; his grandfather had bought them for his daughter-in-law – Mr. Bennet's mother – who never read them. Mary thought they were a family treasure because they were a gift from her great-grandfather to her grandmother.

At Darcy House, Georgiana and Mary had masters who suggested courses of reading; these volumes were then placed together for reference and convenience in the library. Georgiana, Mrs. Annesley, and her new literature master were now exposing Mary to Shakespeare, Robert Burns, William Wordsworth, and more modern writers. *The next time I see Lizzy or our father, we may have some books in common to discuss,* Mary thought, although she doubted her father would ever take time with her.

Darcy's longtime family solicitors had made the arrangements to rent the house in Ramsgate. After the Ramsgate debacle, the Johnsons had found, interviewed, and recommended Mrs. Annesley. Since then, old Mr. Johnson – who had known the Darcy family even longer than Mrs. Reynolds – checked on Georgiana whenever her brother was out of town. "She is like my godchild," he said to his son, but he would never presume such familiarity with the Darcys. He knew he was only a mere tradesman.

On occasion, old Mr. Johnson would send his son to make sure everything was well at Darcy House. Mr. Daniel Johnson was his father's clerk, so he knew about Mr. Wickham's failed attempt to elope with Miss Darcy. He had also helped prepare the marriage settlements for Mr. Darcy and Miss Elizabeth Bennet, Mr. Bingley and Miss Jane Bennet, and Captain Carter and Miss Lydia Bennet.

"Are you interested in reading religious topics?" young Mr. Johnson asked on one visit, after noticing Mary's copy of *Fordyce's Sermons* on her shelf in the library.

"Oh. Yes, although I do not read religious books exclusively." Mary had almost forgotten the book was there; she had been reading so many new books

"Of course not. I expect you must occupy yourself in the actual doing of good deeds, not merely reading of them. My father says Lady Anne was like that; he has told me many tales of Lady Anne's work with the poor. What sort of charitable works are you involved in?" He thought he was making polite conversation, expecting all the ladies of Darcy House to be of a similar nature.

"Oh, I – ahh –" Mary was flustered. She had never helped orphans or visited the sick because Meryton did not have any hospitals or workhouses, although she sometimes went with Lizzy to deliver soup and medicine to sick tenants. Only now did she wonder who would make those deliveries, with all five Bennet girls gone and Mrs. Bennet interested only in fashion, gossip, and her friends. Mary had thought of herself as virtuous, and now she was realizing she was a mere hypocrite – all talk, no action.

"Miss Bennet has not had time to become involved in charities, as she is still new in Town. Her family is from Meryton, as you know," Georgiana interjected.

"Then would you be interested in helping with the same charities that Lady Anne sponsored? I would be happy to assist you."

The ladies were eager to hear about Georgiana's mother. Mr. Johnson described each charity that Lady Anne Darcy had sponsored in London, Lambton, and Kympton. He knew the names of her friends who were still active, and the charities that received donations from Mr. Darcy each year.

"I did not know my brother did this."

"Perhaps he was waiting until your come-out, Miss Darcy. Helping the less fortunate is a privilege, my mother always said."

"'No act of kindness, no matter how small, is ever wasted.'"

"Aesop's fable about the lion and the mouse. Excellent quote, Miss Bennet," he said, as Mary blushed at the compliment. "My own favorite quote is, 'The only thing necessary for the triumph of evil is for good men to do nothing.' Edmund Burke was a Whig statesman from Ireland; I admire him greatly."

Mrs. Annesley said she would look in the Darcy House library for Burke's writings; she was certain Mr. Darcy owned several volumes but did not know whether they were at Pemberley or London. The rest of the clerk's visit passed by without Mary feeling further embarrassment.

Mr. Johnson came by the next week to take them – and two burly footmen – on a tour of several workhouses and the Foundling Hospital. Mary and Georgiana were impressed by the work and the need, and immediately asked Mrs. Annesley to help them become volunteers with those charities; at the least, they could sew clothes for orphans.

Mary also enjoyed dancing lessons. Georgiana or Mrs. Annesley played the piano as the dance master danced with Mary. When she needed to learn a dance that had two couples, young Mr. Johnson came by to help, pairing with Georgiana. He was slight in build and studious in appearance; he was not a man who would catch your attention unless you spoke to him and discovered he was very intelligent.

While Mary enjoyed having Georgiana as her friend, there were times she liked her privacy. One day when Georgiana and Mrs. Annesley had an errand, Mary stayed home. Thanks to hearing Georgiana's voice lessons with Signor Peppino, Mary now recognized her vocal deficiencies. She still loved to sing, so today she was happily singing alone for her own pleasure. She was in the middle of "Joy to the World" – even though it was not Christmas – when she heard a floorboard squeak.

Mary stopped singing and snapped her head to see the doorway. "Mr. Johnson! What are you doing here?"

"I am returning from a delivery to the Old Bailey courthouse and decided to stop by to see if all is well with you and Miss Darcy."

"Oh. Yes, we are both well. Miss Darcy and Mrs. Annesley are at the dressmaker's. Would you care for tea?" She shut the fallboard over the piano keys and stood in embarrassment.

"Please do not stop singing. I enjoy hearing carols and hymns sung with enthusiasm."

"My music master says that I cannot sing."

Mr. Johnson paused thoughtfully. "Your voice is weak, but this is not a large room with a large audience. I say your voice is adequate. If singing brings you pleasure, then you should sing. My own voice and manner are not adequate for a courtroom so I have not sought to become a barrister, but I am more than capable of conducting a negotiation in an office."

"You are only being polite, sir."

"I would never lie to you," he said solemnly.

She pondered his words, then sat at the piano and resumed playing and singing. But now that she had an audience, she used a different vocal style – stiff, unnatural, exaggerated, showy.

He stood by the keyboard and raised his hand, signaling her to stop. "Please, use your natural voice – the way you sang before you knew I was here."

Mary thought of what people in Meryton had said about Lizzy's singing – "pleasing, though by no means excellent." She herself had tried to be excellent to make up for being the plainest Bennet daughter, yet this man was saying that her idea of excellence was wrong.

"If that is what you want, I will comply," she finally said. She began the song, singing as if she were alone. To her surprise, he joined in on the chorus. Both of their voices were less than stellar, but together, they seemed to fill in each other's weak spots.

She still believed that he was only humouring her. *Mr. Darcy must pay him a great deal*, she thought.

When young Mr. Johnson had met Miss Mary Bennet, he noticed all the books she had on her bookshelf. He had heard her practicing at the piano. *She is very well-read, and she works hard at her accomplishments,* he thought. He had seen her struggle with dancing lessons, but she never gave up. He admired her tenacity.

He greatly respected the Darcy family, known widely for their charity and impeccable reputation. He had been intrigued by Mr. Darcy's marriage to Miss Elizabeth Bennet, the daughter of a gentleman, the granddaughter and niece of solicitors, and niece of a tradesman. He also knew of Mr. Darcy's friendship with Mr. Bingley, a tradesman's son.

He wondered what Mr. Darcy would think of him – a law clerk training to become a solicitor – as a possible suitor for Miss Mary Bennet. Would Mr. Darcy think a law clerk was being presumptuous? The new Mrs. Darcy was one step removed from her tradesman roots, and Mr. Bingley would become a landed gentleman as soon as he bought an estate with his wealth, but a solicitor would always be a tradesman, one class below the gentry.

"If we loved each other, would that be enough for her parents and Mr. Darcy?" he whispered to himself.

~*~*~*~

October 1812 – Gardiners' home in Cheapside, London

The curate was still trying to draw out Miss Kitty in conversation. He thought she was afraid he would mock her as her father had, so he tried to add humor in their conversation.

"When you spoke just now with your Aunt Gardiner, you seemed excited about something. What is it?" he asked.

"In school, I am going to start learning how to prepare for Court presentation. I am eligible to apply because my father is a gentleman. We have practice gowns, and ostrich feathers for our hair."

"Ahh, you will learn how to curtsy in a hoop skirt and walk backward with a long train," he said with a smile. "Why is this important to you?"

"Being presented at court means I will be recognized as a member of society with all the privileges attending," she said, obviously reciting what she had been taught in school.

He grinned. "Just be sure you do not drop your flowers or trip on your train."

Her smile faded and she walked away, even as he tried to apologize for being a dunderhead. *Of course, it sounded like I think she will fail!* He knew he had hurt her feelings, but she avoided him the rest of the visit so he could not apologize, and an unmarried man could not send a letter to an unmarried woman. How would he ever know her well enough to see if she would accept a lowly curate as a suitor? He did not have enough money to marry now, but one day that would change, if she was willing to wait for him.

As for Kitty herself, she did not want to talk to her sisters or aunt or schoolmates about her feelings. *One day, I would like a husband who is not afraid of my being poor or silly*, she thought. But there was only one Mr. Darcy, and he was Lizzy's husband.

~*~*~*~

October 1812 – Hunsford Parsonage, near Rosings, Kent

"Charlotte, may I tell you another secret? This one is very serious."

Charlotte smiled and held out her little finger to Anne. The close friends recited their vow, to "never ever break friends" – never break each other's confidences.

Anne gathered her courage. "My cousin, Colonel Fitzwilliam, and I have told our parents that we are engaged. But the truth is: we are not engaged. It was my idea, because I do not want my mother to find me a husband."

"Are you interested in another man?"

"No. I will never marry; I could not survive childbirth."

Charlotte felt sad. "You have a home, but I cannot bear to think of you alone all your life, with no brothers and sisters, no husband or children."

"I have you as my friend, and I want to leave my estate to the Colonel. One day, when my mother is dead and I am truly free to be mistress of Rosings, he may resign his commission and live here with his wife and children. Then I will not be alone."

"He and your mother do not know your intentions?"

Anne nodded. "The colonel and I are cousins, and we have only ever looked at each other as cousins. He deserves a love match."

~*~*~*~

Christmas 1812 – Pemberley, Derbyshire

Kitty, Mary, and Georgiana enjoyed the carriage ride north from London to Derbyshire. They had stopped by Longbourn to deliver small gifts and pick up a basket of Lizzy's favorite mince pies.

When Mrs. Bennet saw their escort, Colonel Fitzwilliam, she gave Kitty a wink and a nudge. "He is an unmarried officer," she reminded her daughter, again.

Mr. and Mrs. Bennet would not be alone for the holiday; the Bingleys were leaving Scarborough and would stay at Netherfield until the Season began in London.

Kitty and Mary were goggle-eyed at everything they saw on their first trip to the East Midlands, their first stay at an inn, their first look at the Peaks. The Colonel and Mrs. Annesley smiled as Georgiana became her friends' tour guide, talking excitedly as she shared her love for her home county. She was no longer the shy, withdrawn girl from earlier this year.

Mr. and Mrs. Darcy were happy to have three girls and the Gardiners at Pemberley. They had plans for many activities with all their guests, but Darcy still took time in his library to meet with his cousin on business.

"You agreed to marry our cousin Anne?" Darcy was incredulous. "If I had known you wanted her, you could have spared me years of pressure from our aunt."

"Anne said that she does not ever want to marry, and she too wishes to avoid her mother's pressure. This is only a ruse Anne devised on her own, modeled after your own delay tactics."

"Elizabeth and I had planned to go to Town in February for the Season. You need to create another way to postpone your imaginary wedding. I must remind you of the bard's warning – 'what a tangled web we weave, when first we practice to deceive.' Things may become more complicated than if you and Anne tell the truth."

"Please, Darcy – just give us a few months to think of a way. You know what my father and her mother are like."

Darcy hesitated. "Very well. We shall postpone our trip until April. But I will not participate in deceiving your father, and you shall have to tell my wife yourself."

The Colonel agreed.

Darcy felt he understood why Anne had no wish to marry. *She must realize she is not physically capable of childbearing*, he thought. As for her hopes and dreams, he had no clue if she even had any.

~*~*~*~

February 1813 – London

Kitty's school was in Queen's Square, Bloomsbury, less than three miles from Gracechurch Street. Like her sisters, she was accustomed to walking freely; little Meryton had fewer than 3,000 residents, and everyone knew each other. Some of the other students were also from the country, so they walked together to shop on their afternoons off, escorted by school matrons.

On this particular day, she wanted to buy some ribbon to make a rose for her hat. Several girls had returned from the Christmas holiday with new dresses and hats, and Kitty had been inspired. She decided to go to a particular store that all the schoolgirls liked, make the purchase, and quickly return to school. Some of the older girls often sneaked away for hours; it was perfectly safe – or so she thought. The school's teachers warned that ladies should never walk alone in London. But Kitty did not have a maid or a sister to go with her, and her friends at school were too lazy to walk that far. In Meryton, Kitty sometimes walked alone to Lucas Lodge; Lizzy was famous for walking alone everywhere. *Lizzy walked alone three miles to Netherfield, so I can walk alone three miles to a shop*, Kitty thought.

She arrived safely at the store and approached the clerk for assistance.

"I want rose-pink ribbon. I am learning how to make ribbon-roses at Ladies' Eton School. My sister says this is a good color for girls my age. She is Mrs. Darcy of Pemberley, and they have a house in Grosvenor Square." Kitty thought she would get more attention by mentioning the Darcy name. She was correct: the clerk suddenly became very accommodating and helpful, eager to show her more.

"I recognize you from your past visits with the Ladies' Eton School girls; such lovely girls," the clerk said politely. "This gold lace is from Belgium – very elegant, perfect for a ball gown for this Season. It is difficult to get things from the Continent due to the war, you know. For you, this lace is only 20 shillings."

Had Mr. Goodman been present, he would have stared at the price. Twenty shillings was a week's pay for a curate!

"I shall ask my aunt to get it for me when I next visit her," Kitty said loftily, pretending that 20 shillings was nothing to her. She looked longingly at the lace before getting distracted by other items in the store, which had greater selection than the few stores in Meryton. While the clerk assembled a selection of ribbons in different shades of rose-pink, Kitty touched bolts of fine silks, velvets, and brocades; ostrich feathers; spools of satin ribbons; and pieces of lace, but it was the one card of gold lace that kept drawing her attention. It looked like it was made of threads of real gold. She was nervous because there was a man in the store who kept looking at her.

The clerk finally gathered a selection of ribbons for her review. Kitty made her choice, but as the clerk cut her piece of ribbon and wrapped her package, Kitty went to take one last glance at the gold lace. She was interrupted when the clerk called out, "I am done, Miss." So Kitty took her package and returned to her school safe and unmolested. She thought she could easily describe the lace to her Aunt Gardiner; it was the only card of gold lace in the store, and having it would make her feel like a duchess, not that she had ever seen a duchess.

A few days later, Kitty was in Newgate Prison, charged with grand larceny – a hanging offense.

She was distraught. Kitty knew she needed help, but neither her parents nor married sisters were in Town. On the rather dubious and unsolicited advice of some of the women with her in the cell, she wrote short notes to her Uncle Philips, Sir William Lucas, and her sister Mary, asking for their help and confidentiality – something she would come to regret.

Chapter footnote: the "tangled web" quote is from Canto VI. Stanza 17, of Marmion, published in 1808, written by Sir Walter Scott.

No lace. No lace, Mrs. Bennet, I beg you!– Pride and Prejudice, 1995 BBC mini-series

PART FOUR: LACE AND LOOSE THREADS

February 1813 – London

There had been a nervous tension in Darcy House ever since the messenger had arrived from Newgate with Kitty's note to Mary. Mary could only stare speechlessly at the note, so Mrs. Annesley had taken it from her to read. She then ordered a basket packed with food, water, medicines, and blankets; sent a note to summon Mr. Johnson to Newgate; and efficiently bundled up Mary and Georgiana to visit Kitty and find out what happened.

Mrs. Annesley did not want to expose her employer's sister, or sister-in-law Mary, to the filth and disease of the prison, but his sister-in-law Kitty was already imprisoned there. Mrs. Annesley did not know Kitty well and doubted her own presence would be as comforting as Mary's and Georgiana's. Had Mary or Georgiana said they wanted to stay in Darcy House or the carriage, she would have gladly let them, but the girls wanted to visit Kitty. Mrs. Annesley could only guess what Mr. Darcy would say, but she did bring several muscular footmen for protection.

It was the ladies' first time inside Newgate, and it was everything they and their footmen had feared. Kitty had to wear the filthy rags issued by the prison, until Mrs. Annesley paid the money so Kitty could wear her own clothes. The cells were redolent with sweat, exhalations, urine, and excrement, and were overcrowded with convicted and untried prisoners together. In the darkness, relieved by only one small high window, some women and children were sleeping naked on the floor, as they had no clothes or bedding, not even furniture. One woman looked ready to give birth on the floor. The convicted prisoners had plenty of horror stories to frighten the sheltered girl from Meryton – "behave or they will whip you in public!" By the time Mrs. Annesley arrived with Mary and Georgiana, Kitty was shaking with terror and cold, as the cells had no fire for heating.

"I stole away from school last week to buy ribbon and when I returned, I found the lace in my bag," Kitty sobbed hysterically. "When I could get away from school again, I walked back to the shop to return the lace, but before I could say anything the man asked if I had paid for it. I told him no, and he brought me before the magistrate, and then I was taken here. I must stay until the trial, unless somebody can post bail for me. I had to pay my last three shillings for the entry fee, I have no more money, and my jail rent is due next week! The next quarter-sessions are not until the end of March.

"Please, Mary, do not tell the Gardiners – they would tell our parents, Mama would tell Aunt Philips, and everyone in Meryton would know, just like when Lydia ran off with Wickham. And then that horrible Mr. Collins would come to condole with us. Only Mr. Darcy can help me; you remember how he helped Lydia – her husband thanked Mr. Darcy over and over for everything he did for them."

Georgiana listened wide-eyed. *The girls are afraid of telling their parents? Their own mother and aunt revealed Lydia's trip with Wickham?* She was thankful again for her brother.

Both Mr. Johnsons arrived and were introduced to Kitty. The solicitor shook his head regretfully. "I am sorry, but the judge was deaf to our pleas and refused our request for bail."

"Not even for Mr. Darcy? His uncle is an Earl!"

"But Mr. Darcy is not yet here to intervene."

"He is coming, but it will take at least four days, Miss Catherine," Mrs. Annesley said reassuringly, "if the weather allows."

Kitty cried even louder, holding Mary tightly like a lifeline.

The Johnsons had to excuse themselves, as they had more work to do. "May we escort you ladies outside?"

"Mary, please stay with me!"

Mary looked at the younger Mr. Johnson and thought of the scripture about visiting those in prison. She also remembered James 2:17: *Faith, if it hath not works, is dead.* She took a deep breath and gathered her resolve. "I will stay with you, Kitty."

The Johnsons, Georgiana, and Mrs. Annesley gasped. "Are you certain, Mary?"

"Yes. I will not let my sister stay alone in this dreadful place." Mary looked at Georgiana. "I would stay here with you, if you were in this cell."

But after the sisters were left in the locked cell with strangers, they cried. Utterly alone, they feared asking of their cellmates any information – such as whether they had been brought in for being thieves or prostitutes, or even worse.

Meanwhile, Mrs. Gardiner had a visit in her Cheapside home from the headmistress of Kitty's school.

"Ma'am, we are fortunate to have more than 200 pupils, but we noticed that your niece, Miss Bennet, is missing and has not been seen for hours. Do you know where she might be?"

Mrs. Gardiner immediately thought back to when Lydia nearly eloped with Wickham just months earlier. Even when they were children, Kitty had always followed Lydia's example, but would Kitty have eloped?

"I do not know where my niece is. May we speak with girls at your school who are her friends?"

"We have already done that, ma'am."

"They may be willing to speak more freely with another girl their age. Kitty's sister could interview them."

Georgiana sent her brother a note with the solicitor's express rider and looked worried, but back at Darcy House, Mrs. Annesley was sympathetic yet firm with her charge.

"My dear, I understand that Mary and Kitty are your friends, but should you not tell their family where they are?"

"Kitty and Mary begged me with their last words tonight."

"I know, but if I had a child who was missing, I would want to know where she is, even if she were in jail."

"My brother will take care of everything. I know it."

"Yes, but he will not be here for at least four days. Do you want the Bennets to worry until then? Perhaps their Uncle Gardiner could help; he is her guardian in Town. You met them at Pemberley last summer, and again at your brother's wedding."

Georgiana nodded uncertainly. She'd always relied on her brother, and she almost got in trouble last summer in Ramsgate because he wasn't there. *What if I decide to tell the Gardiners and it is the wrong decision? Or is it the right decision? Will the Gardiners be like my brother, or will they be like Mrs. Bennet and her sister Philips?*

Mrs. Annesley sat watching her charge, seeing her indecision and her desire to do the right thing. She did not know about Georgiana's younger years, but she sensed the girl was still unsure whether to trust her new companion. *Perhaps the previous companion did something wrong.* So she told herself to give Georgiana a little more time to decide, as it would be good experience for her to solve the problem. *If I must, I will tell the Gardiners myself and risk Mr. Darcy's anger.* She was older than the girls but she was only an employee.

The housekeeper knocked at the door. "Miss Bennet's aunt and uncle to see you on urgent business."

Mrs. Annesley turned to Georgiana, who she could see was still thinking. "If you were missing, I would tell all your family so they could help find you."

The Gardiners entered the room, looking worried. "Miss Darcy, please excuse us for the late visit, but we need to speak with Mary. It seems Kitty is missing from school."

"Kitty and Mary are in Newgate. Kitty is charged with stealing lace, and Mary is staying with her. It is a dreadful place!" Georgiana blurted out. As she realized what she had just done, she hoped they were truly as kind as she remembered from Pemberley.

It took several minutes for the Gardiners to recover from their shock and hear the information, but they did not condemn Kitty. "Some shopkeepers, more concerned with greed than honest commerce, make such accusations to get money for their silence. Kitty may have been a victim of such a swindler, or perhaps she simply accidentally walked out with the lace."

"But she came back to return the lace. If she had stolen it, why would she return?" Georgiana asked.

"The shopkeeper may accuse her of wanting to steal more. What matters to the judge will be the fact that she admitted to having lace she did not pay for; every thief who is caught insists it was an accident and wants to return the item. Kitty may think it a simple misunderstanding, but under the law, the theft of anything over one shilling is grand larceny, which you know is punishable by death or deportation."

"My brother can make this right, I know he can."

"We share your confidence, but until he arrives, we must give Kitty and Mary all the support that we can."

~*~*~*~

Newgate Prison

Georgiana insisted on accompanying the Gardiners to Newgate. She and Mrs. Annesley and several footmen brought more clothes, blankets, food, and medical supplies for Mary and Kitty, now that they had seen their accommodations and their cellmates.

As Georgiana had feared, Kitty was shocked to see her bring the Gardiners.

"I begged you to not tell them!" Kitty wailed. It perhaps was rude, but her school had not taught her any prison etiquette.

"We are afraid this could be met with behaviour similar to last summer when Lydia ran off with Wickham," Mary told the Gardiners.

"I remember," said Mrs. Gardiner. "Your parents were immobilized by shock, and gossip spread throughout Meryton. Everything would have been easier had Lydia's situation remained secret."

Mr. Gardiner had to shake his head. He and his wife – and Darcy – still kept many secrets from Lydia's near-elopement with Wickham, but Mr. Bennet was Kitty's father and it was necessary that he be told certain things.

"We are relieved to know where you are and that you are safe, if not comfortable," Mr. Gardiner said. "You might be out on bail within days, and there is little your father can do for you if he were told. But you are not yet of age. You, Kitty, could be ruined by the shopkeeper's accusation, and you might not be able to return to school, as all the other girls know you were missing. This incident could damage both your chances of a good marriage, and your lives might now be forever changed. I must tell your father, but I hope to wait until Mr. Darcy arrives in Town, when he can speak to his solicitors. With luck, Kitty might even have departed Newgate by then."

"Until he arrives, we shall pay your jail rent each week," Mrs. Gardiner assured them, "but we are certain Mr. Darcy will be here in only a few days to arrange bail. Now, what about telling the Bingleys – they might be in Town now."

The girls and their aunt looked around at the squalor of the cell and thought about how shocking Jane would find this.

"Not Jane," said Kitty. Even as young girls, she and Mary had known that certain secrets could be shared with Jane, but other secrets only with Lizzy. Newgate was a Lizzy-secret. Lydia could never keep a secret; she always slipped up and said something. *Jane would probably maintain that the shopkeeper was a dear man inclined to forgetfulness – hah!*

The Gardiners, and Georgiana and Mrs. Annesley – sometimes escorted by young Mr. Johnson – daily visited Kitty and Mary. They brought food from Gracechurch Street and Darcy House; otherwise, Kitty and Mary would have had only the prison ration of bread, and sometimes a bit of cheese and an onion. The girls shared their supplies with their cellmates, thus creating an uneasy peace.

The Gardiners also sent their parish's curate, Mr. Luke Goodman. On his first visit, he tried to encourage the Misses Bennet with scripture, but it was ineffective; all they wanted to know was when Mr. Darcy would arrive – when could he post bail for Kitty. By now, Mary had vowed to discard her comfortless copy of *Fordyce's Sermons*. Admonitions about "a sober mind and gentle manners" were of no help to women in Newgate.

The curate thought about how he would feel to be imprisoned. *In such a lonely place, I could use a friend,* he decided, and that is what he set out to be now.

"Would you like to talk about dancing, Miss Kitty?" he asked.

She looked at him and blinked.

"When you get out of here, I will be glad to dance with you. We can discuss the dance and the other dancers, and the amount of lace on ladies' dresses."

Kitty gasped in shock. "Lace!" she barely whispered. She did not know whether to cry or scold him for being offensive, but she certainly did not expect a curate to taunt her. She was in Newgate because of lace!

Mary noticed her sister's reaction to the word "lace" and was ready to give the curate a sour look.

"I mean to encourage you with thoughts of what you will do when you are free," he said, realizing that he had said the wrong thing.

Eventually, Kitty smiled faintly. "It is nice to have a visitor here with a friendly face."

"You and your family are friends. For you, I am unafraid of the dark and cold," he assured her, grateful for her quick forgiveness. He began a light conversation, such as the upcoming first concert of the Philharmonic Society of London; this led Mary to mention her favorite Beethoven symphony, and they discussed music for a while.

Kitty wondered about the war against Napoleon and how her sister Lydia was faring, but she decided the war was not a good topic in prison. *Mr. Goodman is so nice to Mary,* Kitty thought as she watched them. *He talks to her with respect. I wonder if he would ever speak that way with me.*

After he left, Kitty and Mary agreed that the curate was not at all like Mr. Collins, who had written to them after Lydia's near-elopement. "The death of your daughter would have been a blessing in comparison of this," Mr. Collins had said. No, Mr. Johnson was not as unfeeling as that.

"I think he visits because he pities me," Kitty decided.

"At least he is not being paid to visit," Mary said. "I am sure Mr. Johnson is coming because Mr. Darcy is paying him."

Mr. Johnson was not being paid by Mr. Darcy to visit Mary and Kitty in Newgate. Mr. Johnson came because he was worried about them; Newgate was a rough place, and it broke his heart that he and his father could not get them out on bail.

Yet each time he saw Miss Mary in the cell, he was impressed with the fact that she voluntarily stayed there to help Kitty. The sisters took turns sleeping so one would always be watching.

It was not proper for gentlemen to buy presents for unmarried ladies, but he could bring flowers. He brought large bouquets of strongly-scented flowers.

"These flowers will help you endure the stench," he said. He could not say anything that hinted of romantic feelings, as he did not have permission from Miss Bennet's family to court her. And he was acutely aware that he was a mere tradesman, even though Mr. Gardiner was also in trade.

On their second night in Newgate, Kitty and Mary were stunned when one of their cellmates gave birth on the floor. With no physician or midwife present, they did as much as they could to help. Now Kitty and Mary understood why Aunt Gardiner had left them with a small supply of cloths and blankets, string, scissors, and soap.

"Yous did sound as a pound," one woman told them afterwards. "We made wagers ed which o' yous would faint, but yous didn't."

"Thank you," said Mary. A compliment was a compliment.

"I do not think I want to return to school," Kitty later whispered to her sister. "Dancing and curtsying no longer seem important."

Neither of them found it necessary to state the obvious: if a girl or woman wished to be presented at court, she had to be of good moral and social character. With Kitty's arrest record, many in society would now consider that questionable.

~*~*~*~

Three days after Kittys' arrest — Pemberley, Derbyshire

The Darcys were busy doing things that newlyweds do behind locked doors when their housekeeper startled them with a sharp rapping.

"Mr. Darcy, an express has arrived," Mrs. Reynolds called through the library door. "He says it is from your solicitor, sir."

"In a moment," he said, as they quickly adjusted their dress. He knew his solicitor would not waste an express on anything trivial.

There were two notes, each dated two days ago. The Darcys could scarcely read Georgiana's, written in evident agitation.

"Brother, a shopkeeper claims Kitty stole a card of lace, but she says she does not know how it got in her bag. The magistrate sent her to Newgate, and Mary is staying with her to keep her company. They are both very frightened. Please come quickly."

Mr. Johnson's note was clearer but with no better news.

"Sir, we need your instructions. Miss Darcy says the Bennet girls beg us to not tell their family; we can advise you on this matter, but we cannot act further without your authorization. Because of our years of acquaintance and service to your family, we believe that you would post bail for your sister, Miss Catherine. We went to Newgate to try to post bail on your behalf, but we were denied."

Elizabeth looked distraught; it reminded Darcy of this past summer in Lambton, after she had learned of her sister Lydia's elopement.

"I will go alone. This should take only a few days, and then I will return to Pemberley."

"Because if you are in Town any longer, your Aunt Catherine might hear of it and insist you attend the wedding of Anne and the Colonel. I remember our promise to him," she said with a small smile. She liked the Colonel and had agreed they would stay at Pemberley until April; however...

"My dear William, you remember that I once trudged through three miles of mud to tend to a sister with a severe cold. Do you believe I would want to stay here in comfort while Kitty is in prison, where she could use the comfort of another sister?"

Darcy hesitated. "Many gentlemen would quake at visiting Newgate."

She gave him a sharp look.

"But not my Boudica," he said fondly.

"With you, I am stronger. How could I not remain with you in time of trouble, especially when this is for one of my sisters? We are married now, and my place is with you."

"For better, for worse," they said together as they embraced for a few moments. Then they set out to prepare for their journey.

Five days after Kitty's arrest – Longbourn, Meryton

Mr. Gardiner traveled to Meryton to inform Mr. Bennet of his daughters' stay in Newgate. He thought that Darcy might stop at Longbourn on his way to London, perhaps to leave Lizzy to comfort her mother; if so, it would not be fair to leave the task to the Darcys who knew little of Kitty's situation, having been in a carriage for two days with no information. But Mr. Gardiner timed his visit to Longbourn for the fourth day, so that the Darcys might arrive within hours of the news – instead of giving Mrs. Bennet (and her nerves) days to fret over everything.

The Bennets had actually been rather calm when Mr. Gardiner told them about the shopkeeper's accusation. They expected that he and Darcy would help Kitty just as they had helped Lydia. No one in Meryton knew of this, so there was no public disgrace, and Mr. Gardiner explained clearly – and repeatedly – that Kitty's secret must remain a secret.

Unfortunately, it appeared that a frightened Kitty had listened to her cellmates' advice and sent other letters before Mary and Georgiana had arrived. Mr. Gardiner sat in horror as many visitors arrived to "comfort" the Bennets. It was a nightmare.

"Kitty's letter said that I need to hire a barrister to plead her case. How much money can you afford?" asked Uncle Philips, a small-town solicitor who had never had a client charged with grand larceny. He was as useless now as he had been when Lydia ran off with Wickham.

"Attorneys owe their clients secrecy," Mr. Gardiner scolded him. "Kitty wrote to you in confidence."

"She is not old enough to hire me, and she has paid me nothing. She wrote to me as her uncle," Mr. Philips said defensively. "Besides, I only told my wife, who is Kitty's own beloved aunt."

"Of course my dear husband will be glad to testify on your daughter's behalf at her trial in March," said Lady Lucas. "Kitty wrote to him, saying she needed witnesses to attest to her good character."

"And perhaps I will then have the opportunity to visit the Court of St. James again. I understand Mr. Darcy's uncle is an Earl; perhaps I might meet the Earl there since we now have a connection," said Sir William Lucas.

"I also wrote to my daughter Charlotte, so that she might ask her husband's patroness to help your Kitty," added Lady Lucas, who had never met Lady Catherine or heard her low opinions of the Bennets. "Charlotte is a minister's wife – she knows how to keep confidences. I expect you will send food to Kitty in Newgate."

"Newgate?" Mrs. Bennet shrieked, then turned to her brother. "You said it was only a card of lace that she found in her bag. The shopkeepers in Meryton would never send anyone to Newgate for a bit of lace. Kitty is supposed to be in that fancy school!"

"Perhaps I was too delicate in my explanation," said Mr. Gardiner. "Kitty is being held in Newgate only until Mr. Darcy can arrange for her bail."

"Why did you not arrange for bail, brother?"

"Her request for bail was denied, but Mr. Darcy should have better connections."

"Bail was denied? Hill, Hill!" Mrs. Bennet called for her housekeeper, Mrs. Hill, in order that she might be fetched a calming medicine, probably something with brandy.

Into this chaos entered Mr. and Mrs. Darcy. With one disapproving glare, he cleared the room of visitors.

After Mr. Philips and the Lucases finally left, Mrs. Bennet took to her bed and moaned that they were all ruined.

Lizzy sat in her mother's bedroom, trying to calm her.

"I blame the school for not taking care of Kitty. And why is Mr. Darcy's sister not at the same school with her? Why is my Kitty not preparing for a Season in Town?"

"Georgiana has already finished her schooling, Mama. She will not be ready for a Season until she is eighteen."

"Lydia was out at fifteen!"

"Things are different in Town, Mama."

"Where are Jane and Mr. Bingley? He could help. He has money."

"They do not know what is happening; we have only found out ourselves from Uncle Gardiner. We can be in Town two hours after we leave here."

"Why can you not stay here with me, Lizzy? You selfish girl."

Lizzy was ready to pull out her hair. She had scant desire to remain here to feed her mother's need for attention, not when she had sisters in Newgate who needed real comfort.

Downstairs, Mr. Bennet had briefly been amused over the "fuss" for a bit of lace, but he became deeply concerned, not knowing if Mr. Darcy had a limit to his patience. He knew that it must have been expensive to outfit Major Carter and Lydia for their travel to the Spanish Peninsula, and Mr. Darcy's 10,000 pounds could only be stretched so far. He let his brother Gardiner lead the discussion.

Mr. Gardiner revealed to them everything he had learned about Kitty's case. Mr. Darcy believed his solicitors could resolve things legally, but the problem now was that the gossip had spread throughout Meryton and perhaps even Rosings.

"I must say, you truly love your wife, to rescue another sister," Mr. Bennet said to his son-in-law.

"Your daughter is worth everything to me. Besides, tribulations of this magnitude could have materialized for my own sister." He said no more on that matter.

Darcy promised that he would take care of the entire matter, and then he, Lizzy, and Mr. Gardiner left for London. In the privacy of a carriage, the three were able to discuss their next moves.

Meanwhile, Kitty's aunt, Mrs. Philips was already industriously spreading the news of Kitty's arrest to all the ladies of Meryton. It did not matter to her that this would harm her niece; in a boring town of fewer than 3,000 residents, any news had the potential for excitement. She had provided the same service after her niece Lydia had eloped. To Mrs. Philips, the word "confidentiality" meant "tell only one person at a time until everyone knows."

As for the Lucases, the news took on a more competitive nature. Mrs. Bennet and Lady Lucas had known each other since they were young tradesman's daughters in Meryton, both competing to win the attention of the Longbourn heir. Mrs. Bennet (née Gardiner) triumphed thanks to her youth, beauty, and exuberance – which had distracted Mr. Bennet from noticing her lack of intelligence, culture, and good taste. But Mrs. Lucas – a very good kind of woman – won points when her tradesman husband had been knighted by King George III himself, sometime after the monarch lost the American colonies and before his mental illness took him from the business of knighting tradesmen. If Mrs. Bennet was seen curtsying to Lady Lucas, it was perhaps a mere half of a half-inch, but it was enough to gall Mrs. Bennet.

Marriage had not ended their battle for preeminence. Lady Lucas had prevailed in the baby wars by producing several sons, while Mrs. Bennet produced only daughters. The latest salvo had been won by Lady Lucas, whose eldest daughter, Charlotte, married the current Longbourn heir after Elizabeth Bennet had emasculated him, butchering his ego and serving it like last night's pigeon pie.

Now that Mrs. Philips was spreading the gossip, it was clear that there was no longer any secrecy involved. Lady Lucas meant to ask all of Meryton to pray for Miss Kitty Bennet who was in Newgate. If someone did not know about it, Lady Lucas was only too sorry to be the bearer of bad tidings – or to embellish what they had heard from Mrs. Philips. "Yes, Mrs. Long, I said Newgate! She must be sharing a cell with murderers. Please tell your nieces about it so they can pray for Kitty."

Eventually, Mrs. Philips would tell her sister about this highly embroidered story, and Mrs. Bennet's nerves would be overcome, and Mr. Bennet's eardrums would suffer.

~*~*~*~

Five days after Kitty's arrest – London

Upon their arrival from Longbourn, Lizzy settled in at Darcy House, where she was apprised of where things now were. She then quickly decided to go with the others – and the robust footmen – to visit Kitty and Mary in Newgate.

Darcy and Uncle Gardiner went to his solicitor's office. Darcy was confident that he – as a well-connected member of the upper levels of society, whose uncle was an Earl – would be able to remove Kitty from Newgate, pay off the wounded shopkeeper, and make the problem go away. He hoped not to need help from his Uncle Matlock, as knowledge of his presence in Town would strip Anne and Colonel Fitzwilliam of their last excuse to delay their wedding.

Two days after the Darcys' arrival, Kitty was released on bail; Darcy would guarantee her appearance at the trial or else forfeit the money. He had also paid the departure fee from prison.

As soon as Mary and Kitty stepped out of Newgate, they breathed in fresh air, thanked their brother Darcy, and proceeded eagerly to Darcy House for baths, food, and a most welcome period of sleep after almost a week with little at all. But when they woke the next day, they discovered that their parents and all of Meryton had learned of what happened.

"Why did Uncle Gardiner tell my parents?" Kitty cried. "Did they truly need to know?"

"Yes, because you are not yet of age," Darcy explained. "Also, you foolishly wrote letters to your Uncle Philips and the Lucases, who visited Longbourn and disseminated the information in Meryton."

"Oh." Kitty felt embarrassed; so much had happened, she had forgotten writing those letters when she first arrived at Newgate and had heeded her cellmates' advice. "Where can I go now? I cannot go back to school."

"Where would you like to go?" Darcy asked in a gentler voice. "At Pemberley, no one knows of this incident, and your reputations are untarnished there. However, if you stay in Town, you can have access to music masters and any masters you wish; you may even attend concerts and the theatre, where you will be only one face in an entire audience. Remember that, in several years, with newer scandals forever erupting, society will forget that any of this happened, and your reputations here will recover. Your friends at school will be more concerned with their come-outs and their own first Seasons."

"But am I ruined?" Kitty whispered.

Darcy hesitated. "For now, perhaps. Always remember that one million persons live in London, and your name is not widely known."

"And the war against Napoleon should be more important than a silly bit of lace," Georgiana added.

Kitty smiled at Georgiana and patted her friend's hand. "I am envious of your good fortune; you have never been at risk of ruining your entire life as I have."

"But I have been at risk," Georgiana admitted. "I have made mistakes of my own. I almost ruined my life last summer when I was just fifteen, and only my brother saved me. Had someone not told him where to find me in Ramsgate, I would have eloped – with George Wickham." Georgiana now related to Mary and Kitty how her previous companion, Mrs. Younge, had conspired with Wickham to plan the elopement so he would have full control of her fortune. "My brother would have done anything to save me, just as he would for you. Somehow, our lives will not be ruined forever."

Mrs. Annesley suddenly understood her charge's cautious behavior. *How despicable, for a companion to want to steal 30,000 pounds from an orphaned fifteen-year-old girl!* Now Mr. Darcy's warnings had greater meaning – when he had hired her, he had expressed concern for his sister becoming a target for fortune-hunters. He had provided no details, but said enough so that she was not completely surprised by this revelation.

Mary and Kitty each grasped one of Georgiana's hands. "You truly are our sister. Including Lydia, the four of us were almost ruined and now are spared because of your brother," said Kitty.

"I am afraid that Mr. Wickham will appear and say something about me, and then no decent man would want to marry me," Georgiana said softly.

Kitty gasped and started digging through her reticule. She pulled out a letter and held it out to Georgiana. "Lydia wrote this from Portugal. She saw Wickham's body being buried."

Everyone except Mrs. Annesley was shaken. Georgiana could not look at the letter; she handed it to her brother.

Darcy read it silently, then aloud:

> As we retreated from Spain to Portugal, I walked past a burial site and spotted Wickham's body. I do not know how he died; perhaps he seduced an officer's wife and died on the husband's blade, or he deserted and was shot. I am glad I did not marry Wickham. I could have been a widow and stranded in Spain!

They were all silent for a few minutes, letting the news sink in.

"You no longer need fear Mr. Wickham," Lizzy said, as she and her husband embraced Georgiana.

"Lizzy, did you know about this business with Wickham?" Mary asked timidly.

"Yes, but nobody else knows except Colonel Fitzwilliam, the solicitors, and those of us in this room, and it must remain that way. Not even the Matlocks and de Bourghs know, nor do Lydia or Jane," Lizzy replied. "Georgiana has shown exceptional trust in telling you this secret; you know how important it is for a woman to be of good reputation."

"If I must go to trial, will it be in the newspaper?" asked Kitty.

"No, because I am working with my solicitor to negotiate a deal with the shopkeeper. We will succeed, and there will be no trial and no newspaper articles. You will soon be free." Darcy did not mention how many of his connections he would need to use, or how much he would probably pay the shopkeeper to withdraw his case.

"I would like to stay in London," Mary finally spoke. "We have been granted an opportunity to help others. After being in prison for just a few days, we should have more compassion on the imprisoned and poor. Georgiana and I were barely starting to be involved in Lady Anne's charities."

Darcy was touched to hear this. "My mother also had charities in Derbyshire, if you would be interested."

"Lizzy is already assisting there, and Derbyshire has fewer people. It is the work in London that needs more volunteers, especially prisons," said Mary. "You should visit Newgate... for an hour or so."

"Even I visited Newgate," Lizzy said with a challenging look.

"How could I refuse such a charming invitation," is all he could say without laughing.

~*~*~*~

Two weeks after Kitty's arrest – Law Offices of Johnson and Sons, London

Darcy would have preferred working with old Mr. Johnson, who had known Darcy's father, but the solicitor wanted to let his son, Daniel, conduct today's negotiations with the shopkeeper who was accusing Kitty of the theft of the lace. Darcy had known the young man since he had begun working as a clerk for his father; both Johnsons had known about George Wickham's extravagant ways and had prepared the papers when Wickham had renounced any claim to the Kymptom living in exchange for 3,000 pounds.

"My son has apprenticed with me for almost five years and will soon come before a judge to be examined and sworn in. He needs the experience of conducting this negotiation, Mr. Darcy, but I will be here to supervise."

Darcy understood this and regretted that his own father had died before he could watch his son become Master of Pemberley. He noticed how the Johnsons communicated wordlessly, with only small changes in their posture or body movement.

At first, the young Mr. Johnson seemed as bland and harmless as a bowl of vegetable broth.

"I agree, it can be very difficult to find good help," Mr. Johnson began, seeming very sympathetic, speaking as one tradesman to another. "Your clerk swore a solemn oath that she did not give Miss Bennet the gold lace. Now when did your clerk leave your employment?"

The clerk was still speaking in a conversational manner, watching as the shopkeeper grew more at ease.

"Do you have her address in Town? Did you check Mrs. Smith's references? Might I see her recommendation letter, sir."

"I... I do not have the information on hand," the shopkeeper stammered.

"I expect you have it in your records, sir." Mr. Johnson gave him a small reassuring smile. "Please tell me about your clerk's appearance – yes, she sounds very pleasant-looking. Now what did Miss Bennet say when she entered the shop – did she give you her true name or a false name?"

The shopkeeper began perspiring. "I do not remember."

"She gave you her address at the school and you had seen her before with the other schoolgirls, all of them well dressed and from good families. On this particular day, you say you watched Miss Bennet look at the gold lace, but did you actually see her put it in the bag? Can you swear positively that it occurred? Sir, you are the only witness – did you know your clerk has left the country?"

As the law clerk conducted the interview, he slipped Darcy a note with the shop clerk's address: it was Mrs. Younge's boarding house in Edward Street. Darcy had heard the shopkeeper's description of the shop clerk – it sounded like Mrs. Younge herself.

"It seems like your shop clerk was in error, generously giving away your lace to a customer who was already promising to send someone to pay for it," Mr. Johnson said sympathetically. "Have you found money missing from your store since your clerk left your employment?"

The shopkeeper froze. "How did you know that? The money went missing just four days after the lace vanished."

"Such a coincidence. Miss Bennet could not have taken the money as she was in Newgate at the time. She gave you her real name and address, which a true thief would not have done. She did hurry out of the store, not because of guilt but because she needed to return to her school before dinner."

Then Mr. Johnson suddenly turned on the shopkeeper like a snake. "Miss Bennet is sister to Mr. Darcy, who is the nephew of the Earl of Matlock. The entire family and all their friends would be very disinclined to frequent a shop where a young lady had been falsely accused of theft. The Darcys are known for their honesty; you will find no tradesman who has complained of unpaid bills.

Also, the Earl – as a leading member of the House of Lords – would be upset to hear that Miss Bennet might have been wrongly deported all the way to Australia at great cost to the government, all for a card of lace that cost only 20 shillings.

"Have you heard of a charge called 'perverting justice,' sir? It is when you falsely charge someone with a felony. You are GUILTY of perverting justice, and it is punishable by death or deportation – Australia for you, sir, if you survive the prison hulks," he almost shouted at the now trembling shopkeeper.

"I strongly suggest that you take the 20 shillings, withdraw your charge of theft, declare Miss Bennet innocent, and thank God that Mr. Darcy may agree to not charge you with perjury. Australia, sir – think of it, but think quickly, before Mr. Darcy withdraws his kind offer."

Darcy displayed his most arrogant look. The shopkeeper cowered and agreed to all terms, signed everything, took the 20 shillings and left with his tail between his legs.

The younger Mr. Johnson returned to his normal self, breathing slower until he was calm and quiet. As he had told Mary, he was more than capable of conducting a negotiation in an office.

"Well done, Daniel," his father said. "Excellent negotiation. You showed him point-by-point that he had no case and no witness, then you put the fear of God in him."

"When did you know about the shop clerk?" Darcy asked.

"I had her investigated and watched. I knew everything before the shopkeeper came here, but I needed to surprise him. She has paid for her fare to Liverpool, where she can get on a ferry to Ireland, and I doubt she will return here to testify – or be arrested for theft – or cause trouble for Miss Darcy."

"You would make an excellent barrister. I could see you in court, defending your clients," said Darcy.

"Barristers' training is expensive," the clerk said softly.

"Being a solicitor is a fine profession. My wife's maternal grandfather was a solicitor, as you know. There is no need to become a barrister unless you wish to become a judge or be presented at Court."

The father and son looked shortly at each other. The son took a deep breath. "A man in my situation naturally looks for happiness in the marriage state. I hoped that my future wife would be satisfied with a solicitor."

Darcy realized that the clerk had been as fierce in his defense of Kitty as a man might defend his wife. "Do you have a lady in mind?" he asked suspiciously.

"Yes, sir, Mr. Darcy, sir. It is... she is... I have grown to admire your sister, sir."

"Which sister?"

"Miss Bennet, sir. Miss Mary Bennet, sir."

"Not Miss Catherine?"

"No, sir. I scarcely know that sister as she has been away at school, but Miss Mary and I have enjoyed many discussions since she began living in your house, sir. She is a good reader and listener, is incapable of any act of dishonesty, works hard, and has a sincere desire to be a good Christian and help the poor, just as your mother and my mother did. Because of her compassion for her sister, she was willing to stay in Newgate – there are grown men who fear that place!"

"Yet you visited her there."

"How could I stay away when the woman that I... that I admire was there?"

"Does she know of your interest in her?" Darcy remembered that his own Elizabeth had not expected his proposal at Hunsford; it was a joke now, but not then.

"I have said nothing directly, sir. I thought I should wait until I am licensed as a working attorney, which should be this summer. I will continue to work here with my father, of course, so I will have sufficient income to support a wife."

"Are you asking for my approval to court her?" Darcy asked.

"Yes, sir. Mr. Bennet has final approval over his daughter, of course, but if this is presumptuous of me, then... then I should resign, in order to not harm my father's ability to continue serving your family, sir."

Darcy looked at the elder Johnson – a man who had known and served Darcy's own father, prepared his parents' marriage settlement. The man's face looked impassive as a good solicitor should, but there were signs of tension. Darcy thought of the clerk's offer to resign before he completed his apprenticeship – would that hurt his career? He conceded that he needed more time to decide.

"It is not necessary for you to resign," Darcy said. "I have complete confidence in your firm's ability to serve as my solicitors, and your willingness to not approach my sister for courtship until you have her father's approval. As for my own approval – I believe I should discuss this with my wife."

"Thank you sir," the younger man said, echoed by his father. They stood silently as Mr. Darcy left. He was one of their most influential clients, a man whose recommendation for or against them could change their lives.

The father patted his son's shoulder. "Try to not worry too much. You have done all you can. You have been a man of honour and integrity, presenting your case to him instead of going around his back. Now it is up to him and Mrs. Darcy, and then the Bennets."

"I feel dreadful," said the clerk who wanted to be Mary's husband.

"If it is meant to be, then nothing can stop it," his father encouraged him. "Remember Jacob in the Bible, who labored fourteen years before his father-in-law let him marry Rachel."

In the carriage, Darcy considering telling Elizabeth about Johnson's interest in courting Mary. *Perhaps Mary might not even be interested in Mr. Johnson. Having a respectable solicitor for a brother would be better than Wickham – even better than Major Carter. Elizabeth's Uncle Gardiner is a tradesman, her Uncle Philips is a country solicitor. Wickham's father had been an honorable solicitor but his wastrel son was considered a gentleman. Would a solicitor be acceptable as brother-in-law if Mary truly loved him?*

"Mr. Darcy, you should take Kitty and throw her in the way of other rich men," Mrs. Bennet had told him. She clearly wanted a rich man for a son-in-law. But what of Mr. Bennet's views? As father, he had the last word for his unmarried daughters.

Darcy realized his thoughts were jumbled. He had to speak with Elizabeth. But he would not embarrass Mr. Johnson by revealing his name.

Darcy House

That evening, Darcy enjoyed announcing to his family that the charges against Kitty had been withdrawn and she was now free. His sisters were excited. Darcy told Kitty, Mary, and Georgiana to take the carriage to share the news with the Gardiners and Bingleys.

After the girls left, he asked his wife to join him in his study.

Lizzy saw his expression and was frightened. "I thought Kitty was safe from prison."

"She is safe, but I have been considering a serious matter. Elizabeth, would you have married me if I had been a tradesman – perhaps a solicitor?"

"If Lydia had not been found, I might have been glad for even a shopkeeper's attentions, if he had been a decent man. Why do you ask?"

"Would your parents accept a tradesman as a son-in-law?"

Lizzy felt conflicted. "I hope my sisters can do better than that, but I realize that Jane and I were extraordinarily fortunate; there are far more pleasing young ladies with no dowries than there are gentlemen of fortune willing to offer for them. In a family of five daughters, it is unlikely to happen again! I suppose I should show more liberality since both my uncles are in trade." She looked at her husband. "Has a solicitor approached you about marrying Kitty or Mary? Is it Mr. Johnson?"

He shook his head in exasperation. "I was trying to spare him from embarrassment by not telling you his name, but I should have known you would identify him. Yes, it is Mr. Johnson, and he is interested in courting Mary." He told her about their discussion that afternoon.

"Does he love her?"

"Yes, I believe so."

She paused to think. "My mother might complain, but she has never had high expectations for Mary. My father would not mind a solicitor for a son-in-law if the man had money to support a family, but he has never been overly concerned with anything Mary does. William, what should we do? Do we encourage Mr. Johnson, ask Mary if she is interested, or let my father decide?"

"I do not know," Darcy admitted.

Gardiners' home in Cheapside, London

The Gardiners were excited for Kitty's freedom. They sent a message to Mr. Goodman to join them for an impromptu celebration; the curate had visited Mary and Kitty daily in Newgate, so he should appreciate the news.

"This means you still have chances of a good marriage," Mrs. Gardiner said happily, as she watched Georgiana play with the Gardiners' children.

"Who would dare marry us? We have no money," said Mary, as Kitty nodded in agreement.

"Look at Jane and Lizzy," Mr. Gardiner reminded his nieces. "Come, let us send a letter to your parents with the news."

The sisters would never say this aloud, but Mary was thinking of a certain solicitor who was the most honourable man she had ever met.

Kitty wondered if a certain curate was a good dancer. *He still thinks I am silly*, Kitty thought. *Perhaps he would think better of me if he knew that I sew clothes for children in the workhouse. I have improved after Newgate – at least, I hope so.*

As he walked to the Gardiners' home from his small set of rooms in Cheapside, Mr. Goodman pondered his own future. *I am a gentleman, but I do not have enough money to support Miss Kitty*, Mr. Goodman thought. He prayed, *Lord, I cannot remain a curate forever. I need a living as rector.*

The Darcys and Bennets might accept a curate as Kitty's husband, but not if he only had 50 pounds a year.

"Have faith," he reminded himself. "If she is supposed to be my wife, I will have a parish of my own one day. Every pot has a lid."

~*~*~*~

Irish Sea

Far away on a ferry ship to Ireland, the shopkeeper's clerk was off to her new life. Mrs. Smith – formerly called Mrs. Younge, Mrs. Olds, Mrs. Weeks, and Mrs. Day – had worked only briefly at the shop to supplement her boarding house income. Like Wickham, she was resentful of the spoiled scions of the ton with more money than sense; for weeks, she had watched the schoolgirls wander in the shop, dropping things that she had to pick up, making her curtsy to them. Like Wickham, she was an opportunist; when Miss Kitty Bennet walked into the shop alone and said she was Darcy's sister, Mrs. Younge – no, Mrs. Smith – jumped at the chance to cause trouble for Darcy. All it took was a bit of lace dropped into a bag, and a hint to the shopkeeper.

She was still angry that Darcy had spoiled her and Wickham's plans to take Georgiana's 30,000 pounds. Darcy had ruined her ability to find a new companion's position; if not for him, she might have caught another rich heiress for Wickham. She was angry that Wickham died in Spain; she had learned of his death from Wickham's friend Denny of the militia, who heard it from his friend Captain Carter, who heard it from his brother in Spain, the very same one who had married Darcy's sister Lydia, who had seen Wickham's body. To her resentful and irrational mind – she who was formerly Mrs. Younge – it meant Darcy must have been behind George Wickham's death.

There was nothing good for her in being near to Darcy. She sold everything she had, and took some money from the shopkeeper. In Ireland, she would open a new boarding house and change her name to Mrs. George. *In Ireland, there will always be plenty of food,* she thought. Unknown to Mrs. Younge, the Great Famine would hit Ireland, causing a period of mass starvation, disease, and emigration between 1845 and 1852; she would lose every bit of money and property she had ever gained, and die in poverty.

.

FANTASY

G.E.O.R.G.E.

Tagalong story

What if Jane Austen's favorite couple traveled through time?

PART ONE BY AIMÉE AVERY

"Oh! Oh! Oh!" Frances Bennet shouted as she rushed to catch up with her husband. But Ward Bennet was in no mood to be caught up by his wife's need to communicate the rest of the community's business. He quickly maneuvered himself into the drink queue at the Meryton Pub's Sunday all-you-can-eat brunch.

Only it didn't work.

"Ward Cleaver Bennet! Oh, how you delight in vexing me!" Frances shouted. "Why did your mother have to give you such a silly name?"

Ward sighed. He didn't really want to go into his mother's penchant for early television programs. Not again anyway. And definitely not in the middle of a crowded pub. "It beats being called 'The Beav.' What is it, Fran?"

"Betty Long just informed me that the big complex at the Netherfield Industrial Park has finally been leased!"

"I'm thrilled, dear. I bet the city council is dancing a jig, knowing they can now blow our tax dollars on themselves and not on empty buildings."

"Oh, Ward! Don't you see? The girls can all get jobs! Move out maybe!"

"Fran, Kitty and Lydia are still in high school. I don't think they'll be moving anywhere."

"You know I mean Jane and Elizabeth!" Fran said in exasperation. "Well, Jane is a sweet, beautiful creature, but Elizabeth..."

"Oh, don't start on Lizzy! It's Sunday, and I want to relax."

"Well, the right man could tame her! She needs to get out and find one. And a job at the Pemberley Corporation just might be the place for her to start."

"The Pemberley Corporation?" Ward turned to face his wife.

"I knew you'd be interested. You're always talking about them."

"Well, yes. They are the company where Joshua Wick and Robert Hamm work. You know, the scientists working on the Genetically Engineered Organic Robot Growth Experiment!" Ward said with awe. "They're featured constantly in my *Popular Scientist* magazine."

"Yes, I know. I know. G.E.O.R.G.E.," Fran said with a touch of annoyance. "That is why I thought you would be interested. In fact, they're hosting the next chamber of commerce mixer in the community center assembly hall!"

Two weeks later...

"You know, Jane, I don't mind that mom rushed me over to fill out an application for a job at the Pemberley

Corporation, but this dress!" Elizabeth took hold of a handful of material on the prom-style dress. "She bought it at Save-mart, Jane! Save-mart! At least yours came from a real department store. But this!"

"Oh, Lizzy. You actually look really great in it. The blue brings out your eyes," Jane said, trying to appease her sister.

"If you hadn't made the alterations you did, I wouldn't be wearing it right now! I swear my own mother hates me!"

"She doesn't hate you, Lizzy. She just doesn't understand you!"

"Well at least I have an interview for the job, that is if me wearing this rag doesn't offend anyone from the company at this stupid mixer."

Frances Bennet skirted through the crowd toward her two eldest daughters. She had plans, big plans. She had been speaking to Betty Long once again, and had found out more interesting news.

"Girls!" Fran said in a loud whisper. "I've just had it from Mrs. Long. A Mr. Charles Bingley is the manager for this division of the Pemberley Corporation, and he's single! Just think, if one of you marries him, then it would mean no more dresses from Save-mart! Though finding that gown at fifty percent off at Ford's for you, Jane, was a stroke of luck. He makes $500,000 a year! Net!"

"How on earth do you know how much he makes, mother?" Elizabeth asked with her hands firmly sitting on her hips, elbows akimbo.

"Well, he's renting one of those fancy condos in Meryton. You know, the ones that Betty manages. She had to do a credit check."

"Isn't sharing that kind of information illegal?" Jane asked

"Whatever… it's informative is what it is," Fran said as she looked around the room, trying to spot the newcomers.

"I swear, Mom! You're going to get thrown into jail for some of the stuff you do! It's just not honorable. Don't you have any integrity?" Elizabeth said with exacerbation.

"I didn't do anything! Betty did. Oh! Here they are. Look girls!"

The women turned to see four men and two women enter the assembly hall.

"The blond man is Charles Bingley, according to Betty," Fran whispered. "Oh, no! They are going over to meet the Lucases. Crap."

"Mom!" both girls exclaimed.

"Well, I have plans!"

"Mom! You can't plan the lives of others," Elizabeth admonished.

"Elizabeth, why must you always contradict me?"

"Oh, I give up!" Elizabeth said as she massaged her temples. "Here comes Charlotte!"

Frances Bennet groaned just as the plain young woman approached.

"Hi, Charlotte! You look great in that dress!"

"I was going to say the same thing to you, Lizzy! Where ever did you find that dress? It looks sensational on you! The color brings out your eyes!"

"Oh, forget about Elizabeth's dress," Fran interrupted. "Tell us about Bingley and his friends!"

Charlotte smiled and then quietly pointed out each member of the group.

"The two women are Bingley's sisters, Louisa and Caroline. The bald man is married to Louisa, the blonde. The one in orange is Caroline. She's single, from what I gather. The shorter of the two good looking men is George – I didn't get his last name – and the taller is William Darcy."

"William Darcy?" Fran asked. "THE William Darcy? President and CEO of the Pemberley Corporation? Why, he makes at least $10 million a year, if you can believe what you read in the financial section of the paper!"

"Shh, Mom! They're coming this way!"

"Good evening, ladies. I'm Charles Bingley, and you are?" he asked as he took Jane's hand. The two stood and stared at each other until Fran cleared her throat.

"It's so nice to meet you, Mr. Bingley! I'm Frances Bennet. This is my eldest daughter, Jane, and my second daughter, Elizabeth."

Bingley smiled at Elizabeth then turned back to Jane, keeping a hold of her hand.

"I'm George!" said the shorter dark-haired man. "It is a very good pleasure greeting your acquaintance."

"I believe he means, 'It's a pleasure to make your acquaintance,'" Darcy said quickly. All three Bennet women and Charlotte smiled at George, who wore a big grin as he nodded and pointed first to Darcy, then himself and finally to the women.

"If you'll excuse us," Darcy said as he took a hold of George's arm and dragged him off to the far side of the room.

Bingley escorted Jane onto the dance floor while Fran and Elizabeth gaped at the retreating dark-haired gentlemen.

"That was strange," Charlotte whispered.

"Yeah," Elizabeth laughed. "It is a very good pleasure greeting your acquaintance? And what was all that pointing he was doing?"

"Well, I've never seen such a thing," Frances Bennet stated with displeasure, then turned to abandon the two younger women.

"What is up with your mother?"

"Oh, Char, you really don't want to know!"

"Uh oh!" Charlotte said in the middle of a laugh as the two made their way to the food table.

"Lizzy!" Ward Bennet raced over to his daughter as she picked up some cheese and placed it on her plate.

"Hi, Dad! You want me to fix you a plate?"

"Thanks, but no. I've been talking to one of the Pemberley scientists. He said they have made great strides in their organic robot program. They actually clone human tissues for their robots."

"Isn't that illegal?" Elizabeth asked her father.

"What? No! You can't clone a human, but you can skin and things like that. They actually use quantum acceleration to make the cells grow faster. He wouldn't give me any more details. I would *love* to see their operation."

"Quantum acceleration? You mean time travel? Dad, that isn't possible," Elizabeth looked at her father as if he'd lost his mind.

"Lizzy, do I need to explain the Planck Constant to you again? The constant between the energy of a photon and the frequency of its associated electromagnetic wave ..."

"Dad! Really, no!" Elizabeth put her hand over her father's mouth. "I was just ..." Ward Bennet tugged his daughter's hand away and interrupted.

"Tissue acceleration, Lizzy! I know you think all this is science fiction, but ..."

"I'm sorry, Dad. I know you love this sort of thing. And I grant you, it can be very interesting, but ..."

"I'm sorry, Lizzy. I'm just so excited."

"Hello! I hope you will vindicate me," a smiling George said as he tapped Elizabeth on the shoulder. "I have enthusiasm to pirouette. May I solicit your acquiescence?"

"I beg your pardon?" Elizabeth asked, but George just smiled broader. "Are you asking me to dance?" George nodded exuberantly, and Elizabeth couldn't resist his boyish excitement. "Sure, it would be my pleasure. Dad, will you take this?" Elizabeth said as she handed off the plate.

Upon reaching the dance floor, George stood and mechanically took Elizabeth's hand in his as he placed his other hand on her waist and began a very precise box step.

Elizabeth couldn't resist George's smile, and began to grin as well, even though she felt as if she were back in her third-grade dance class.

"So, George, what's your last name?"

"I do not comprehend. Explain 'last name.'"

Elizabeth stared at the man she was dancing with and thought maybe he was joking, but when she saw the earnestness in his looks, she replied, "Your surname."

George continued to stare blankly.

"Your family name. You know, your father's name. My father is Ward Bennet, I'm Elizabeth Bennet."

"I have deciphered *last name* -- reference falling in last position of fathers' designation. My *last name* is Wick Hamm.

"George Wickham. That is a very nice name," Elizabeth said, wondering at the oddness this man exhibited, but couldn't deny she was having a good time in his company.

"I gift you with gratitude," George replied, and crushed her to his body.

Elizabeth giggled and returned the hug, only pushing her dance partner away when she heard a very stern "George!"

"George, go over to that side of the room and wait for me." William Darcy pointed to the far side of the room near the front entrance.

George nodded, but turned to Elizabeth and said, "I have gratitude for our pirouette." He smiled at Elizabeth, then at Darcy, and with a quick nod, he took William's hand and said, "I possess his male copulatory organ. He gifted me his erectile tissue. It is very impressive." George shook Darcy's hand and quickly walked to where Darcy directed.

William Darcy mumbled something under his breath, then said, "I would appreciate it if you would keep your distance. I don't need you confusing things. He is too valuable to me to have mediocre input damage him."

"We were just dancing! And I am *not* mediocre," Elizabeth said through her teeth. "You and your boy-toy can go exercise your 'impressive' organ in the back seat of your car for all I care. Don't give me your drama queen attitude!"

The fire in her eyes mesmerized Darcy. It was only as Elizabeth turned and stormed off did he realize how she had interpreted his words. "Great! She thinks I'm having a homosexual affair with a robot that has a cloned version of my manhood. If it weren't against my ethics, I would jump into the quantum chamber for a do over. I really don't do well around regular people."

Darcy walked over to George and escorted him out of the building.

"Did I do well?" George asked.

"Yes, George. But we still need to work on your vocabulary and what is appropriate to say and what isn't,"

Darcy answered. "Joshua and Robert will help you tomorrow. I'll take you back to the lab so you can sync to the computer."

"Joshua and Robert have last names. They are Wick and Hamm. They are my fathers. My last name is Wick Hamm."

Darcy smiled as he helped George into the Pemberley Corporation van. "That's right. Did Joshua and Robert tell you that?"

"No. Elizabeth Bennet dispensed information for proper deciphering."

Darcy closed his eyes and winced. If she could get George to comprehend such a concept in the few minutes they danced, then he definitely put his foot in his mouth. He closed the van door and walked around the front of the vehicle to the driver's side. "I definitely don't do well around regular people."

Darcy climbed into the van and started the engine.

"Darcy?"

"Yes, George."

"Can you provide information?"

"For what, George?" Darcy replied as he turned onto the main road leading to the industrial park.

"Justification for change in erectile tissue?"

Darcy stepped on the brakes hard, making the van skid to the curb. "What change?"

"This change," George said as he pointed to the tent at his groin. "It commenced upon connection of my skeletal form to Elizabeth Bennet."

Darcy groaned. He wasn't sure if he was up for an explanation of the birds and the bees, especially since he also suffered from the same change in his erectile tissue.

PART TWO BY ENID WILSON

Two months later...

"Come, Elizabeth Bennet, I have 98.6945% of yearning to show you my birth chamber." Wickham grinned as he pulled Elizabeth along some unknown corridors in Pemberley Corporation.

"Wait, George, you're going too fast! And what are you talking about? Birth chamber?" Elizabeth shook her head at the enthusiasm of the strange, handsome man. She had worked at Pemberley Corporation for the past two months as a public relations Vice President. The job put her in daily contact with Darcy and Bingley. She didn't like the overbearing and arrogant Mr. Darcy one iota. He stared at her all the time, to find fault most probably, and kept trying to separate the charming George from her. Wickham might have strange vocabulary and manner, but he was polite, gentlemanly and had the hots for her, the exact opposite of Mr. Darcy's treatment of her. She teased her CEO verbally whenever she had the chance, which seemed to be a lot of time, as Bingley was dating Jane, and they usually invited Darcy and her to tag along.

"There!" George stretched out his hand, gesturing to Elizabeth to admire the magnificent setup in front of their eyes.

Elizabeth's mouth gaped open. Inside the room was an enormous circular structure, the size of a football field and height of 7-storey building, resembling the interior of a spaceship from a science-fiction movie, with countless computers, electronic devices and monitors. While the machines blinked and processed data busily, the room was devoid of occupants.

She stepped outside the corridor to make sure it wasn't her imagination. No, it was real: from the Pemberley Corporation corridor, this was just an ordinary room, but once she stepped through the door, it was a huge structure. Lizzy was reminded of a British television show about an alien who traveled inside a police call box that was really a spaceship.

"What is this place?" She cranked her head, trying to read the nonsensical content on the wall-to-ceiling computers as she moved into the room.

"You enquired about my birthplace yesterday." George brushed an unruly curl from his forehead in front of a monitor and said, "This is the Quantum Chamber, where Joshua Wick and Robert Hamm, what did you call them, yes, *my parents* procreated me."

Elizabeth whirled around to stare at George, from a distance. While her feet had taken her deep into the chamber, George was still stationed by the door. "You meant your parents conceived you here? But that can't be true! Pemberley Corporation only moved here two months ago. And Joshua and Robert couldn't conceive you. They are men. Did you mean they adopted you?"

"I'm an honourable man! I tell the absolute truth. My *parents* worked for Darcy."

"I know that."

"I was procreated from a minute small portion of Darcy's tissue using quantum acceleration inside the crystal palace in Derbyshire in 1821."

"Crystal palace?"

George turned to press a few buttons on the wall by the door, and the banks of computers on Elizabeth's right hand side parted open to reveal an inner chamber with a sparkling pagoda-shaped structure, larger than her entire house, in crystals. A high-back reclining chair, fit for a king, also made in eye-blinding crystals, occupied the center of the pagoda.

A palace inside a chamber? Did Mr. Darcy name them? Strange choice, she thought.

With mouth gaped open again and feet seemingly moved by magnets, Elizabeth walked inside the *crystal palace*. She had never seen so many crystals in her life, and every one of them looked to be perfection under the spot lights. Tracing her fingertips along the surface of the wall, she thought about what George had just said.

Did he mean he was not human? He was apparently created by G.E.O.R.G.E., the Genetically Engineered Organic Robot Growth experiment her father spoke a lot about. Darcy in 1821? From Derbyshire? Did George mean Mr. Darcy was a man from nineteenth century England who funded G.E.O.R.G.E. and time travel? That couldn't be true. Elizabeth was speechless, and sat heavily onto the chair.

"No!" Darcy's high-pitched voice startled her. He charged towards her like a raging bull. Elizabeth swirled the chair to avoid the flying man, but he knocked the breath out of her. She felt dizzy and in great pain. What had Mr. Darcy done to her? Did he kill her with his sheer masculine weight because she had discovered his crystal palace? She could feel his virile body pressed hard against her. Her eyes flashed with sparks, but she saw nothing. Her body felt like it was splitting up, disintegrating into millions of particles, yet she could feel every inch of Mr. Darcy's skin in her mind. After what felt like hours or days, the faintness stopped.

"This shouldn't be happening."

Mr. Darcy's husky voice made Elizabeth pry open her eyes. They were nose to nose. His mouth was inches from hers. Their bodies were pressed together, with her lying on top of him. He was holding on to her for dear life.

"This can't be happening," he murmured.

She scrambled off his body and fell to the ground. The unfeeling man with no manners left her there and walked out of the *crystal palace* and stood in front of some computers.

"Computer, how did Elizabeth travel through time, intact, without pre-programming?"

She stood up, followed him and looked around. Was he crazy too? And where was George? The other man was no longer in the Quantum Chamber, unless he was hidden somewhere behind those banks of computers and high-tech pieces of equipment.

A mechanical voice spoke out. "Mr. Darcy, your feelings will not be repressed, despite your concern of the inferiority of Miss Bennet's connections and total want of propriety of her family. You love and admire her ardently. You plan to ask her to become your wife today. Your constant thoughts of Miss Bennet and regular body contact with her in the last 59 days 8 hours 39 minutes 11 seconds means that the time travel program recognizes a majority of her genetic makeup that you specified in 1821. Also, your body was present during her quantum leap. Your tight grip on Miss Bennet's body ensured her body particles regrouped successfully in present time, even without pre-programming."

He turned to stare at her, his face bright red.

"But who activated the time travel?" he said to the computer again.

"George."

Darcy tightened his jaw. "Why?"

"He was just playing with the controls."

His lips thinned. "What is the present time?"

"Year 2820."

"And where are we?"

"Planet Austen."

"Process external data and provide us with appropriate clothing."

Elizabeth stood like a stone statue, unable to accept what the computer had said. Mr. Darcy loved her? How could that be? He only stared at her to find fault. He found plenty of defects, *in her connections and her family's improper behavior*. Who still talked like that? Like in old English? And she had traveled through time to an unknown planet.

Crap!

She felt a shiver down her spine and found that her blouse, long A-line skirt, bra and panties had been ripped off her body.

"Shit!" She swore and raised her eyes to look at the tall man in front of her. His six foot four inch potent body was also stripped naked at that moment. Wow, her eyes moved from his red face, to his broad shoulders, six-pack abs, with hair tapering to his...

Wow, he had a huge arousal, and his perfect male body part was so well endowed that she couldn't stop from swallowing. Or was she salivating over her arrogant boss?

He turned around, probably to hide his arousal from her. But the gesture exposed his toned pert ass to her devouring eyes. While she took in every single hot inch of his back, she felt heat radiating in her body again. She looked down and found herself now wrapped in a tight top made of thick silk-like fabric in gold and a mini-skirt of similar style. She glanced at Mr. Darcy. He was now wearing a dark green body suit similar to hers. He drew in a few deep breaths and turned around to face her again.

"Miss Bennet, would you like to explore Planet Austen, with me?" Since the computer revealed this time travel thingy, Mr. Darcy acted like a man from the nineteenth century.

"Hang on a minute. Are you saying I've really traveled to the future?"

"Indeed." He nodded. "Computer, pray show Miss Bennet outside."

"Affirmative."

The banks of monitors turned into one giant screen. Elizabeth was taken to a virtual tour. Green parks with lush trees, rainbow-colored flowers and birds adorned the planet. Stone mansions and ultra modern multi-storey buildings hung in mid air. The camera zoomed to one of the magnificent estates. Inside a glittering ballroom, a host of well-dressed and bejeweled men, women and aliens – with several heads, eyes, ears or other body parts – chatted, danced and drank. But all of them were dressed in Regency clothing, in various states of attire. Some were dressed very decently, in full-length empire dresses. But some wore only breeches, while another wore just a bonnet!

She swallowed hard and dragged her bulging eyes from the aliens. "Are you really from the 1800s?"

He nodded.

"Show me." Her voice shook.

"Computer, pray show Miss Bennet my estate, Pemberley, in 1821."

The image on screen changed to a large, handsome stone building, standing well on rising ground, and backed by a ridge of high woody hills. And in front, a stream of some natural importance was swelled into greater, but without any artificial appearance. Then the camera focused to the *crystal palace* deep in the woods behind the building, to a man in traditional clothing, cravat, breeches and all, caressing the crystal throne chair.

It was Mr. Darcy, dressed like a Regency hero!

"If only you could bring me to my destiny, a woman of character and strength." The 1821 Mr. Darcy murmured.

Elizabeth darted her eyes to the modern Mr. Darcy by her side, then back to the *ancient* Mr. Darcy and to this Mr. Darcy in a body suit.

"Is this a pre-recorded April Fool's joke?" No way could someone from Regency or Victorian England be so scientifically advanced.

He shook his head. "I am eight and thirty in 1821, with immense wealth and a noble mien. Mothers and women in London and the Continent court my attention. But no one interests me with their wit and character."

"Vain and proud!"

"Yes, vanity is a weakness indeed. But pride, where there is a real superiority of mind, pride will be always under good regulation."

She rolled her eyes.

"I met Wick and Hamm and was fascinated by their quest for cloning and journeying to the future. They were well into the advanced stages of their experiment, and only required the final push of funding. I sponsored building the crystal palace in Pemberley's woods, and even offered a tiny part of myself for the experiment. And we have been traveling through time for well over a year, although at first not with so many of us or on such a grand scale. This is the first time we have brought George with us."

"Crap! What do you do when you arrive in another time or dimension? Aren't you careful about time paradoxes, becoming your own grandfather or something?" She wasn't Ward Bennet's favorite daughter for nothing. She was as curious as her father about time travel, aliens and flying saucers. She just balanced her life better than her father, with modern day pursuits like watching movies, traveling and playing sports.

"The inventors often closet themselves inside Pemberley Corporation to learn as much as possible about a new place or planet. I prefer to explore and interact with locals."

"But you look down on us!"

"I seldom rattle away. I am ill-qualified to recommend myself to strangers, especially because of the changes in English idioms. You Americans speak a very different English than my time."

"You just didn't take the trouble to practice."

"I shall take your reproof to heart."

His smile and intense gaze unsettled Elizabeth. He looked like a man passionately in love, and with her. That scared the hell out of her. Mr. Darcy was from the past. He was condescending about her family. She had had no clue he loved her. She didn't even like him at all, though she admitted that he was smart and hot. It might be nice to screw him for a night, or a few nights, but to spend the rest of her life with him and travel through time and space? Holy shit! She wasn't ready to shake hands with aliens with six eyes and three heads yet. And what about children? Could they have children, him from 1821 and she from 2012? What was she thinking? Children? No way! She blurted out, "I'm not marrying you!"

His brows frowned together. "Did I make you an offer of marriage?"

"Your computer said so."

He drew in a deep breath. "It is wrong. Ignore it."

"Negative." The computer barged into the human conversation. "Mr. Darcy, you practiced the speech to ask

Miss Bennet to marry you just before you entered the Quantum Chamber. 'In vain I have struggled. It will not do. My feelings will not be repressed. You must allow me to tell you how ardently I admire and love you.' You decided you would not tell her about your time travel until after you can trust her."

"Desist!" He demanded the computer to stop.

Elizabeth flashed her angry eyes at Darcy and then turned to the machine. "Mr. Computer, can you take me to the ball? I need a stiff drink." Then like a whiff of air, she flew through a bright light tunnel. Mr. Darcy's voice echoed in it. "I shall ask Wick and Hamm to rewire you after I return, Disobedient Computer."

Two hours later...

"Come, Miss Bennet, you are drunk. You need to lie down." Darcy pushed Elizabeth gently onto the huge bed inside a hotel suite that was probably the best on Planet Austen.

"Am not. I want to talk to Austen aliens. The blue one in the empire dress with eyes on her forehead made me shiver. She talked about making galaxy bucks all the time."

"You can talk to them tomorrow. You should rest."

"But some of them are leaving tomorrow. They're going on a road trip – no, a space trip to Planet Rebel. They have big plans, to kidnap people from there back to Planet Austen."

"You are not making sense. You have consumed too much alcohol."

"I am too! I know I want to jump you." She dragged him down with her and flipped him beneath her. Then she rained kisses over his mouth, jaw and earlobes.

"No, Elizabeth. We should not. You do not know your mind."

"I do too! I know you're hot." Her hands moved down his body, along his hard chest. "See! My hands are burning."

He drew in deep breaths. "I shall not take your virtue, until we are married."

"Told you I won't marry you. I just want to screw you. And I'm no virgin. Lost it when I was seventeen. Not very enjoyable though. He was small, not like you." Her fingers reached for the waistband of the trousers of his body suit as she rubbed against his arousal. "You're unbelievably hot and deliciously large."

"No, I shall not trifle with a gentlewoman who is not my wife."

"Forget the English gentlewomen! I'm a liberated American chick."

Elizabeth pulled his tight trousers down and palmed his velvety skin. He gasped out loud. She felt giddy. He was losing his battle to maintain propriety. Unbuttoning her top, he squeezed her breasts and raised his head to lick her nipples. She gulped for air. Their moans were loud and their hands were busy, until Elizabeth rose to sit on him.

She threw her head back as he invaded every inch of her inner muscles. His hot, hard and strong body linked with hers.

"I love you, dearest, loveliest Elizabeth. Marry me."

She stared at him. As he thrust up into her hot core slowly, again and again, his words transcended time and space. The universe consisted only of them. She felt deeply connected to him, both physically and emotionally. And yet, she could not forget his conceited words about her family and his readiness to hide his time travel from her. She reached her peak and collapsed on top of him, uttering a loud "NO!" that pulled Mr. Darcy's body tense and tight.

PART THREE BY JUNE WILLIAMS

"'No?' What do you mean, 'no?' I realize that was too fast, but I swear I will do better next time," Darcy said desperately, pulling up his trousers.

"I mean no, I will not marry you," Lizzy said, as she moved off the bed and started to dress herself. "That computer said you were concerned about the inferiority of my connections and the total want of propriety of my family. They may be lower middle-class, but they are all the family I have."

"But your connections and family will not matter when you and I live at Pemberley in 1821."

"What! You expect me to leave everyone and everything behind to live in the past? You don't even have flush-toilets or central heating, and your idea of medicine is barbaric."

"We can use the Crystal Palace to travel back and forth."

"I don't know if I can do that to our children. They would be uprooted constantly, and we would have to keep secrets from our friends."

"But everyone has secrets. There must be things you don't even tell your sister Jane."

"Yes, but, well, that's different," Lizzy sputtered.

He gave her a questioning look.

"Very well, I cede that point. But how would this work – you're from 1821, I'm from 200 years in your future, and I like it in my time. Women have few rights in 1821 England. I mean, as my husband, you could beat me with a stick and not go to jail."

"But I would not do that," he said urgently. "We do not need to be at Pemberley more than a few weeks every year; we could say that we are traveling – which would be the truth."

"You don't mind living with me in the 21st century?"

He touched her hands. "For you, I would do anything. Have you not wondered why I named it the Crystal Palace?"

"The pagoda thing inside the Quantum Chamber?"

"I called it a palace because it was meant to find my queen: you. The throne chair is programmed to search through time, to find my ideal woman of character and strength. The time travel program analyzed your psychological and genetic makeup, and the monitors showed me key moments of your life – the time you saved a child from drowning, your debates with college professors, your thesis on women's rights, your volunteer work on behalf of the poor. The last two months have only confirmed that you are the right woman for me."

"The crystal chair is programmed to find me?"

He nodded and blushed. "The search subroutine is called W.O.M.A.N. – Wife Of Many Accomplishments, Noble."

"You think I'm noble," she said with a grin.

His eyes looked shiftily.

"Or were you looking for a Wife Of Many Accomplishments, Naughty?" she teased him.

Now he really blushed.

"Caught you!" she said with a laugh. "I suppose women in your time don't jump into bed with a man after two months."

"It is one of many things that surprised me about this time," he muttered.

"So why did the chair bring us to Planet Austen?"

"When I told the computer I was going to ask you to marry me, it searched the galaxy and determined that Planet Austen would be a romantic destination for after our engagement – after you took your place on the throne of my heart. It seems men and women from my time and yours – and the future – believe Jane Austen is the ultimate authority on marriage."

"Because marriage should be built on a foundation of love, not money. 'Anything is to be preferred or endured rather than marrying without affection,' she once wrote to her niece. Jane Austen was revolutionary for her time," Lizzy said pensively.

"And that is why I could not find a wife in my time – I had to find you 200 years in my future."

She stared at him. "How did you and Wick and Hamm build all this stuff? It's very advanced technology for 1821."

He was silent.

"Wait, you're not actually an alien from the future who is disguised as a human, are you?" Lizzy demanded. Without waiting for an answer, she stormed out of the hotel suite. "Computer, you made a mistake – we are not yet engaged."

"Elizabeth, please wait! I am a human just like you are. I love you," Darcy called out as he followed her.

She turned around and held out her hands to stop him. "I need some time to think on my own. I'm going to sit in the time-travel gizmo and ask the computer questions."

In the hotel lobby, Lizzy quickly realized she had acted hastily and impulsively. She figured the time-travel device was still here on Planet Austen, but she had overestimated her ability to find it. *Maybe I can ask the hotel concierge for help*, she thought sarcastically.

Being a strong and independent woman, she first tried to solve her problem on her own. She found an empty bathroom – which had some interesting stalls designed for alien bodies – and locked herself in a stall for humans.

"Crystal Palace, beam me up," she called out. Nothing happened. "Quantum Chamber, transport me now." Still nothing happened. "I guess the Quantum Chamber is smart enough to be small on the outside yet big on the inside, but it doesn't come to you – you have to find it. I'll have to ask Darcy to invent a voice-operated remote, if I ever speak to him again."

Lizzy made her way back to the ball, which was in the same hotel. Outside the ballroom door, she saw the blue alien in empire dress with eyes on her forehead. "Excuse me, have you ever traveled to Earth? I'm looking for a ride."

The alien touched her, and Lizzy found herself frozen – unable to move, but able to see and hear. *Oh no, I am in huge trouble now*, she thought frantically.

"I make big galaxy bucks with you," the blue alien said, then turned to someone. "You pay me galaxy bucks now."

Caroline Bingley stepped in front of Lizzy and smiled smugly. "Miss Eliza, fancy meeting you here. I hate your time, and I hate this time. Nobody here appreciates a woman who can paint tables, cover screens, and net purses. All the songs and dances I know are out of fashion except on Planet Austen, and I am not staying here."

Lizzy thought back to Darcy's words – "We have been traveling through time for well over a year, although at first not with so many of us." She could not speak, only making grunts and groans with her voice.

"I assume you are wondering if my sister and brother and I are from 1821. We are, and we are going home to England as soon as I can convince Mr. Darcy that he made a mistake by choosing you," Caroline said. "I was very uncomfortable hiding amidst those horrible computer machines, where I overheard everything you said in the crystal pagoda. Once we are back in 1821, Mr. Darcy will no longer admire you ardently, and I will ensure this invention can never again travel through time." Caroline turned to the blue alien. "Take us to the time-travel device."

Caroline was able to enter the Quantum Chamber, which accepted her commands since she and her family had traveled in it with Darcy. The blue alien used a strange device to float Lizzy's still-frozen body and place her in the Crystal Palace.

"Computer," Caroline called out. "Miss Bennet refused Mr. Darcy's offer of marriage."

The monitors displayed the memory from the hotel suite when she shouted "no" to his proposal. "Confirmed," the computer voice said. "She is no longer his ideal W.O.M.A.N."

Lizzy felt her heart sink. *I'm no longer Darcy's ideal woman? What have I done!*

"Computer, you need to send Miss Bennet back to Earth," Caroline commanded, then addressed Lizzy. "I did not come all the way here to see Mr. Darcy marry a hussy like you. You refused him, and now I will have him and Pemberley."

"And his galaxy bucks," said the blue alien.

"Since you are so primitive in your behavior, you might as well go to a primitive time," Caroline said haughtily, before leaving with the blue alien and giving the computer a final command.

Again, Lizzy flew through a bright light tunnel. She had only known Darcy for two months and needed more time before agreeing to marry him, but she knew instinctively that he was a man of honor and integrity. He would never lie to her about being a human or loving her, and he would rescue her – but only if he knew where she was.

When she finally stopped moving through time and space, Lizzy found herself on Earth, but it wasn't the right time, judging by the dinosaurs stomping on the open ground in front of her. She tested moving her arms and legs. Fortunately, she was now able to run for her life, so she climbed up a steep rocky trail on a hill and into a small cave. She could now look down at the dinosaurs.

"Flat teeth – possibly a vegetarian dinosaur, but still able to smush me with its weight." Then she saw another dinosaur bite the herbivore dinosaur. "Oops, that one is definitely a carnivore."

She was too intent on survival to waste time screaming in fear. Lizzy looked around the cave – it was more of a large hole in the rocks, but it was safer than out there, and the dinosaurs were too big to fit their jaws through the opening.

"Lizzy, you will not become a snack for dinosaurs," she lectured herself. "You will not let your skeleton be found in the future with dinosaur fossils. You are not going to alter the timeline, or the time-space continuum, or whatever it's called."

She touched her silky gold mini-skirt and tight top. "I look like a reject from a B-grade caveman movie. Wait, Dad used to make us watch those movies with him, so he could laugh at the bad science. Wasn't there any way a person could realistically survive dinosaurs?" She thought of the *Jurassic Park* movie, in which the survivors managed to escape from the island.

"So could I escape by telling Darcy I will marry him after all? That's not a good reason to marry," she said to herself. "I don't know him well enough to know if I could love him." She thought back to what the monitors showed her – Darcy at Pemberley, talking to the crystal chair; he looked lonely. *Well, he was probably bored by women who only knew how to paint tables and net purses, whatever that was.*

She was still thinking of Darcy and how he had searched for her, when she heard her name being called. Dinosaurs don't talk, so she knew it had to be a human – or alien? She stuck her head out to look.

The Quantum Chamber was at the foot of the hill. The door was open, and Darcy was outside calling for her.

"Miss Bennet, where are you?"

"Here!" She ran down the trail, struggling to not slip on the rocks.

Then she saw a dinosaur start toward the Quantum Chamber. She didn't stop to see what kind of dinosaur it was; it still weighed enough to smush Darcy and the chamber. She didn't want Darcy to die – he was risking his own life to save her, and he'd had to search through eons of time to find her here.

"Watch out!" she yelled at him, and raced faster. When the dinosaur stretched its neck towards Darcy, she started throwing rocks at its eyes. "Get inside!"

Darcy saw the dinosaur, but he would not enter the Chamber without his W.O.M.A.N.

She started sliding down the trail out of control. "Get inside, get inside!"

Darcy grabbed her and pulled her into the time-travel device. "Computer, take us back to Pemberley Corporation, one minute after George activated you and sent us to Planet Austen in 2820." He held her tightly.

Again, her body felt like splitting up, disintegrating into millions of particles.

When she felt things stop moving, she ran out of the Quantum Chamber to the corridor of Pemberley Corporation, then went to a window. She looked out and saw familiar surroundings – Oakham Mount, her parents' home, the stores with her neighbors' cars in the parking lots. She saw the billboard that was still being erected this morning, when she came to work. Relieved to be back in 2012, she stepped back into the Quantum Chamber to face Darcy.

"When I travel through time, why does it sometimes feel like I'm being torn apart, but other times it feels like I'm flying through a bright light tunnel?"

"Wick and Hamm are still fine-tuning the device. It is complicated, since it performs time-travel as well as teleportation," he murmured. "Elizabeth, you have just escaped from dinosaurs, and that is the first question you have?"

"I am a very curious female, but curiosity is a sign of intelligence."

He smiled. "I was terrified that the dinosaurs would kill you."

"I was afraid for your life," she murmured. "You stubborn man. I told you to get inside."

"Do you care for me?"

"Yes, but I'm not ready to agree to marry you – you've been looking for me for a year, but I've only known you for two months in my time. What if I agree to time-travel with you? We can get acquainted then."

"Excellent idea, Miss Bennet. We could attend Queen Victoria's coronation in 1838, and there is a Great Exhibition in London in 1851 that you might enjoy."

The door opened and George entered with Jane and Charles Bingley.

"Miss Elizabeth, has Mr. Darcy taken you to see his home yet?" Charles asked, his eyes directed to Darcy.

"Lizzy, your arms and legs are scraped. Have you been climbing trees again?" Jane asked.

"Not quite," replied Lizzy. "Do you know what this thing is?"

"I told her," said Charles, as Darcy nodded at him. "I just want to show her that I really do come from 1821."

"And your sisters come from 1821 as well. Caroline kidnapped me and sent me back to the dinosaur-age."

Charles and Jane were shocked.

"Caroline is so very bad! It is almost beyond belief," said Jane.

"Mr. Computer, can you show us what happened when Caroline sent me to the dinosaurs?" Lizzy called out.

The computer complied, and displayed the moments on a bank of monitors.

Charles and Darcy looked grim. They agreed to discuss matters later, after Charles and Jane returned from visiting 1821, and after Darcy added more safeguards – including security passwords and DNA scans – to prevent the device from being hijacked by anyone.

Lizzy, Darcy, and George stepped outside into the corridor to watch the Quantum Chamber disappear with Charles and Jane.

"George, what have you been up to, and why did you play with the controls, sending us to Planet Austen in 2820?" Darcy sounded firm, but not angry.

"I watched the future on the computer's monitors and discovered that you and Miss Bennet will marry, but she had objections – such as the lack of flush-toilets and central heating, having to travel back and forth so many times to Pemberley – so I fixed them," George said. "It was my destiny to send you to the year 2820."

"Wait, you can watch the future on these monitors? And the past?" Lizzy asked in amazement. "No wonder the computer area is the size of a football-field."

"We only store the recordings of certain persons," Darcy said. "You, me, anyone who has been through the time-travel device. But the computer does not display anything too personal or intimate."

She thought of how the monitors had displayed only her face – not her half-naked body on the bed – when Caroline saw her refuse Darcy's proposal.

"It was how I found you," Darcy said softly. " I waited for you in the hotel on Planet Austen, but you did not return after several hours, so I searched for you. Only Mr. Wick, Mr. Hamm, and I have a recall device to summon the Quantum Chamber to us. I was terrified when the computer showed you with the dinosaurs, but you proved again that you truly are a woman of character and strength."

"You wouldn't leave without me."

"Never."

She smiled at him as they looked at each other for several moments, appreciating their safe return from the dinosaurs. For Lizzy, it was still perhaps a bit early to say she loved him, but she knew she cared for him, and that love would probably grow after they got to know each other.

Darcy remembered that George needed a lecture. "George, you know that we do not look at the future. If Miss Elizabeth truly did not want to marry me, I would have let her go. I only looked for her because she was not on her own planet or her own time."

"I am sorry, sir, but I wanted to know my own future – which affected the past, present, and future," George said. "If you look at your records for 1821, you will find that Pemberley had a steward named George Wickham; that was me. In 2012, Pemberley's steward is George Wickham the Sixth, which is still me, but in this period's clothing. I travel back and forth through time to take care of Pemberley, so that you and Miss Elizabeth – your wife – will not have to travel to the past as often, which was or is one of her concerns."

"I don't want to see dinosaurs again, but I would like to see Pemberley in your time. We do travel occasionally to the past, won't we, George?" asked Lizzy.

"Yes, mostly so you can visit your sister, Jane."

Lizzy was still gawping when the Quantum Chamber returned with Charles and Jane, who embraced her. Jane was dressed in a gorgeous Regency outfit of embroidered silk and lace trim; she had obviously been in 1821 longer than a few minutes.

"You and I each have wonderful men to spend our lives with," Jane said. "In addition to every other source of happiness, Lizzy, you and I will always be within thirty seconds of each other with time-travel and teleportation."

"You will truly be happy living in the past?"

"What better time and place for me, Lizzy, with my college degree in eighteenth and nineteenth century literature, and a minor in art history."

Lizzy looked at Darcy. "You never did tell me how you and Wick and Hamm built all this, with technology from 1821."

Suddenly, Mr. Wick and Mr. Hamm appeared, checking their timepieces.

"Just in time, of course," Mr. Wick said.

"Mr. Darcy promised to not tell anyone who we are. We are from your future. In 2820, we went back a thousand years to 1820, but we damaged some of our equipment, and were stranded for a year looking for someone to help. Mr. Darcy saved us after we demonstrated time-travel, although with our broken equipment we could only travel through time by a month. He paid to build the Crystal Palace in Pemberley's woods, and enabled us to travel back to our own time and continue with our experiments."

While they were speaking, Lizzy was wondering if Wick and Hamm were human or alien; she quickly decided it was not important to her, but then she realized they had said something. "What year did you say you are from?"

Mr. Wick looked a little embarrassed. "We come from 2820, the year you just visited. Actually, thanks to you, my partner and I have just been inducted into the Planet Rebel Order of Honor. In our time, the Planet Austen people are unusual because they still believe in love and commitment."

Lizzy remembered the aliens she'd met at the ball on Planet Austen. "Some Austen aliens were going on a space trip to Planet Rebel. They wanted to kidnap people from Planet Rebel and take them back to Planet Austen."

"Yes, they wanted to evangelize us about Jane Austen, who believed true love can endure through time and trouble. Captain Wentworth's love for Anne Elliot endured seven years of separation, a long time considering the human lifespan."

Mr. Hamm stepped in. "In 2820, we think we are far advanced over you, and yet you have proven that we are only advanced in technology – not in matters of the heart. When Mr. Darcy was given access to powerful technology and time-travel, he did not use it for money or power; instead, he used it to find the woman he loved. That makes him a rebel in 2820, but he is also a romantic hero on Planet Austen. For once, the ideals of Planet Rebel and Planet Austen coincided – so the Planet Austen people called off their plans to invade Planet Rebel. That is why Mr. Wick and I received the Order of Honor – for saving Planet Rebel."

"I was a rebel in 1820 as well. I believe love is more precious than all the technology in the world, greater than social connections and material wealth, more important than family obstacles – even opposition from my Aunt Catherine," said Darcy.

"Am I only a piece of technology, or can I find my own true love?" said George, who had been listening quietly.

His creators looked at him. "You were cloned from a bit of Fitzwilliam Darcy, so his DNA is in you. Go use the time-travel device to find the queen of your own heart."

Darcy, Lizzy, Bingley, Jane, Mr. Wick, and Mr. Hamm stepped outside into the corridor to watch the Quantum Chamber disappear with George.

"Where shall we travel to first, queen of my heart?" Darcy said to Lizzy.

She smiled naughtily. "To bed."

As for Caroline Bingley, she didn't have any galaxy bucks to pay the blue alien for kidnapping Lizzy. So the blue alien – whose real name was Luce Ironcarbon – put Caroline to work, catching and cooking horqvathkas, which are grouchy blue animals that taste like chicken, swim like a squid, and are the size of grizzly bears. Charles rescued his sister... eventually.

The Witch, the Loch and the Laird

By Enid Wilson

What if our heroine faced two predicaments?

Run.

Run!

Ignoring the pain, Matilda urged her body to leap and bound along the rugged lane. Her tiring feet tripped on a small rock that sent her flat, face down, onto the ground.

"Shit!" she hissed.

Thump!

The terrible swinging sound of the Loch Ness Monster told her the giant animal would hit her any minute. She rolled her body twice on the ground, narrowly escaping being crushed by the tail of the sea creature. Whoever claimed there was no Loch Ness Monster in Scotland should be shot.

"An eye for an eye!" she muttered. Jumping up, she grabbed the tail of the monster with one hand, then wiggled her arse and swatted it three times. "Fiery and Fury, I command you to turn into jelly!" she commanded, praying that the magic words she uttered would work. As a learner witch of only a year, Matilda Mason's trade was sporadic. She had to practise every day to keep up with her grade, even when she was holidaying in the Highlands. Today's training by the lake had awakened the monster. If this didn't work, her arse would be kicked, or she would be swallowed alive by the giant beast.

A second later, the hard, muscular tail of the creature transformed. The dark grey skin, which had looked like a foul day's clouds, turned so transparently clear that Matilda could see the green grass underneath it.

She released her hold on the tail and pumped her fists up. "Yes!"

The monster stood, stunned, breathing fire onto its transforming tail. Matilda took the chance to run as far as she could, into a ruin she saw a few kilometres away. The stone castle, no matter how dilapidated it was, would provide some protection, she thought.

Once she was deep in the centre of the castle, she rested against a wall and panted.

"You'll be trapped here." The mechanical voice of the monster startled her. "Forever!"

When Matilda looked out of the window, she could see the monster staring at her with a wicked expression.

It's trying to lure me out, she told herself. But she tested the nearest window anyway. It wouldn't open. She jerked the next one. The same. All of the openings in the ruin were jammed or barred by invisible doors, preventing her from leaving.

"Let me out!" Matilda called, fighting panic.

"Not unless you surrender your treasure."

"What treasure?"

"The Margaritifera."

Why did Loch Ness want the silver-coloured freshwater pearl shell she had found by the lake? She patted the treasure in her jeans pocket. Would the monster let her leave, after she surrendered it? When she darted another glance at the sea creature outside, the evil glint in his eyes told her to hang on tight to the pearl shell.

"Not on your life!" she said.

"Then you will spend the rest of your life in the McMillan ruin." Laughing, he slid his gigantic body across the grass and slipped back down into the lake, sinking down until only his eyes were above the water, staring at Matilda.

She continued knocking and pushing all of the windows and doors, charging into empty openings for another half hour, but it was all in vain, leaving her bruised and exhausted.

"Mother, where are you? Come help me!" she shouted. Where was her mother when she needed her? "I must get out." She closed her eyes in frustration.

When she opened them again, the sun was setting in the sky. Darkness would come soon. Would Loch Ness be more powerful then?

Her thoughts of the monster brought him up to the surface a few more inches. His mouth curled up, as if laughing at Matilda's predicament.

She shook the windows and doors again. When that didn't work, she sat down and thought hard, reviewing all that she could recall of the books and lessons she had experienced at the Academy of Wizard in the past year. Was there any anti-curse against imprisonment? Was there any curse against monster Loch?

Nothing came to her mind.

"Even if I can't solve this, someone else must be able to." Her mind ran through all the famous wizards she knew about, and she started chanting, to call for them in her mind. From A, B, C, she called out for help. But no wizard seemed to be in the vicinity or willing to help a 25-

year-old learner witch stranded in a Scottish castle ruin by a monster.

Her voice was hoarse by the time she finally gave up and returned to her exploration of the ruin. The remaining bricks, beams, wood, broken chairs, tables and other items spoke of the splendid past of the place. Perhaps she could return it to its former glory. Loch Ness might not have inhabited the loch in at that era.

She envisioned the reversal curse, wiggled her arse and swatted it three times "Fiery and Fury, I command you to return to your glory!"

With the blink of her eyes, Matilda saw that the ruin had returned to its former splendor. The walls were hung with rich tapestries and hunting trophies. The place where Matilda was standing now appeared to be a bedroom.

At that moment, the door swung open. In walked a six-foot-six-inch muscular man, shirtless, dressed in a dark-green and black kilt.

He stopped and gazed at her with wide eyes. "Who are you?"

"Who are *you*?" She eyed him with caution, inching herself along the wall.

"Disrespectful lass." He tossed his long, curly, chocolate-brown hair away from his face as he shut the door.

"Arrogant jerk!" Matilda muttered.

"Jerk? What language do you speak? You are in my bedchamber, within my castle. I won't allow such rudeness."

"Well, you're not *my* lord." She moved towards the entrance. "And I'm leaving now."

As she attempted to walk past the lord and out of the room, he grabbed her by the waist. "Not so fast."

She swung her hand against his chest and tried to twist her body out of his hold. "Let go of me! I've to leave now."

"Upon my honour, you're a feisty one! You will stay here until you answer my questions." He swung her over his shoulder and carried her toward the bed.

She screamed and thumped his back with her fists, but he was as hard as the monstrous Loch. Worse, he was more difficult to get rid of, because of his hands and legs. He easily tied her to his bed with some cloths he found in a pile by the bed.

"Now, who are you?" He stared down at her in a thoroughly unsettling manner.

"I don't have to tell you."

He lowered his mouth and kissed her neck. "You smell good, like flowers," He said, his voice growing thick.

"Let go of me."

His mouth moved to the neckline of her T-shirt. "Where did you come by such strange clothing?"

She bit her lip and glared at him as he drew the T-shirt up and exposed her bra, which was adorned with a sunflower pattern. As his fingers explored the contours of her breasts, a shiver raced down her spine.

"Strange, strange clothes..." he murmured. His pupils dilated and his voice lowered still further in pitch. "Again, what is your name?"

She clamped her mouth shut, refusing to reply.

His hand tightened around the fabric between the two bra cups. "Answer me or I will tear this off."

She drew in a deep breath, glaring at him, and said, "Matilda Mason. And what about yours, *my dear Lord?*"

"Laird McMillan. Where did you come from?"

"Australia."

He frowned. "Where is this Australia?"

"In the south."

His face twisted tight. "You are English?"

"No. Scottish, many generations ago."

"So you have English blood now."

"No, Australian."

"And this Australia is not in England?"

She raised her voice and her chin. "There is a whole world outside of England."

At that, he smiled. The expression softened his face, making him look like a twenty-year-old. He traced his strong fingers along her jaw, making sparks on her skin. "Why are you here?"

"You won't believe me."

"Try me."

"I was chased by Loch Ness."

He threw back his head, laughed and lowered his mouth to nip at her lip. "Adorable creature."

"He's a monster!"

"I'm not talking about Nessie. He's harmless. I meant you, Redhead."

"I am a woman, not a creature. And don't call me Redhead!"

His hands palmed her pert breasts through the bra's fabric, then traced down her abdomen. Appearing puzzled by the button and zip of her jeans, he fingered them for a few seconds before smoothing his hand farther down from the waistband.

"What have you got here?" he asked, patting her pocket. He had found the pearl shell!

Matilda twisted her body, trying to dislodge his hand and prevent him from retrieving the shell from her pocket, but her hands and legs were tied. He drew out the silver shell...and gasped aloud, staring down at it and then at her.

Finally, giving himself a shake, he tugged her T-shirt down again and called out for his servants.

"Dress and guard this lass. Her name is Matilda, and she and I will marry in an hour's time."

"What?!" Matilda cried out. "I don't want to marry you. I have a boyfriend in Sydney. Let me go!"

"The bearer of the silver Margaritifera shall bear seven immortal heirs to the McMillan clan, according to the legend. Your friend who is only a boy must go."

"I'm not going to marry you or have your heirs. Seven children? Are you a horny bunny? No way! Get that idea out of your thick skull, Laird McMillan!"

"Call me Gavin. Gavin McMillan. I have been waiting for you for years. I am honoured to take you as my wife. I look forward to enjoying your burning body."

Matilda swore. Perhaps it would have been better to be kick-arsed by Loch Ness than ravished by this arrogant Highlander.

What would be the fate of the Learner Witch? Could the Highlander force her to marry him? Was she truly the woman whom the legend had foretold?

Ah, but the answer to those questions is another story, to be revealed some time in the future...

MODERN

Blind Leap

By Aimée Avery

What if Elizabeth didn't realize Darcy's identity?

"Oh Lord! No!" Elizabeth screamed as her car hit a patch of ice, slid into a ditch and stopped with the aid of a rather large tree trunk.

Though everything went black, Elizabeth could feel a sharp pain in her head and the sound of someone knocking on the window.

"Miss? Miss? Can you hear me?" A man's voice repeated over and over.

Elizabeth tried to tell the man to stop yelling, but it only came out as a grunt. She was more worried about the car. It was her uncle's new sedan, and she knew that there was more than just a scratch she was going to have to talk her way out of. Not to mention that her Uncle Edward didn't even know she'd borrowed the vehicle.

This was supposed to be a good deed, not a way of becoming good and dead! But Elizabeth was never one to live on the dull side. Even if dull was what she really needed at this time in her life.

Edward and Madeline Gardiner had invited their niece to join them on this winter's trip to get her away from her dysfunctional family. At home, Elizabeth spent most of her time mediating disagreements between her parents and bailing her youngest sister out of trouble. Things had reached an all time high ever since Jane Bennet, Elizabeth's older sister and best friend, had married and moved out of the area. But removing Elizabeth from a house whose occupants were in constant need of lobbying one's interests with another's, didn't take Elizabeth desire to help away.

Unsolicited help was what got her into this mess. Only she wasn't sure just how much of a mess she was in. Her head hurt too much, and she couldn't seem to open her eyes to figure it all out.

And that *damn* shouting!

"Shut up!" Elizabeth finally croaked out.

"Well, at least you aren't dead!" The male voice said with a touch of humor. "Are you hurt?"

"My h..head..."

"Okay, okay. Relax. I need to get this seatbelt off of you. Good thing you were wearing it, or you might have jumped the airbag and gone right out the window."

Why does he keep talking? It's making my head hurt more! Elizabeth thought.

"Can you please shut up? I want to go to sleep!" Elizabeth said.

"As soon as I get you out of this car, sweet cakes, I might think about it."

"Don't call me 'sweet cakes' unless you want me to slug you!" Elizabeth weakly waved her hand.

"Good luck with that!" The man laughed, and Elizabeth felt herself starting to float. "Okay, you are out of the car. Now to get you to someplace warm."

"I'm not cold."

"You aren't totally conscious either, sweet cakes! But that isn't going to stop me from getting you out of this snow drift."

"I told you..."

"My you're feisty in a semi-conscious state. Are you like this when you're totally awake?"

"Shut up!" Elizabeth wanted him to stop talking. Concentrating on the conversation made her head hurt worse. "Where were going in such a hurry anyway?"

Elizabeth's pride began to swell as she remembered the sweet older couple that she spoke with earlier in the day at the Lambton Diner. George and Caroline Wickham were in an uproar over their landlord raising their rent. They said they could barely pay as it was, and he raised it so high that they would have to sell their store and move away.

How could someone do that to such a nice elderly couple fighting to keep their movie rental shop afloat? They were so sweet and kind as they introduced themselves that morning in the diner.

"Hello, miss!" The older woman had said. "Are you new in town? We've seen you here for the past three mornings."

"I'm visiting. My aunt is from here, and she came to help out her family. I came along for the change of scenery," Elizabeth answered.

The couple sat down next to her. "Well, my name is Caroline Wickham, and this is my husband, George."

The three visited for a couple of hours. When Lizzy mentioned her troubles with her family, it didn't take much for the Wickhams to confide their troubles regarding their twenty-year-old movie rental business and the evil landlord that was trying to cheat them out of their hard-earned money.

Elizabeth leaned into the warm embrace of the man carrying her to safety. "I was going to give a greedy old bastard a piece of my mind."

"Ah! Well, I'm afraid that is going to have to wait until a bit later. Neither you nor your car are in any condition go anywhere. Not to mention, the snow is coming down pretty hard and the road is closed."

Suddenly a gust of warm air hit Elizabeth. It was enough to rob her of what faculties she had, and she fell into a deep sleep.

~*~*~*~

Elizabeth woke and looked around at the strange surroundings. It resembled a ski chalet or something similar. It was an A-framed structure, with a beautiful stonework fireplace. She was lying on a comfortable plush couch, and there was a heavy quilt with an intricate pattern covering her. Something smelled wonderful! Food! Wonderful smelling food! Images of an expensive restaurant in Los Angeles came to mind. She remembered the wonderful food she had eaten there. Too bad it had coincided with a bad blind date with Bill Collins!

"Well, hello!"

Elizabeth turned to meet the eyes attached to one gorgeous man. *Oh my God! I've died and gone to heaven!*

"Do you remember what happened?" The man said as he approached and then sat on the coffee table in front of the couch.

"The car!" Elizabeth suddenly remembered and rapidly moved to sit up.

"Whoa! You took a good whack to the head. I wouldn't move so fast if I were you."

Her head spun quickly, and Lizzy slowly dropped her head back onto the pillows.

"Who're you?" she asked the man she couldn't stop staring at.

"My name's William, but call me Will."

"Will?"

"Mmm hmm. And you are?" Will asked.

"Elizabeth. My name is Elizabeth."

"Happy to meet you, Elizabeth'

"Lizzy!" Elizabeth suddenly shouted.

"Excuse me?"

"Lizzy. Everyone calls me, Lizzy," she added quietly.

Laughing, he replied, "O-okay."

He lightly touched the bump on her forehead.

"Are you hungry?

"Starving!" She took a deep breath. "Something smells delicious."

"Good. Hunger is a good sign! I have some soup, and if you feel up to it, there's some garlic chicken, salad and pie for dessert."

"Thank you."

"You're quite welcome," Will answered. "Let me fix you a tray. Don't go anywhere now!"

"Right!" Elizabeth whispered sarcastically as she slowly sat up.

"Here we go!" William sat a tray on Elizabeth's lap and promptly sat back down on the coffee table. "I'd start with the soup first, if I were you. You hit your head pretty good, and might have a slight concussion. Don't want you to get sick on top of it."

"Mmm. This is good."

"Thanks. Those home economics classes in junior high paid off," he said with a smile.

"Are you always so... so... weird, or is it just for my benefit?"

"Lost your sense of humor?" Will asked.

"You could say that."

"So when I was carrying you in here, you said something about being on your way to give someone a piece of your mind. Where were you headed?"

"I was going to rip a greedy old rich guy a new one for taking advantage of an elderly couple!"

"Out here? I think maybe you took a wrong turn. There aren't any greedy old rich guys living out here."

"Well, I might have taken a wrong turn, I don't know. I was headed to some place called 'Pemberley.'"

"Pemberley!"

"Yeah. You know it?"

"Yes. Very well. I, uh, work there."

"Oh, so you must know the greedy old rich guy. His name is Darcy."

"I know him. But what makes him so 'greedy' anyway?"

"I met this nice old couple at the Lambton Diner this morning, and they told me how this guy raised their rent so high that they can't afford it anymore."

"The Wickhams?"

"Yeah. You know them?" Elizabeth looked at the handsome young man, wondering if she'd found herself an ally.

"I do, but, you might want to hear both sides of the story before you go 'ripping a new one' for anyone."

Elizabeth's hope fell as quickly as it had risen.

"Oh, you just want to protect your boss so you don't lose your job. Who cares who he hurts! You're just as bad!"

"Calm down, Lizzy! I'm just saying that there might be more to the story than George and Caroline didn't tell you."

"How do you know what they did or didn't tell me?"

"I don't, but I *do* know them. I've known them my entire life, so I might have a better idea of what they might tell some stranger to get sympathy."

Elizabeth lost her appetite and pushed the tray off her lap and onto Will's.

Will looked down at the food on the tray for a moment before he picked it up and placed it next to him.

"Okay. So, how much did their rent go up?" Will thought maybe he should take an objective stance for the moment. He didn't want this pretty girl with the beautiful eyes falling prey to the town's resident con artists.

"Um... I... er... They didn't tell me."

Will's eyebrows rose, but he didn't say anything sarcastic, even though he had really, really wanted to. After a few moments, he asked another question.

"Did they even tell you how much rent they pay?"

"No." Elizabeth hung her head. *Maybe I was a bit rash. I should at least know some of the facts before I go storming some old codger's door.*

"Let's forget about all that for now. Okay, Lizzy?"

"Sure."

"Now, I assume you aren't a resident of Lambton?"

"No. I came with my aunt and uncle. My aunt is from here."

"Really? What's her name?"

"Madeline Gardiner."

"Gardiner. Gardiner. That doesn't sound familiar to me," Will said softly.

"Oh! Her maiden name was Reynolds!" Elizabeth quickly added, and Will's eyes flew up to meet hers.

Smiling, he said, "Reynolds? Madeline Reynolds? Her brother's name is Alfred, and she has a sister Renee?"

"Yeah! You know them?"

"I know Alfred very well. His wife is... a... well... she works at Pemberley too."

"Oh," Elizabeth was beginning to feel a bit ashamed of her anger over the Wickham's problems. "I feel so stupid."

"Why?" Will asked in a soft voice.

"Because I drove out here half-cocked, ready to scream at some old guy and not having all the facts."

"Elizabeth..."

"Lizzy. Call me Lizzy."

"Elizabeth is such a pretty name though," Will took her hand and left his seat on the coffee table to sit next to her on the couch. He put his arm behind her and wrapped it around her shoulders. "And I think it's quite an admirable to take up someone's cause. True, you don't have all the facts, but it takes guts to do something like that."

"I'm glad I didn't make it to Pemberley and start screaming at this Darcy guy though. He probably would have called the cops!"

Will laughed and gave her a hug.

"I doubt it."

The two sat there quietly for a couple of minutes before Will got up and grabbed the tray off the table.

"Are you sure you're done?"

Elizabeth nodded.

"Well, I'll put it in the refrigerator just in case you want it later. By the way, where are your aunt and uncle staying? We might want to give them a call so they know you are all right. You were asleep for three hours."

"Oh God! They will be out of their minds with worry. I need to get back to the Inn!"

"Whoa! Whoa! Slow down!" William ran to Lizzy as she tried to stand and head for the door. "First of all, your car isn't going anywhere at the moment. It will take a tow truck to pull it out of the ditch, and then it's going to need some major work."

"Oh God! I am so dead!"

"Why?"

"It's my uncle's *new* car!"

Will chuckled.

"It's *not* funny!" Elizabeth chastised him, even though she was fighting her legs to keep standing. She just wished she knew if her inability to control her legs was because of the bump to the head or the fact that Will was standing so close to her. *He is **so** handsome. And he smells **so** good!*

"I think he'll just be happy you're okay. I assume you're staying at the Lambton Inn?"

"Yes."

"Your uncle's first name is...?"

"Edward."

"Okay. Let's get you back to the couch, and let me give him a call and let him know what's happened. Then I'll get the snowmobile out and get you back to them."

Will sat her back down on the couch and wrapped the quilt around her before grabbing his jacket, his cell phone and heading to the door. He mentioned that he was going to give her uncle a full report on the damage to the car as he explained everything and that she should stay where she was.

As soon as Will closed the door behind him, Elizabeth let her tears fall. She felt so stupid for having believed the Wickhams blindly. She normally spent too many hours getting both sides of the story with every disagreement her sisters, and even her parents, had. And yet she followed the elderly couple blindly, she wrecked her uncle's car and she could have hurt herself worse. Even died.

And she looked like a fool in front of the best looking guy she'd ever met! Nicest too. *I wonder if he has a girlfriend? I'm sure he does. I bet he's a great kisser.*

By the time Will returned, Elizabeth was imagining lying naked under the quilt she was wrapped up in... on the floor in front of the fireplace... with Will lying next to her... naked... kissing her. She blushed scarlet as soon as she saw him.

"Are you okay?" She nodded. "Your uncle wants to talk to you," he said as he handed her the phone.

"Hi Uncle Eddie," Elizabeth said in a meek voice. "Yes, I'm fine. My head hurts, but I'm fine. I'm sorry about the car... Oh, I don't think I should do that... It would be imposing, Uncle Eddie..." Elizabeth turned to see Will go into the kitchen, turn on the water and begin to wash the few dirty dishes. "But Uncle Eddie, I don't even know this guy! I can't stay here, he might be an axe murder!... Ugh! Uncle Eddie! I know people don't murder axes! This isn't the time for jokes... Aunt Maddie knows this guy?... Since he was four years old? Really?... Well, if you think I should... Okay... I'll see you tomorrow... I love you. Bye." Elizabeth ended the call and set the cell phone down on the coffee table.

"So, you think you can handle staying here for the night?"

"You heard, didn't you?" Elizabeth was embarrassed. She seemed to be making it a day for rash decisions.

"Yes, but you had very valid arguments. You don't know me from Adam," Will said as he sat next to her.

"My aunt says that you are a man of honor and integrity."

"That's nice of her to say."

"She also said she baby-sat you since you were four."

"True. She and Renee both had that dirty job. Until I was twelve anyway," Will said with a faraway look in his eye. "Then my sister was born, and I got to do the baby-sitting."

They both sat quietly again until Elizabeth broke the silence. "You don't mind if I stay here tonight, do you?"

"Not at all," he said, putting his arm on the back of the couch behind her. "If you should need medical attention, which I doubt, the hospital is actually closer to here than the Inn. And I can take you by Pemberley on the way back into town tomorrow," he said with a sly smile as he removed his arm and rose from his seat. "I'll get something for you to sleep in."

~*~*~*~

Elizabeth wasn't sure if she should be embarrassed that Will wanted to take her by Pemberley in the morning or that he had a woman's night gown for her to wear. He had offered her the bed, but she adamantly refused, saying that she preferred the couch. In actuality, she didn't want to sleep in a bed that his girlfriend slept in.

Crap! I bet he's married! The great looking nice guys always are, she thought jealously, and cursed the Wickhams for getting her all riled up.

As she thought about her conversation with the elder couple, she realized that they had egged her on after she'd innocently said she felt like driving out and giving the old coot Mr. Darcy a piece of her mind. In fact, they had given her the directions. All that after the waitress at the diner had told Elizabeth that she should use extra care when driving, since the car didn't have snow tires or chains. In fact, Elizabeth remembered offering the couple a ride since they would be going in the same direction, and Mrs. Wickham turned her down, saying that she didn't like the road conditions!

"Why didn't they try to stop me?" Elizabeth whispered to the fire still crackling in the fireplace. "I could have been killed, and all they cared about was themselves. And I'm such a fool!"

Elizabeth put the pillow over her face and let out a quiet scream. She let out another one when she remembered she was wearing this really nice handsome guy's girlfriend's or wife's nightgown.

She turned, placed her head back on the pillow and stared at the flames in the fireplace. Her head still ached. And she felt so foolish for believing what complete strangers had told her, for wrecking her uncle's car and for being too late in meeting a man that not only did she feel comfortable with, but also was known and well-like by the members of her family she admired.

Elizabeth knew there must be some sort of lesson in all this, but she was too tired for any type of analysis, so she closed her eyes and fell fast asleep.

She awoke to a roaring fire and the smell of brewing coffee. Her headache was gone, but her body felt like she had been tackled by at least three football teams. Some vacation this turned out to be.

"Good morning, sweet cakes!" Will said holding two mugs of fresh coffee. "You take anything in your joe?"

"Well, I usually I put in fresh ground cinnamon, but..." Will didn't let her finish as he turned and went back into the kitchen. He returned seconds later with both cups and a peppermill.

"You put pepper in your coffee?" she asked looking at him as if he were from another planet.

"No!" he said with a chuckle as he sat down. "I put cinnamon sticks in a plastic bag and hit them with a hammer until they are the size of peppercorns, then I put them in this peppermill. Fresh ground cinnamon, my favorite coffee additive."

"Well, GMTA!" Elizabeth couldn't believe he also added the spice to his morning brew. Great minds really did think alike.

"Great minds and great coffee!" He smiled. "Sounds like a commercial." They laughed then sat quietly and sipped their java.

"I'll make some breakfast, then we can head out," Will said as he rose and made his way toward the kitchen. "Why don't you hop in the shower. I ran your clothes through the washer last night. They're sitting on the dryer, behind the door to the right of the bathroom."

"Thanks!" Elizabeth sat her mug on the table, buddled up in the quilt and made her way to the bathroom muttering, "Really nice, really hot and really taken. It's all right, Lizzy, old girl. It's just as well, you're really gullible, really stupid and really SOL. I really need to stop speaking in acronyms."

As she stepped into the shower, she tried to figure out a way to convince Will not to take her to Pemberley before heading into town. She'd tried convincing him last evening over dinner, but that hadn't worked. She didn't want to yell at old man Darcy now, especially after her epiphany the night before. After rinsing the shampoo from her hair, Elizabeth finally decided to tell the old gentleman about meeting the couple and listen to his side of the story.

And so was her plan when she climbed aboard Will's snowmobile.

The ride across the snow and tree covered hills was magnificent, as was the sight of the beautifully situated and immense log cabin that they stopped in front of.

"This is Pemberley," Will said as he removed his helmet. "I was able to restore the exterior before the snow came, but I'm afraid the inside isn't finished yet."

"You're restoring it? You do excellent work!" Elizabeth said, amazed at the condition of the structure. It was obvious the house had been around for some time, yet Will's repairs looked as if they were original.

"Come on inside." He grabbed her hand and pulled her up the front steps.

"But Mr. Darcy isn't expecting us, and..."

"It's no bother. C'mon."

They entered through the front door, and Elizabeth again was taken aback at the grandeur of this magnificent structure.

"As you can see, there is a lot of work to be done yet, but the beauty still shines through."

Elizabeth looked beyond the broken and dilapidated bits, and saw the splendor of the hand-carved moldings and railings, intricate inlays and all the details that had once made this more than a beautiful home.

"I remember when I was a child, this place was amazing. I adored being here. Then my mother died, and we moved to the city." Will said as he shook his head.

"What happened to this place? Who would be so callus to allow all this damage?"

"Caretakers that didn't take very good care."

"Didn't anyone ever check up on these people?" Elizabeth asked in disgust.

"Not well enough," Will said angrily.

"How could someone not? What is wrong with this Mr. Darcy? He paid them to let this happen?"

"Like you, he believed the Wickhams."

"*They* were the caretakers?" Elizabeth asked, already knowing the answer.

"Yes! God knows everything they did here, but they would send photos of the place showing it in mint condition. It wasn't until the last set of photos they sent that they were found out. They took old photos of the house and superimposed them onto newer shots of the exterior, only they forgot to Photoshop out the television aerial and substitute the satellite dish. That and the curtains in the window of what had been..." Will stopped and took a deep breath. "Anyway, they were told they could stay, but had to pay in full for the repairs, an estimated ten thousand dollars worth, and submit to physical inspections every six months or get out. They couldn't leave fast enough."

"Has Mr. Darcy brought charges against them?" Elizabeth asked. "This is criminal!"

Will stepped quickly up to Elizabeth. He smiled as he grabbed her shoulders and kissed her soundly. He then grabbed her hand and led her back to the snowmobile.

~*~*~*~

The ride into Lambton took fifteen minutes, but to Elizabeth, it lasted mere seconds, and a lifetime.

She didn't know what to think. Her lips were still tingling. Oh, how she wished he wasn't already spoken for.

They entered the Lambton Inn, but Elizabeth hardly noticed. Her mind was still reeling with all she'd learned about the older couple she so fervently believed in just yesterday.

"Elizabeth!" Madelyn Gardiner yelled as she ran to greet her niece. "Oh, we're so glad you're all right!"

"Oh, Lizzy," Edward Gardiner added.

Elizabeth couldn't hold back the tears as everything that had happened in the last twenty-four hours assailed her. "Oh, Uncle Eddie! I'm so sorry about the car," she cried.

"No! No! No harm done. You're okay, and that's all that matters. Cars are replaceable, nieces aren't." Edward Gardiner smiled.

"Oh, Will! How can we ever thank you?" Madelyn asked, hugging the younger man.

"There's nothing to thank me for."

"Of course there is. Ed, come meet Will," Madelyn said. "Edward Gardiner, William Darcy."

"What?" Elizabeth screamed.

Will quickly grabbed Elizabeth's hand and said, "I took Lizzy to see Pemberley on the way over."

"Oh, Lizzy! Isn't it the finest house you've ever seen? Wouldn't you just love to design the interiors?" Madelyn gushed.

"You're an interior designer?" Will looked at Elizabeth in surprise.

"Yes."

"Have I got a job for you!" he said joyously.

Elizabeth would have jumped at the chance, but she knew she would become even more attached to the owner, the owner who already had someone who kept a nightgown at home away from the restoration home. "Well, I don't..."

"Oh come on, Lizzy! You could see the beauty right through all that disgusting mess. For heaven's sake, you take cinnamon in your coffee, how more perfect can you be?" Will enthused.

"I don't know."

"Please? The project scared my sister away," Will rolled his eyes. "She saw the mess and fled so fast she left half her clothes. Lucky for you she did, or you wouldn't have had anything to sleep in last night."

"Excuse me?" Edward Gardiner bellowed.

"Wait! That was your sister's night gown?"

"Yeah. Who did you think... Oh!" Will smiled.

"Just what went on last night?" Edward Gardiner asked.

"Nothing inappropriate, sir. I think your niece just thought I had a girlfriend."

"You don't?"

"No sir. But I hope I will soon," Will said and took Elizabeth's hand.

Handsome Harry

By June Williams

What if our hero didn't choose the prettier sister?

The overpriced coffeehouse had only a few other customers, so Jane dragged two tables together. *Good thing I wore my comfy jeans and sneakers*, she thought. She set up her laptop on one table, put her purse and phone on the other table, and got online; it could be hours before she looked at the time. She was busy typing when someone stood near her and made harrumphing noises.

"Thank you, but I don't need any more coffee," Jane said.

"I'm not a waiter," said a friendly male voice. "You're sitting at my table."

She looked up and frowned. "Excuse me, but they don't have reserved tables here. I was here first."

"But I always sit here. This table has enough power outlets so I can plug in all my toys."

"I was here first," she repeated. "And I'm a big girl. I need room to spread out."

He bent down to look at her monitor.

She closed her laptop so he couldn't see what she was typing.

"Oh, you're looking at porn." He grinned.

"Am not."

"You sound guilty to me."

Jane turned to look for an employee. "Excuse me, is this table reserved for special nosy customers?"

"No, it's Harry's table," a waitress answered.

"But I was here first, and the table doesn't have a 'reserved' sign," Jane protested.

The waitress scurried over with a power strip with six outlets. "Will this do, Harry? You know you're our favorite customer." She winked at him.

"You're a sweetheart. Thank you, doll." Harry beamed at her, then plugged in his toys – MacBook, iPad, iPhone, camera – at the table next to Jane's, where he could glance over to see her monitor.

She turned her laptop around, moved her chair, and resumed typing, while keeping an eye on the intruder. Jane didn't stare at him, but she noticed he was attractive. Handsome, even. No wedding ring, but that didn't mean anything.

"Go ahead and look. I'm used to women staring at me."

"Yeah, it's been a while since I've seen an ego the size of Milwaukee."

He froze. "Milwaukee? How did you know I'm from Milwaukee?"

Jane groaned. "Of course you're not from Milwaukee. I was just making a point about the size of your ego. Milwaukee is the largest city in Wisconsin, and the name sounds funny; that's why I used it. Mill-wockey. Now go play with your toys and leave me alone."

He was silent as she typed, until the waitress brought him a drink and a plate with a bread slice.

"The zucchini bread is fresh today," she chirped.

"I know," he said conspiratorially. "I plan my entire week around today's delivery of chocolate zucchini bread. And I know who's working each shift today."

The waitress laughed and walked away.

Jane ignored him and kept typing – until her stomach growled. "Drat! I haven't had chocolate zucchini bread in eons. Would you finish eating it so I don't have to smell it?"

"But it's my reward for finishing my work. I won't eat it until I'm done with my report."

"You haven't even started it yet. You've just been sitting here, bothering me."

"I can't start working until I've had my coffee."

"So drink it already!" Her stomach rumbled again and she groaned. "I'm getting my own piece." But when she got to the counter, there was no chocolate zucchini bread, and no waitress or waiter in sight. She walked back to her table and sat down.

Harry sipped his coffee and watched her. "Your typing doesn't sound right. You're upset."

She ignored him and kept working.

"Your typing sounds worse."

"I was fine until your chocolate zucchini temptation reminded me that I haven't had breakfast. And I didn't hear you order anything – how did she know what to bring you?"

"I'm their favorite customer. I have an account. I'm here so often they all know what I drink and eat. When there's a new staff member, my order is part of their employee training."

Jane did not want to laugh or smile at him. She knew from sad personal experience that handsome men were all bad; there was no need to encourage one. She kept typing.

Harry turned his head and waved at a waiter, who brought him another piece of chocolate zucchini bread. Harry slid the plate next to Jane's hand, as he sipped his coffee.

"Do you have your own secret hand-signals with the staff?"

"Yes."

She pursed her lips to stop herself from smiling. *Don't encourage him*, she reminded herself.

"Are you waiting to eat it after you finish your work?" he asked politely.

"Yes, and I don't want you to see me inhale it and then lick the plate." She made pig-like snorting sounds.

He laughed. Unfortunately, he ended up snorting hot coffee through his nose. "Ouch!"

"Oh, no, I'm so sorry." Jane jumped up to get paper napkins, then wiped his toys, which were still shut. "Good thing you haven't started working yet. I shouldn't have done that. I'm such a klutz. I never say the right things. I should buy you a new coffee. Did you get coffee on your zucchini bread? Here, take my bread."

"Jane, are you attacking that poor handsome man?" A soprano voice rang out.

Harry looked up as a gorgeous blue-eyed blonde walked in, her ivory dress clinging to her curves, her stiletto heels tapping out a sing-song message: *I'm so pretty, look at me-eee.*

The newcomer stopped at their tables and smiled. "Is there room for me, sugar?"

"There are other tables here," he said neutrally.

"Oh." She pouted, then turned to the chubby brunette who was concentrating on her typing. "Jane, aren't you done yet?"

"Almost. I'm still updating your links." Jane tried to type faster, but it was hard when she had two people watching her. "Talk to the man, Jackie."

She looked irritated, then turned a brilliant smile to Harry. "My name is Jacqueline." She pronounced it the French way – zhak-LEEN – rhyming with "queen."

"Good morning," Harry said, his hackles raised instinctively.

"Do you know my twin sister?" asked Jacqueline.

"We're acquaintances."

Jacqueline looked at him expectantly.

Harry stared back. "What?"

"I said Jane and I are twin sisters," said Jacqueline, obviously waiting for a response from him. She was still standing, the better to display her long legs. You can't look statuesque when you're sitting down.

Jane didn't even stop typing. "She's waiting for the usual response. We're obviously fraternal twins, not identical, so most people say things like, 'Wow! You sure don't look like twins.' And if they're especially rude, they add, ' It's easy to see which of you got all the good looks. Too bad you lucked out in the gene pool, Jane.' Aren't you going to say something, Harry?"

"No," he said, although he wanted to say a lot of things. "Jane, do you often help Jackie with her work?"

"She just got a manicure and can't type. That's what she told me," Jane said resignedly, still trying to type in front of her audience.

"Some of us are meant for better things," said Jacqueline, still trying to get an admiring look from the handsome man. Jane hadn't noticed, but Jacqueline noticed the man's Rolex watch. She tapped on the watch face, which sounded like crystal and not glass. She noticed the watch letters and numbers were sharp and detailed. The watch looked real, not fake, and if she could get it off his hand, she could analyze it under her jeweler's loupe. Jacqueline lightly ran a fingernail over the top of Harry's hand and up his arm, which almost always got a reaction from a man.

Harry drew his arms to himself. "Jane, I can help you type if you dictate the words to me."

Jacqueline preened. "Of course you may read my resume."

Jane turned her laptop so he could type.

Harry quickly read the resume and fixed a few typos. "What are you adding, Jane?"

"Click on the browser – see those tabs? – those are links to videos of her latest commercials."

"Got it." Harry added the information to Jackie's resume, following the same format as the other links. If the fashion model said anything, he wasn't listening. He didn't even notice that she was still striking alluring poses, trying to get his attention.

Jacqueline handed him two business cards. "New references. Recognize the names?"

Harry looked at the names of two well-known party animals – *rich* party animals. "Yes," he said simply, then added their names, phone numbers, and e-mail addresses to the references section of the resume. He turned the laptop back to Jane.

"Uploading this file to your website." Jane murmured as her fingers typed more easily. "Done."

Jacqueline handed her a flash drive. Jane copied the file to it and returned the drive to her.

"Goodbye," said Harry, handing the business cards back to Jackie.

Jacqueline frowned at her dismissal and left in a huff.

"You're welcome," Harry called to her, but the model didn't even stop. "Is she like this all the time, Jane?"

"Yes. I love her; despite her faults, she's my sister. She's not any different than our brother and parents. They're all very attractive, but I look like my dad's father – and even he preferred Jackie and my brother."

"They expect the world to fall over them because of their good looks?"

Jane nodded, eyeing him suspiciously.

Harry stared back, then smiled in understanding. "You're judging me. Or you've already judged me but now you're thinking you're wrong."

"Yes," she said softly, unable to look him in the eyes. "I'm sorry. It's just that – you know – handsome guys like you prefer my sister. In fact, all guys prefer her because she's prettier, taller, skinnier, everything better than me."

"But she expects things handed to her on a silver platter. Jackie isn't the one who interrupted her day to meet her sister. She couldn't be bothered to drive to your house, I take it."

"How did you know?" She finally looked up at him.

"When I got here, your clothes were still damp, like you'd taken them out of the dryer in a hurry. You don't normally do that; you're very organized and methodical. You didn't even stop to comb your hair, which is still damp from a shampoo." He leaned toward her head and sniffed. "You didn't even take time to rinse out your hair conditioner."

Jane groaned in embarrassment. "Nailed. Jackie said it was an emergency, that her revised resume had to be online by eleven o'clock so a new model agency could look at it. She wanted me to meet her here because it's on her way to an interview."

"Hmph. She still could have thanked you."

Jane shrugged. "Could I buy you a new coffee?" She pushed her slice of bread to him.

"It's okay." He put his hand over hers to stop her, then picked up Jane's cup. "This is full. You haven't touched it; it must be cold. I'll get you a fresh cup."

"Erm, I actually don't drink coffee. I just ordered it because I was using their free wi-fi."

He stared. "You don't drink coffee?"

"I don't even like the smell of coffee. Not even if you add it to chocolate."

He was stunned, then burst out laughing.

Jane look at him. "It's not *that* funny, is it?"

He nodded, still laughing. "Jane, I own this coffeeshop – and six other locations. Coffee is my life."

She turned red. "Oops."

"It's okay. We still have chocolate zucchini bread in common – and a lot of other things, I bet." Harry patted her hand. "Do you even know the name of my store?"

"No. Jackie told me to go to the coffeeshop on the corner of Austen and Regency."

He showed her a sign on the wall and read it out loud. "Handsome Harry's Coffeeshop. Our slogan: ' Coffee so strong it puts hair on your chest.' Headquarters: Milwaukee."

She groaned. "And that's why they gave me a graduate degree in English, because I can't read what is in front of me."

"And if you open the menu, it has my picture in it." He showed her the picture – it was a hand-drawn cartoon caricature of a man working at a coffee-roaster. You would recognize him only if you knew it was supposed to be him. "You're a genuine person, Jane. You could have lied to me just now, pretended that you like coffee, but you didn't. You're a woman of honor and integrity. You don't treat me differently because I have a bit of money."

"No, I'm rude to everyone."

"No, you're not rude, Jane. You have a sense of humor. You're very sensitive to others' needs and hurts, you're forgiving of those who hurt you, and you would give away your only piece of chocolate zucchini bread to a stranger. But you're also learning to stand up for yourself – a hard lesson for you, I imagine."

She nodded.

"How about it, Jane? Would you be willing for us to get to know each other? I know this great coffeeshop where you can order chocolate desserts off-menu, but only if you know the owner."

She grinned. "I will even help you with your report."

"It's a date."

The Prince's Private Eye
By Enid Wilson

What if Darcy was a prince who caused a racket?

Britain was shocked with the sudden death of tennis champion Mr. Frederick Hurst today. Hurst, a four-time Grand Slam winner in the 1970s and a family man, suffered a sudden seizure during Britain and Belberley's Davis Cup match at Wimbledon. He was taken to Parkside Hospital, but doctors were unable to revive him.

Hurst was the outgoing coach for Britain's Davis Cup. At two rubbers all, Britain was set to capture the trophy for the first time since 1936 with Britain's No. 1 tennis player, Charles Bingley, tipped to take the final deciding match against Belberley's Mathis Lee.

Bingley, whose sister was married to Hurst, was believed to be shaken by the event which happened about an hour before his match, and lost to Lee in straight sets. Once again, the Davis Cup was loosened from the grip of British team. Belberley's first Davis Cup victory was watched on by their Crown Prince Fitzwilliam Darcy, who works as a Chief Financial Officer in Britain's Standard General Bank. Hurst, 49, was survived by his *wife, Louisa and two daughters from his previous marriage. – London Evening Gossip, Saturday, 6 August 2011*

69 Grove Park Gardens, Chiswick
Thursday, 1 September 2011

"Are you certain about the address?" Prince Fitzwilliam frowned. The corner detached house in the leafy suburb, which could be well worth more than two million pounds, looked too good to be the office of a private detective.

"Yup. Richard said Bennet makes his money from the shares market and only works as a private detective part time."

"Is that wise to hire such a person? With the credit crunch, he may be busy saving his arse, instead of helping you. I can talk to someone in Scotland Yard and get you a full-time professional."

"No wonder my arse tingles," the cheerful voice of a young woman startled them. They turned. "Someone's talking about it."

Where were his security guides? Darcy frowned as he examined the woman and his face felt warm – 5 feet three, around 100 pounds, dark chocolate hair, small build, wearing a non-descriptive black track suit. Very ordinary, except for those fine eyes. She glanced at him with her lips curled up before turning her attention to Bingley.

"Elizabeth Bennet. Sorry about your family loss, Mr. Bingley. Richard, the Deputy Commissioner didn't tell you I'm a woman?" She extended her hand to Bingley.

Bingley shook hands with her. "Thank you, Miss Bennet. No, Richard didn't mention it. And this is…"

"His Royal Highness Prince Fitzwilliam Darcy of Belberley, your friend," said she, before opening the front door with a remote, neglecting to extend her hand to Darcy or curtsey to him.

As Bingley chatted with Miss Bennet, Darcy noticed his security guards running towards the house in fast strides, red-faced. He waved them away and followed his friend into the house. It was decorated in excellent taste, homely, country and yet modern. Photographs of beautiful people from around the world hung on the wall. She led them to the kitchen.

"What would you like?" said she, to Bingley.

"Tea will be good."

She busied herself preparing the tea and gave Darcy a silent glance. Bingley shifted his weight, uneasy with the unconventional treatment Miss Bennet was giving his friend. Usually when women met his handsome and single, royal friend, they swoon, drool, scream or fall all over him immediately. When she was not looking, with a gesture, he urged the scowling Prince to speak.

"I'd like to have a glass of wine," said HRH, in a displeased voice.

"Help yourself," said she, indicating the wine on the racks and taking two cups of tea to the patio through the kitchen.

Darcy's lips tightened. After he had poured himself a glass of vintage merlot from France, he joined them, sitting directly opposite Miss Bennet. He would not be ignored.

"Who is contesting the will?" said Miss Bennet, continuing her discussion with Bingley.

"My sisters Louisa and Caroline, separately."

She raised her eyes and typed the information into her iPhone. "Why?"

Bingley sighed. "They were in a screaming match, said Hurst made a new will, or wills a year or two ago, promising them separately one-third each of his estate, to be shared with his two daughters."

"But his lawyer doesn't have either of these wills?"

"No. Frank Churchill, his lawyer, only has a will that was drawn up five years ago, before Hurst married Louisa. In this will, Augusta, Hurst's first wife, who hadn't remarried then, is named the third beneficiary. He had urged Hurst to rewrite the will, but my brother-in-law never came round to doing it, at least not with Frank."

"Miss Bingley was sleeping with Mr. Hurst."

"I don't know," Bingley shrugged. "Caroline said Hurst promised her part of the estate because she took good care of his daughters, much better than Louisa."

She nodded. "What do you want me to do?"

"Find the wills, if there are any."

"And investigate Hurst's murder?"

"Bingley didn't say Hurst was murdered," said Darcy.

"I know the case is treated as suspicious."

"You're very good with police information, Miss Bennet," said Bingley.

"Call me 'Elizabeth'. And how do you propose, Mr. Bingley, to bring me into your life to find the suspected lost wills?"

"Call me, Charles. You can pretend to be my girlfriend." He smiled. "As for Hurst's death, I'll leave it to the police to investigate."

Elizabeth shook her head. "You're not my type. Difficult to pretend. I wouldn't mind kissing a Prince though," said she, licking her lips as she gazed at HRH, sitting tensely opposite her.

Darcy's face turned cold. Before he could reject her vulgar proposition, she said, "My sister Jane can pretend to be your girlfriend." She flicked her iPhone and brought up a photo for Bingley to have a look. His eyes went wide. "She's stunning, like an angel!"

"It's decided then. I'll set you up for two dinner dates, and then you can invite Jane and I to your brother's estate in Berkshire next weekend."

"You're very well informed."

She nodded. "Our fee is 500 pounds per person per hour, travel and expenses on top."

Bingley nodded. Darcy was extremely annoyed with her. She had practically ignored him throughout the entire meeting and then teased him with a proposition. Now, she was pushing Bingley into a quick decision with the lure of her beautiful sister. And her fees were exorbitant, perhaps just because Bingley was his friend.

"And why do you need His Royal Highness in this meeting?"

"Umh, I..." Bingley was lost for words.

"He wants an honest second opinion," Darcy jumped in, "to ascertain your professionalism. Do you have a past client with whom we can check on your work?"

"Charles didn't ask for it. It's more for your peace of mind."

"I'm trying to look out for his welfare."

"The recommendation from the Deputy Commissioner isn't enough for Your Royal Highness?"

"Richard can be susceptible to flattery by pretty girls."

Elizabeth laughed a genuine hearty and loud laugh. "Thank you for the compliment. I should tweet about it."

Darcy's face turned grey. He hated to be centre of attention, especially in the mindless social media.

She twirled a strand of unruly curl and said, "I'll tell your cousin what you said. You can expect some tough matches from him."

"You seem to know everything about me," said Darcy. "Even my tennis nights with Richard."

"Very egoistic assumption. I'm interested in everything about Charles, as a client, not in you, Prince Fitzwilliam."

"Or Richard saves your lazy self and feeds you information because of your cheery innocent persona."

"Tsk tsk, someone should be called His Royal Pain in the Arse."

"No, Elizabeth, I'm fine with your suggestion, especially about Jane and me," said Bingley hurriedly. He hated confrontation and, judging from Darcy and Elizabeth's face, this might lead to a fistfight. "I trust Richard and you. And you can call him 'Darcy'. His friends all call him 'Darcy', less of a mouthful. He'll be there next weekend."

Darcy scowled at Bingley, but Elizabeth smiled, rose from her chair and showed them out of her house, with some parting words to Darcy. "I will befriend you on Facebook." That made Darcy want to put his hands on her pretty neck.

The Grosvenor, 282 Coronation Road, Ascot

Saturday, 10 September 2011

"How long have you known my brother?" Louisa Hurst asked Jane Bennet.

"Just a few weeks," replied Jane. Elizabeth had gone through the basic backstory of their 'love interest' with Bingley and her sister.

"You are from Hertfordshire."

"Yes, from a small town called Meryton."

"Have you visited her there yet?" Louisa asked her brother.

"Not yet. Jane and Lizzy live in Chiswick. Darcy and I have been there."

"I like their house," commented Darcy, which caused Elizabeth to raise her eyes. Another compliment from His Royal Pain in the Arse?

"This is a magnificent house," Elizabeth ignored the staring Prince and stepped forward to admire the pictures on the wall. It was a Gainsborough. Genuine? Not really. "You have some very interesting paintings."

"Yes, Frederick liked to collect art," nodded Louisa. "His agent, John, handled all of his purchases."

"John?"

"John Thorpe, or John the Teddy. He's like a teddy bear, big and friendly. Frederick had known him since they were teenagers."

"So, Mr. Thorpe handled Mr. Hurst's tennis career as well as his personal business?"

"Yes, he's a real friend, always looking out for Frederick. Real smart guy. When the stock market crashed the past few times, he always got Frederick out of the hot water in one piece. He will be joining us this weekend too. I want to thank him for helping me through the funeral and the reading of the will, etc."

"Of course."

"And who will be coming too?" said Bingley. "I assume Caroline is not coming."

"Don't mention the orange maniac to me," exclaimed Mrs. Hurst in a raised voice. "Harriet and Henrietta will be here soon."

"Orange maniac?" Jane said.

"Miss Caroline Bingley, my sister, only wears clothes in orange, every hues of it."

"Augusta will drop them off? Harriet and Henrietta are Hurst's daughters from his first marriage. Mrs. Augusta Elton is Hurst's first wife," explained Bingley to Jane and Elizabeth, as if they didn't know.

"You know that woman is not welcome here either. I've sent the driver to pick the girls up."

"Would you like a tour of the house, Elizabeth?" said Darcy. "If Louisa has no objection to my taking you around."

"You know the house well enough to conduct a tour, Your Royal Highness?"

"Darcy has been here many times," commented Bingley. "I think that's a good idea, but I want to head out for some practice. Jane, would you like to join me?"

"As long as you do not expect me to play a match with you," smiled Jane. "I'm hopeless with scoring."

Elizabeth frowned. She would rather have Bingley take her on the tour, as he would know the right place to check for the missing wills, but Charles seemed more eager to sweet-talk Jane than find the documents. Anyway, she didn't expect to find them in the house. She just wanted to form a better idea about Hurst and the other suspects.

Louisa exclaimed, "Oh, Prince Fitzwilliam, let me conduct the tour. I wouldn't like to trouble you."

"No trouble at all. Your step-daughters will be arriving soon. You may prefer to wait here to greet them."

"That's true."

"Where would you like to begin, Elizabeth?"

"Hmm, how about the gallery?"

Darcy signalled for her to proceed to the north side of the house. Halfway through, Elizabeth said, "Let's go to Hurst's study."

"Hmm, he usually used the library."

"The library then."

He didn't engage her to talk, instead walking onward with his hands behind his back. Elizabeth observed the layout of the house and the decoration along the corridor. If His Royal Highness was not eager to talk, she would have no problem at all.

The library was spacious, but the number of volumes was lacking. One of the walls had been converted into a bar. Judging by the number of bottles there, it seemed Mr. Hurst loved his bottles more than his books.

"Did Hurst spend a lot of time here?"

"Yes. I think this is his favourite room. The sofa there can turn into a bed."

Walked to the not-so-mini bar, Elizabeth nodded and pulled it open.

"You expect he hid the wills among the frozen snacks here?"

Insufferable man! She ignored him and looked at the contents. Chocolate, capsicum salsa, Camembert, celery stems, carrots, cucumbers, etc., etc. They all seemed to have passed their expiration dates. Mrs. Hurst apparently hadn't bothered to ask the servants to clear out her late husband's things.

Closing the fridge, she walked to the last row of shelves and examined the books on each level. Prince Fitzwilliam followed her closely. When her eyes scanned the top, he scanned the top level as well. When she browsed the middle level, he did the same. Most of the books were not arranged in any order. They had been crammed in randomly.

Elizabeth folded her arms across her chest. She didn't like someone underfoot, even if he was a handsome prince. "Don't you have some business to attend to? You can leave me here for half an hour."

"I'm quite at leisure this weekend. And I'm monitoring your work, for Bingley's sake."

The nerve on her neck throbbed. She could be sarcastic too. "Is your job real, in Standard General?"

"Very real. My team has to predict shares performance every quarter and seven out of ten, we get them wrong." His mouth curled up slightly.

Was the prince trying to flirt with her? "Why do you need it? You'll be inheriting the throne one day."

"I like some real-world experience. And financial knowledge always comes in handy, to help our economy."

She took out a set of three books that had been put tidily on the third shelf up.

Biographies: JFK, Elizabeth Taylor, and Muhammad Ali.

"Why are you interested in those three?"

"They're neater and without dust."

"So perhaps Hurst had been reading them? Why would he be interested in them?"

"Was he planning on writing one himself?"

"Very smart, Miss Bennet."

Elizabeth's lips curled up. The Prince was definitely flirting, but she wasn't interested. She didn't want to be a notch on the bedpost for a royal, though from her research, the Prince seemed to be living like a monk – not one photo of him kissing any women anywhere. Perhaps he had a harem of women somewhere in his palace. She flipped the pages quickly. Nothing out of the ordinary. Then she passed them to HRH, one after the other. His mouth gaped open and then closed, and then he placed the books back into the empty slots in the shelf. He didn't like to be treated like an assistant. He was a prince!

In this manner, she completed her examination of the shelves and moved on to the desk. Some pieces of paper were stacked on the tray. She scanned through them quickly. Bills, bank statements (minimal cash in this account though), magazine clippings, invitations. Mr.

Hurst was very casual with his paperwork, not bothering to lock them up. Anyone could come in here and measure up his life.

She was pulling and feeling the drawers under the table when she suddenly heard voices approaching the library. She pulled Darcy to hide in the dark end of the room. With their bodies pressed together, she could feel his fresh manly smell and his 6 foot 3 stature. With her heels off, she only reached his torso. The Prince didn't seem to care about the position they were in. He even casually put his hands on her butt. If he moved them an inch, she would kick him where it hurt, prince or no prince.

"Darling, I've been waiting," purred Louisa. "It's a pity Charles brought so many guests this weekend."

The smooching sounds were loud and exaggerated. Then a breathless male voice was heard, "You're one hot, desperate housewife."

"What are we to do, John?" The agent, John Thorpe!

"I'm going to fuck you senseless, that's what I'm going to do now."

A swatting sound. "I meant the will! That bitch Caroline wants my money."

"I'll take care of her, don't worry, babe."

"Then, I'll take good care of little John."

"Oh...." Thorpe moaned. Their low moans and grunting hummed throughout the library. Elizabeth rolled her eyes and hoped the man wouldn't last long. She didn't want to have to hear their passion, especially when she noticed that His Royal Highness seemed to be up as well. Pervert! Getting a high from this voyeurism.

Darcy's hands moved slightly, to rub her butt cheeks. She took them abruptly and pushed them back to his side, then gave him a death glare. Darcy's gaze intensified, and then he lowered his lips to kiss her! She wanted to bite him, but didn't want to alert the other two in the library.

Damn this man! He's one hell of a good kisser. So instead of giving him bodily harm, she raised her hands to his shoulders and kissed him back. They licked and sucked each other's lips and he thrust his tongue into her wet mouth, teasing her inner muscles. They didn't come up for air, until nearly a minute after the other horny couple had reached their peak and left.

"Royal Pain in the Arse!" said Elizabeth breathlessly, before pushing him away and walking out of the library. Prince Fitzwilliam Darcy needed several minutes to cool down. Wow, she was damn hot!

~*~*~*~

Elizabeth was happy to sit so far away from Prince Fitzwilliam. He was a distraction she didn't need. She wanted to concentrate on the persons of interest around the table. They were enjoying a delicious lunch on the patio. Louisa Hurst sat at one end with the Prince and John Thorpe at her sides, Henrietta and Harriet Hurst on either side of them. Bingley had brought back a neighbour and his tennis hitting partner, James Benwick. Benwick was England's No. 2 player at the time when Hurst was No. 1. He had retired due to injury and now worked with Bingley.

Thorpe was a master of disguise, very professional at the lunch table, talking to Harriet like she was his favourite lady friend and to the host like she was his best employer.

Both Henrietta and Harriet were horny twenty years old. They latched onto the gentlemen by their sides with batted eyelashes and seductive smiles. T hey twirled their artificial blonde curls with their fingers in harmony. Elizabeth wondered what their upbringing had been like. The two young women didn't seem to be in mourning, though their father was only dead for a month.

Prince Darcy was bored, Lizzy could see that plainly. His eyes darted to her end of the table constantly. He was polite to Henrietta, but didn't encourage her at all.

"Your Royal Highness, what's your holiday plan? Will you be going to the Caribbean for Christmas?" said Henrietta, tracing her fingers purposely on the neckline of her low cut sundress. At the age of 21, she had a fabulous figure, smooth tan skin and lovely features. If she could cut down on the make-up and fake smiles, Prince Darcy might find her attractive, Lizzy thought.

"I've no plan yet," replied the Prince. His eyes drifted to Elizabeth again.

"Oh, John, don't you think we should go to Nectar Island this year? Cameron was happy to have the two girls and I use it. After this terrible affair with Frederick, I think it would be a great idea to relax and unwind," exclaimed Louisa. So, Britain's billionaire Ian Cameron was good friend of the Hursts. "We'd be honoured if Prince Fitzwilliam were to join us," she smiled. "Of course, Charles, you are welcome to come too."

"I'm not sure," said Charles. He knew Cameron sometimes had movie stars stay on his private island. And Darcy didn't like to stay in places frequented by celebrities. Paparazzi always kept tabs on those islands. "Jane, what would you like to do this Christmas?" Bingley had such a puppy love expression on his face that Elizabeth rolled her eyes. She didn't think she would need that long to find the wills, if there were any. She wouldn't want to impose upon Jane to act as Bingley's love interest for this long. But when she turned to look at her eldest sister, Jane had a blush of pink in her cheeks. She seemed as besotted as Bingley. Elizabeth shook her head. She hoped Jane wouldn't be hurt by his handsome charm.

"I'd love to go to the beach too," said Jane, "but I prefer somewhere nearer."

"But in the Caribbean, we get to be seen," argued Henrietta. "Last year, I was photographed with Leonardo and my friends were so envious of me."

"Talking about the Caribbean," said Elizabeth. "'The Two Women Chatting by the Sea' by Pissarro in the gallery is quite magnificent."

"Isn't it just the most peaceful painting you've ever seen?" commented Louisa.

"I don't see how marvellous it is," retorted Henrietta. "Daddy refused to buy me the diamond necklace from Tiffany but bought that piece of thing instead. Once the will is sorted out, I swear I'll have all the paintings sold and blow them on blinks."

"I agree," said her sister. "I don't know why Daddy liked to collect these boring landscape paintings. He should collect portraits of hunky guys. I blame you, Uncle John. You're always showing him 'exciting' investment opportunities, one after another."

"Nonsense," replied Thorpe. "Masterpieces by Gainsborough, Pissarro, and Monet are very good investments. If you two can hang onto them and sell them in 10 years or so, the value will double or triple."

"Who needs investments when I can have limited collection handbags?" pouted Henrietta. "And some of your schemes didn't work at all."

"Oh yes, I remember," added Harriet. "Those beachside developments in Indonesia. A big wave came in...whoof...and Daddy's millions washed away into the sea."

Imitation artwork and dodgy property investments, Thorpe seemed eager to bleed Hurst dry, thought Elizabeth.

"That's a tsunami," said Louisa. "No one could predict such a natural disaster."

Thorpe raised his hands. "Don't I always look out for you, Harriet? But investment does have its ups and downs. And there is not much risk with masterpieces like this."

"Did you get them from Sotheby?" asked Elizabeth.

Thorpe smiled. "I've my private sources."

"Yes, John knows a lot of people," added Louisa. "Some of the purchases are of such a reasonable price."

"Legal sources," added Prince Fitzwilliam. "I hope." The Prince was insufferable, Elizabeth thought. Why did he have to barge into her investigation? She was leading the conversation in that direction already, without his help. And such a comment wouldn't get anything out of Thorpe.

"Of course," commented Thorpe. "Hurst's lawyer is very careful about these."

Unless Frank Churchill was in cahoots with John Thorpe too, thought Elizabeth.

"I still don't care about paintings," pouted Henrietta. "I love movies much better."

"You love those big...you know what...actors from America," giggled Harriet.

"You're just jealous I've got my way in Hollywood."

"Oh yes," said Louisa. "Warantino's agent approached you after you were seen photographed with Leonardo, didn't he?"

"Yes, I got selected for his latest cult movie. But they are filming in Mongolia. Why would I want to get stuck in that God-forgotten place for three months? Of course, I have to decline."

"As if," sneered Harriet. "You couldn't remember your lines in the audition. And you had to beg the agent to get you in, for it."

"Shut up, little mouse!"

"Wash your mouth, you giant ostrich."

"Girls, girls!" placated Louisa. "Remember your manners. Prince Fitzwilliam is here."

The two young women flustered and glared at each other.

"But seriously, Jane," said Louisa, in condescendingly. "I hope you're not referring to Brighton when you said somewhere 'nearer'."

"Brighton is very nice," said Elizabeth. "Our family spent many of our summer holidays there."

The Hurst women laughed out loud. "How quaint!" "Locals." "Such a country gem!"

"Yes, sometimes things closer to home hold real meaning," said Darcy. His comment stopped the women's chuckle.

"You're correct, Your Royal Highness," continued Elizabeth. "Will you put that line in your memoir?"

"Already writing a memoir, Your Royal Highness?" Thorpe interrupted. "You wanted to rival Hurst? Aren't you a bit too young?"

"Hurst had written an autobiography?" asked HRH, pretending not to known.

"Yes," nodded Thorpe. "He completed the first draft about a month before his death."

"Now that he past away suddenly," said Benwick, "will its publication be affected?"

"No, I've been talking to the publisher. The editing is progressing well. They are going to push it forward. The book will be available before Christmas."

"I've read some of it," said Harriet. "Quite sensational!"

"How come Daddy didn't show it to me?" pouted Henrietta.

"It was after the Wimbledon party that Caroline organised in June. You went to Paris, remember. All of us – John, Uncle Charles, Auntie Caroline – were here except you, sister dear."

"Forget Caroline! John, it's marvellous about the publication date. Book sales always go up before Christmas!" exclaimed Louisa.

Elizabeth arched her brow. Mrs. Hurst seemed to congratulate the timely loss of her husband. Could she have killed him because he discovered she was screwing his agent?

"Will we be promoting his book for him?" asked Harriet excitedly. "Perhaps the publisher will get Andy Morrison to help with the book launch? I'd love to tour USA with a handsome man on my arm."

"Your Royal Highness will be the best person to help launch daddy's book," argued Henrietta. "You look extremely handsome in your tennis gear, Prince Fitzwilliam."

"So, your uncle Charles, Britain's current No. 1 is not good enough for you?" commented Elizabeth.

Crinkling her nose, Henrietta said, "Who wants to be seen with her uncle! That's sick."

"But Darcy is older than I," reminded Bingley.

"He's a prince, you're not."

"Is there any juicy detail from the book, Harriet?" asked Elizabeth. "You said it's sensational."

"Oh, yes, Daddy made a shocking confession, which will piss off a lot of people. But you've read it too..." Harriet's eyes gazed at one of them.

"Ah, Miss Bennet," interrupted Thorpe, with eyes narrowed. "What have you heard?"

Elizabeth wanted to throttle Thorpe for stopping Harriet mid-sentence. "I'm just a share trader, how do you expect me to hear about the tennis circle?"

"Mrs. Hurst said you are Richard's friend."

"Being a friend of a police officer automatically means something?"

"Can you access Scotland Yard's computers?" asked Harriet, sitting up with interest. "I fancy having a dinner date with Britain's most wanted and tweeting about it.

Can you arrange that for me?" She and her sister broke out into giggles.

"You cannot come in!" The frantic voice of the housekeeper cut short the laughter of the young women.

"Why can I not come in?" A woman's sharp voice dismissed the servant's plea.

"The mistress..."

"Stuff her!"

A tall, impeccably dressed woman came out to the garden. "Charles, what's the meaning of this?"

"Caroline, this is Louisa's house." Bingley and the other men rose to greet her. Henrietta and Harriet waved hello as they sipped their wine.

"Oh, Prince Fitzwilliam," smiled Caroline, sauntering to the Prince and trying to press her orange lips to his mouth. With a quick reflex, the Prince avoided the mouth-to-mouth kiss, but the bright orange lip marks landed on his cheek. Elizabeth looked away, trying to hide her smile.

Caroline latched onto the Prince's arm as she continued to complain, "This is Hurst's house, and he never forbade me from coming here when he was alive."

"But you're not welcome now," hissed Louisa, gulping down the wine. "Now go before I call the security."

"Mom, let her stay," said Harriet, popping a piece of canapé into her mouth. "I want to ask her about the Gigi collection in the Milan fashion show."

"See, Hurst's daughters welcome me," smiled Caroline triumphantly. "This is their house too." She left the Prince's side and walked forward, trying to grab a chair to squeeze between Henrietta's and Darcy's. Before she could do so, though, Louisa splashed the content of her wine glass at her.

"Fucking old prune!" Caroline screamed and jumped away. Her orange designer dress now stained with spots of red. "What was that for, bitch? I come to see Harriet and Henrietta, not to argue with you about the will, though I'm sure you've hidden it somewhere." Launching herself at her older sister, she used her handbag to smack Louisa's head as she yelled out.

"You smutty old orange! Screwing Frederick when I was away and daring to contest for his money?" Louisa raised her hand to scratch Caroline's eyes. The catfight caught everyone by surprise. The two women pushed and shoved each other, overturning chairs and smashing dishes to the floor. Henrietta and Harriet hopped away from their seat to avoid being hit. Thorpe and Bingley tried to separate the scuffle. The others stood aside, watching with mixed disbelief to disgust.

Suddenly, Caroline pushed Louisa with such force that the latter backed up onto Harriet, mother and daughter were tumbling to the ground.

Elizabeth stood near the pair. When she pulled Louisa up, she noticed something wrong with Harriet. Harriet's face had turned purple and her eyes very still.

"Call the ambulance!" cried Elizabeth.

Caroline flew forward, trying to hit Louisa again. With a quick duck, her sister avoided the attack. Caroline's hand almost landed on Elizabeth's shoulder, but Elizabeth easily twisted Caroline's arm behind her back with a smooth kung fu move. The assailant cried out in pain. "Let go of me! Who are you? Charles, help!"

"Stop, this moment!" said Elizabeth, loud and stern. "Harriet is injured."

Either the pain or Elizabeth's harsh words registered in Caroline's brain, she stopped screaming and fighting. "Take her away!" said Elizabeth. Prince Darcy came forward and pulled Caroline back.

Elizabeth crouched down to examine Harriet. No pulse. So fast! Damn! "She's dead." Elizabeth was angry that she couldn't prevent the murder. She prided herself as being observant and alert. But she had no clue who the murderer was. How could someone kill someone in front of so many witnesses? And she felt sorry for the young girl. Despite her vanity, Harriet was a sparkling girl with years of living in front of her.

Everyone gasped.

"Harriet!" Caroline shrieked and cried. "Did I kill her?" She seemed to genuinely care for Hurst's daughters.

Shortly afterwards, the ambulance arrived and the paramedics confirmed the death. The police followed. Perhaps because of the presence of a foreign prince, Richard Fitzwilliam, Deputy Commissioner of Police, arrived as well. And a large contingent of media started assembling outside the gate of the estate.

The officer in charge was interviewing everyone one by one in the library. Richard asked Elizabeth to come with him to the entertainment room for a quiet chat.

"Can I join you?" asked Prince Fitzwilliam.

Richard looked to Elizabeth who shrugged.

"I thought you were just trying to locate the wills," said Richard, sitting down on the sofa by the window.

She went to sit on an armchair opposite. "I can't help it when the murderer chose to strike again."

"Again?" Prince Darcy decided to mark his territory and sat on the arm of the chair where Elizabeth was sitting. "It's confirmed that Hurst was murdered?"

Richard nodded as he stared at his cousin's strange behaviour. Elizabeth tried to squirm as far from the Prince as possible.

"Yes, we've known for two weeks but kept a close lid on it. His energy drink was spiked," said Richard, "with one antidepressant too much."

"And he didn't take those pills," Darcy murmured to himself.

"Hmm, the MO is the same," commented Elizabeth. "Harriet's wine smelt different too. Perhaps someone popped some pills into her wine too."

"Who is your chief suspect?" Darcy asked Richard.

"Everyone present today was at the Davis Cup tie too."

"So any of them is possible."

"Including you, Prince Fitzwilliam," Elizabeth murmured.

Darcy's eyes widened. "Why would I want to kill Hurst?"

"Belberley was in dire need of its first Davis Cup," said she with a smirk. "And the Crown Prince resorted to crooked means."

"If that was the case," smiled Prince Fitzwilliam, "I should have poisoned Bingley, not Hurst."

"Or you're madly in love with Miss Bingley," said she with an arch of her brow, "but Hurst was encroaching on your turf."

"Yikes!" Darcy pretended to vomit onto her.

Richard stared at them as they flirted with each other. Well, well, he would never have thought of such a development when he recommended that Bingley ask Elizabeth for help. His stoic cousin who rarely smiled when photographed and who hadn't dated a single woman for the past three years was clearly smitten.

"Did you notice anything suspicious?" Richard hated to interrupt, but he wanted to solve this high-profile case as soon as possible.

"Mrs. Hurst is sleeping with John Thorpe."

"How did you know?"

Both Prince Fitzwilliam and Elizabeth turned a shade of pink. "We just know," said she.

'We', thought Richard, *like a couple*. He let it drop and continued, "So both of them have a motive to get rid of Hurst."

"And Hurst's memoir may tell us who his enemies are," added Darcy.

"Perhaps you can get a copy of its draft," commented Elizabeth. They were finishing each other's sentences. Interesting. Richard noted that in his notebook.

"What about Caroline?" the Deputy Commissioner asked Elizabeth.

"She was sleeping with Hurst but had no reason to kill Harriet. I don't think she's our guy."

"Henrietta will get richer now?" asked Prince Fitzwilliam.

Richard nodded. "Yes, according to the existing and 'lost' wills, on the death of either sister, the other one will inherit the share." He paused for a moment before asking, "And do we have any reason to suspect Bingley and Benwick?"

"They are lambs!" exclaimed Darcy. "I won't believe they would harm anyone."

"You could be surprised," commented Elizabeth.

"Bingley can resent Hurst's military coaching torture," speculated Richard.

She added, "And Benwick just hates Hurst for beating him all the time throughout his career."

Darcy shook his head. "Policemen and private investigators!"

"What?" she said and turned to stick her tongue out at him.

It's time to leave them alone, Richard thought as he quietly slipped out of the room. When she rose to follow, Darcy held her hand and stroked her thumb. "Have dinner with me tonight."

Was that an order? she wondered. His caress sent a strange sensation through her arms. She shook her head. "Busy."

"With what?" Prince Darcy's lips thinned, his fingers moving up to her wrist.

"Louisa said she would return to London and the Police have closed off the estate as a crime scene. I'll talk to Richard and stay here to check where the will is."

"You think it's here?"

"Not sure, but I want to be thorough."

"I'll stay too." He stepped closer.

"No need!"

"I still want to have dinner with you."

"Stubborn!"

"Persistent, that's a good character trait."

"Arrogant!"

"I know what I'm good at," murmured Darcy, before lowering his mouth and capturing her sensual lips. Her mouth was intoxicating, tasting of fruity wine. He liked that she wrapped her hands around his waist when he sucked her lips. She pushed her tongue into his warm mouth and duelled with his tongue, sparking heat in his body, but before he could press her body to his, she pushed him away and strolled out of the room, fast.

I will kiss her senseless next time, swore Prince Fitzwilliam to himself.

~*~*~*~

Grosvenor House

Saturday, 10 September 2011

When Prince Darcy cooled down and went in search of Elizabeth, she had joined the interview in the library. It was Thorpe's turn to be interviewed.

"Here is the table out on the patio," said Inspector Denny, showing the interviewee an image on the iPad he was using. "Where were you sitting?"

"Here, right beside Harriet."

Denny marked Thorpe's sitting position on the screen. "Now where were you when the fight broke out?"

"I was trying to protect Louisa from Caroline's smacking, standing roughly here," Thorpe pointed out a location opposite to where there was a mark, indicating Caroline's position. Miss Bingley had been interviewed earlier, before Elizabeth joined the Inspector.

"So you walked past the victim."

"So?" Thorpe raised his eyes.

Denny typed his note into the iPad. "We will need to see all the recent investments you've been conducting for the victim's father."

"What are you implying? That Hurst's heart attack has to do with me too?"

"According to the victim's sister, Henrietta Hurst, the last conversation around the lunch table was about some of their father's investment having gone sour."

"Henrietta's a waste who has nothing to do, except wanting to get into any man's pants."

"So, she tried to point the finger to you because you refused to sleep with her?"

"For god sake, she's barely 20 and I worked for her father."

"I've seen men sleep with younger."

"You meet mostly perverts, Inspector."

"And you're not, Mr. Thorpe?"

"I come from the upper class. And I wouldn't kill Harriet just for her words. As I said over lunch, investments have their ups and downs."

"And I'm sure she has many words about your bad investment," the Deputy Commissioner said, joining in for the first time.

"Not you too," protested Thorpe. "We play golf together, Richard! You've known me for years. Don't tell me you think I look like a murderer."

"I'm keeping my mind open in this case. After all, you've cost Hurst millions before."

Thorpe jumped up, grabbed Richard's lapels and yelled at him, "Hurst wanted those investments! I didn't force them on him."

Inspector Denny moved to tear him away. "Sit down, Mr. Thorpe! You don't want to be charged for assaulting a police officer."

Thorpe flopped back down onto his seat and continued his rant. "There've been some fucking bad investments in the past. So what? Everyone's losing money these days. If I have to kill every one of my clients for that, I've to round up all the poison in the whole of London."

"But not everyone is sleeping with the client's wife," added Richard.

"Me, sleeping with Louisa? Does the desperate housewife tell you that?"

"Are you denying it?"

"I could have a young, lush 20-year-old Henrietta, why would I need to make do with wrinkled skin and sagged tits like Louisa?"

So Thorpe lied, thought Elizabeth. *Why?*

"You could be sleeping with all of them to keep them happy."

"Didn't I just say I haven't had sex with Henrietta before? And not Louisa either. My dick has higher standards than that."

"Then you won't mind us having a look at your penthouse and office in London?" jumped in Inspector Denny.

"What do you want to find there?"

"You mentioned poison."

"I thought the Met hired smarter policemen. Why would I leave the 'murder weapon' still in my possession? You just want to mess up my belongings and poke your nose in my business papers. Get your subpoena."

"We will certainly do that, Mr. Thorpe," said Denny. "That's it for the time being. Do not leave the country until we say so."

He gave Denny the finger before he exited the room.

"Who's remaining?" asked Richard.

"He's the last one," replied Denny.

"What's your gut feeling?"

"I'm betting on the horny 20-year-old."

Richard stroked his jaw. "Henrietta has a pretty face, but you think she's capable of killing her father and sister?"

"She gets two shares of the money. And she doesn't seem at all upset with both of them dead."

"Where can she get her hands on the anti-depressants?"

"Her mother, ex-Mrs. Hurst, now Mrs. Elton, takes anti-depressants on a daily basis."

"OK, keep tabs on Henrietta's movement. When the autopsy comes back, we will proceed. How about the Bingley sisters?"

"Miss Bingley had some tears for the victim. How genuine, though, I'm not sure. But judging from the witnesses' account, she was in a catfight with Mrs. Hurst. Not sure if she had the chance to poison the victim."

"Couldn't she have planned it beforehand?" asked His Royal Highness. *Perhaps, Prince Darcy wanted Miss Bingley put behind bars.*

"She doesn't benefit from Harriet's death. Louisa either."

"A crime of passion? All fighting for the attention of Thorpe?"

"Miss Bingley said Thorpe was sleeping with Mrs. Hurst and Henrietta but not Harriet."

Richard brushed his jaw some more and said, "Unless she's was killed for talking too much."

"That's possible."

"And Bingley and Benwick?"

"Both were genuinely upset about the victim's death."

"A murderer can be upset too about his or her victim," said Elizabeth.

"Neither benefited from Hurst' and Harriet's deaths. I haven't found any clue that Bingley was in any way involved in incest relations with the ladies in the house. And all the women said Benwick was a bore. So, I think it's safe to rule out a crime of passion with these two men."

"And Hurst's biography?" asked Richard.

"Bingley said Hurst had revealed he had taken steroids and had been sleeping around in nearly every tour stop he visited when he was England's No. 1."

"So Mrs. Hurst could be enraged with him."

"Or Mrs. Elton."

"But she's not here today, unless she has an accomplice."

"Some of the women Hurst slept with were quite famous."

"Such as?"

"Royalty, movie stars."

"And have husbands?"

"Yep."

"Damn, we have to widen the search then."

"Yes, I've already asked for a copy of the biography draft. His publisher is in Australia."

Tapping his jaw, Richard commented, "No London publishing house is interested in his story?"

"He's an Aussie. He wanted to have it published by his compatriot, Bingley said. All the book contracts were handled by his friend in Australia rather than Frank Churchill."

"Check out the friend too."

"Sure, Gov."

Richard rose, and the meeting concluded.

Bingley was waiting for them in the parlour, with Jane and Caroline.

"Are you not coming?" asked Bingley to Prince Darcy. Miss Bingley leaped forward to grab HRH's arms in a tight grip.

"No, I'm helping Elizabeth. The Deputy Commissioner has agreed to it."

"Why does she need your help," argued Caroline. "Surely, Your Royal Highness has more urgent matters to attend to in London."

"I promised Bingley to monitor Elizabeth's works."

"Then I'll stay too."

"Louisa won't allow it," sighed Bingley. "Come now, Caroline. I want to leave now. Don't say another word."

Miss Bingley reluctantly relaxed her tight grip of the Prince and glared at Elizabeth.

Elizabeth ignored the Prince and his loyal follower, bade goodbye to Jane and left for the library again.

Having received authorisation from Mrs. Hurst and Bingley before joining the interview earlier, Elizabeth now undertook a more methodological search of Hurst's business papers in the library. Originally, Louisa and Thorpe were not very happy about this, leaving a private investigator to probe through Hurst's affairs. But Bingley had put his foot down. He wanted the deaths in the family and the argument between his sisters to stop. Faced by threats of withdrawing his financial support in future, Mrs. Hurst had finally agreed and left with Henrietta.

"Have you found anything interesting?" said the Prince, as he closed the door quietly.

"Hurst's money is leaking like an old sink, to his wife, two daughters, his agent and his ex-wife. Luckily, he's still drawing in a lot of sponsorship and appearance fees."

HRH stood by her chair and leaned forward to examine Elizabeth's laptop.

"How did you crack open passwords of his bank accounts?" said Prince Fitzwilliam with a raised brow. The laptop had several Web browsers opened, with the details of numerous bank accounts displayed.

"I have my methods."

"Should I be worried?"

"What for?"

"What if you hacked into my emails and accounts?"

She turned, looking him up and down. "Is there anything to check out?"

He smiled arrogantly. "I've been told I'm quite perfect."

"By Miss Bingley," she shook her head. "She hasn't checked her eyesight since she was 15. Hmm, there is no reason for any of them to kill him."

"Unless it was out of rage."

"Spiking a drink is more premeditated. The only persons who won't benefit from Hurst's death are Frank Churchill, Bingley and Benwick. Churchill wasn't here today, unless he hired someone to do it."

"What if he worked with Thorpe?"

"Perhaps, but the murders are not my concern."

"Why not? Don't you want to help Richard?"

"He wouldn't thank me for doing that. I've been asked to find the will only."

"And did you have any luck yet?"

"I most certainly have now," nodded Elizabeth as she looked at her watch. "But it's too early to call yet."

HRH waited for her to continue, but she just closed the laptop and started packing. "Hmm, too early...to call...Asia...or Australia?"

She smiled but didn't confirm. *He was definitely not a dumb royal.*

"Where are you going?"

"You're sounding like a stalker."

"I'm a Prince! I don't need to stalk women."

"Then you don't need to know where I'm going."

"I just want to offer you dinner."

"Offered and turned down already. Bye, Prince Fitzwilliam."

Darcy followed her out to the garage and managed to kiss her goodbye on the cheek.

Crossing his arms with a scowl, he watched her speed away in her silver green Mini Cooper Cabrio, the roof down. Sitting in his limo a few minutes later, he was sorely tempted to ask his driver to chase her up. He had to be smarter, though, if he wanted her. Did he want her? Yes, definitely, in his bed. But longer than that? He wasn't sure right now. She's smart, beautiful and spirited. But as the Crown Prince of Belberley, he couldn't marry anyone. When did the word 'marriage' sneak into his mind? No, he would bed her and think about the rest later on. But how to get her into his bed? She even refused to dine with him. Overseas call...to Asia...Australia?

Belberley House, Knightsbridge

Saturday, 10 September 2011

He rang Bingley, "What's the name of the friend who handled Hurst's book contract?"

Once Darcy got the details, it was easy to track down Mr. Luke Willoughby, even though he was not in Sydney. After all, who wouldn't answer a call from a prince?

"I didn't know that Hurst has died. My condolences to his family," said Willoughby, from a very bad connection from Tibet. "I'm on a spiritual cleaning holiday. I'll get back to Sydney ASAP."

"Did he ask you to handle other legal matters, besides the book contract?"

"No, he has Frank Churchill on retainer, but Frank is not good with book deal negotiation. That's why Hurst asked me to help. Is there some problem regarding his legal matters? His will?"

"Not that I know of, why would you think his will has a problem?"

"Oh, he mentioned he'll be in a bit of problem with his women when the book came out. So I thought maybe he would draw up something to placate them."

"Thank you for the help, Mr. Willoughby."

"Anytime, Your Royal Highness. May I offer you dinner when you next come to Australia?"

"I'll let Bingley know, if I'm interested."

"Thanks."

After a quick shower at home, Darcy rang Elizabeth from his bed.

"Your RPA, what can I do for you?"

"I prefer you call me 'Partner'."

"Are you offering me a position in your palace, dear Prince?"

I have a position in my bed now, he thought. "I meant Partner in the investigation."

"I don't work with others."

"You work with your sister."

"She's family."

I could be your family too. He wouldn't go there. "I've talked to Luke Willoughby."

She didn't reply, but he could hear her swear away from the phone. He smiled. Good, I stirred her up.

"Smart arse!"

"You seem obsessed with my butt." HRH smiled.

"That's not worth a decent answer. What did he say?"

"After all the trouble tracking him down in Tibet, that's all I get, 'Partner'?"

"I didn't ask you to do so."

"He didn't handle Hurst's will, but Hurst might have been thinking of drawing up a new will to protect his women, due to the disclosures in the memoir."

"I want a verbatim of what Luke Willoughby said."

"We can still have supper, though I'm in bed." *And naked.*

"Come here tomorrow morning, at ten. I will have breakfast with you, only because I don't like to owe other people." Then she hung up the phone. Exasperating woman! Prince Darcy slept badly that night, dreaming of the elusive private detective.

Elizabeth's residence, Chiswick
Sunday, 11 September 2011

When Prince Fitzwilliam arrived at Elizabeth's house with his best-looking casual wear, he was disappointed that he was not the only man there.

"Why are you here?" said Richard, sitting at the breakfast table with a copy of the Sunday paper. Darcy scowled. Had the Deputy Commissioner spent the night?

"Elizabeth invited me," said HRH, grumpily. "Are you two involved?"

"Nah." Richard replied. "Not that I've never tried."

The Prince turned from grim to grin in a second. More and more, he was becoming impressed by Miss Elizabeth Bennet. His cousin had megawatt charm, and he had seldom seen Richard fail to get his woman in their younger years. "Getting old and losing your touch?"

"I'm eager to see you losing yours too, Darcy."

"She's not gay?"

"Definitely not," replied the lady herself. She came in with Bingley, glaring at HRH. "Now that my client has arrived, I'll start. Help yourself to breakfast. Charles, you don't mind His Royal...Highness joining us?"

"No, I always rely on Richard and Darcy's advice."

Using a remote, Elizabeth called up a hidden big screen from one of the walls. With a few more buttons, she hooked up with a CollinsSydney on Skype.

"Thank you, Mr. Collins, for staying late for the meeting."

A round man in his late forties was sitting in front of a cheap-looking banner: Collins and Collins – Offer you thunderbolt and saintly legal advice!

"No worries, luv."

"My client Charles Bingley and his two friends, Richard and Darcy."

Mr. Collins rose immediately and bowed low. "Your Royal Highness Prince Fitzwilliam, it's my greatest honour. I was unaware that you would be joining the meeting. Mr. Bill Collins, your humble servant."

HRH gave him a curt nod.

"And Deputy Commissioner, I've heard many praises about you..."

"You're quite well informed," interrupted Elizabeth.

"Of course, it's my job to learn about all the famous people which may be of use to my cases in the future. And I've been..."

"Let's get back to our meeting. With the presence of the Deputy Commissioner, Mr. Collins, I'll be recording this, as part of the evidence in court. Do you agree?"

"Well, can't we not do it informal? You know..."

"His Royal Highness won't be present if it's not formal."

"True, true. I agree, but..."

"Mr. Luke Willoughby told me his twin brother Larry and you worked for Mr. Hurst occasionally in Australia."

Huh? How did she get so much more information from the Willoughby in Tibet? Darcy thought, annoyed.

"Yes, I've known the Willoughby twins for years. We've gone to..."

"Did Mr. Hurst make a will with you?"

"More than one, throughout the years, usually as he took on more mistresses and their children. Your Royal Highness, you know how Mr. Hurst was, being your friend..."

"How many?" continued Elizabeth.

"Six or seven, roughly speaking, I've lost count..."

"You've a very good memory, Mr. Collins. I'm sure you remember the exact number."

"Nine to be exact. Hurst was a busy and lucky man..."

"Good, and when was the last one made?"

"Early January this year, when he came down for the Australian Open. We had dinner at..."

"Do you keep his original for him?"

"Yes, we've a safety deposit box here in Sydney for all his legal documents."

"What happened to them when he died?"

"I contacted Larry, and he told me Hurst's estate has asked for it, and I handed it to him, about a week afterwards."

"Just like that?" asked HRH.

"Of course, Willoughby always accompanied Hurst to all the meetings. He knew everything and Hurst trusted him."

Stupid lawyer! HRH thought.

"Thank you for your time, Mr. Collins. Please send the meeting fee to my assistant," said Elizabeth, cutting off the connection before Collins could utter more flowery words.

"Bingley has to pay for this stupid man, too?" frowned HRH.

"He's a lawyer. He'll even charge for picking his nose in front of you."

"I didn't know Hurst had so many mistresses!" cried Bingley. "Louisa's no saint, but he's getting too far. I'd kill him, if he wasn't dead already."

"Be careful what you say, Bingley, you're in front of a police officer," joined in Richard. Then he turned to Elizabeth, "So, we've to track down this Willoughby con twin?"

"I've already done that."

"Did you sleep at all, last night?" said HRH, with a concerned look.

"Why didn't he come forward earlier?" asked Richard.

"Officially, he was waiting for his brother to return from Tibet so he could bring the infamous last will to London in person. Unofficially, I think he wants to add his name in as the other executor or beneficiary."

"Who is the executor?"

"Bingley."

Bingley looked surprised.

"And the beneficiaries?"

"Beneficiary, as in one only."

Richard whistled.

"Who's the favourite mistress?"

"Bingley."

"You meant Miss Bingley?"

"No, Charles."

Bingley's eyes widened. "Why did Hurst leave all the money to me?"

"Did you kill him?" asked Richard.

Bingley rolled his eyes.

"No, you don't," added Elizabeth. "Hurst left all the money to you, in trust, to distribute to all his mistresses, existing wife, ex-wife, children, legal and bastard ones. He said you are the kind one and you will treat them all fairly."

"Urgh!!!!" groaned Bingley. "Can I not accept this? To be his executor and beneficiary? Surely it's not right."

"You can consult your lawyer, to refuse or accept. I've arranged to get the original will to be couriered here by tomorrow, for authentication."

"Well done, Lizzy!" said Richard. "You've finished your case much faster than I. Will something be done about this Larry Willoughby?"

Elizabeth shrugged. "Not worth the legal proceeding, I think. And I didn't ask you here, just to scare Collins."

"You've a good lead for me?"

"Someone has rung the good Willoughby, Luke, before, for a copy of the biography."

"Who?"

"Benwick, in June."

"Why?" asked Bingley in a surprised voice.

"Are you implying Benwick..." said HRH.

"No, that can't be true," protested Bingley. "Benwick is the nicest guy in the circle. He's the gentleman player. He wouldn't hurt Hurst."

"Luke Willoughby didn't comply with his request on the spot," continued Elizabeth. "He was trying to confirm with Hurst when Benwick rang back to say that there wasn't any need."

"He's seen the draft of the memoir at the post-Wimbledon party?" speculated HRH.

"Perhaps, but Benwick's voice was agitated in the second call, according to Luke."

"There may be a reason why he asked to see the draft," Bingley said of his friend.

"You could be right," said Elizabeth. "I did a check on the pharmacy sales surrounding London areas from June to now. I've credit card records of Benwick's sister buying several packs of anti-depressants from pharmacies in Brentwood, Dartford and Croydon. She lives in Highgate, which is quite far from the three pharmacies."

Bingley gasped. Richard rose and gave Elizabeth a peck on the cheek. "I don't want to know your computer method. But you're a gem! Still refuse to join me in the police?"

"I don't like to be bossed around."

"You like to boss people around instead."

She smiled to Richard and gave the dazed Bingley a tight hug.

"I still won't believe it," murmured Bingley.

"We're not sure yet. Benwick could have a good explanation for everything." She patted his back, compassionately.

"Yes," agreed Richard. "I'll just follow the leads."

"You better go with your friend, Your Royal Highness," suggested Elizabeth.

A fantasy of breakfast in bed with Elizabeth had long gone from Darcy's mind. And seeing Bingley's distressed face, Darcy had to agree to follow Bingley. He left her with a disappointing peck on the cheek.

~*~*~*~

England's tennis circle is rocked by the arrest of James Benwick, over the suspected murder of former grand slam winner Frederick Hurst and his daughter Harriet Hurst. It's rumoured that Hurst had admitted to taking steroids in important matches throughout the years in his soon-to-be published biography.

When former Britain's No. 2 heard about this after Wimbledon this year, it's suspected that Benwick was enraged by the deception of his friend and long-term rival and planned the murder at the Davis Cup tie. Miss Hurst was murdered at a party two weeks ago, apparently for identifying Benwick as one of the persons who had read Hurst's controversial biography.

Benwick was said to have suffered financial and emotional hardship due to his unsuccessful career. He had lost substantial sponsorship and TV appearance opportunities to Hurst at every turn of his career.

The reputation of Britain's greatest tennis champion, who was branded as the family sportsman, has been marred by the revelation of a string of mistresses and illegitimate children around the world. Details of Hurst's affairs are contained in his biography; however, his sole estate executor and beneficiary, also his brother-in-law, Britain's current No. 1 tennis player, Charles Bingley, is trying to put an injunction against its release.

"Hurst's biography may hurt a lot of women in his life and it has already cost two lives," said Bingley in response to our enquiry. "I don't want to see this book in print."

Hurst's Australian publisher Godwin & Edwin is fighting the injunction, claiming that the world should know about Hurst's genuine and heartfelt confession of his multiple lives that were hidden behind his public image.

The death of the Hursts also captures world headline attention due to the close involvement of the Crown Prince of Belberley, Prince Fitzwilliam. Bingley was a good friend of His Royal Highness and, according to our anonymous source, Prince Fitzwilliam was present in a meeting with the Australian lawyer handling Hurst's last will and appeared to be on friendly terms with a female private investigator hired by Bingley.

Seen here is a photograph of His Royal Highness kissing Miss Elizabeth Bennet passionately before leaving Hurst's Berkshire home after the death of Harriet Hurst. Prince Fitzwilliam's hand was spotted palming Miss Bennet's breast.

The Prince reverted back to his usual scowling face in the next photo after seeing Miss Bennet off. The lady is a financial investor by profession and private investigator by reputation.

ACA will keep you posted of the latest romance of one of the most eligible bachelors in the world with our English rose. They have not been seen in public since the Berkshire steamy encounter, but royalty watchers noted that Miss Bennet has been receiving a supply of Belberley chocolate and stunning flowers daily since. – A Celebrity Affair, Tuesday, 27 September 2011

Not So Scary
By June Williams

What if the scary stuff happened after the scary movie?

"Lizzy, you are my favourite sister," coaxed the voice on the telephone.

"Jane, you are a sweetheart, but I have better things to do than babysit another one of your husband's friends."

"It's just a movie with one of your favorite actors."

"You mean James Isaac? I didn't know he had a new movie out."

"And it's playing at the Meryton Mall Cineplex, the one with fourteen theatres and the comfy chairs with the high backs."

"Jane, what's the catch? Are you trying to matchmake me again?"

"I only want my sister to be just as happy as I am with Charles."

Lizzy groaned. "No, Jane, not again."

"Charles says his friend shouldn't see the movie alone, but we have other plans tonight, and Thursday is the last night the movie is playing in a real theatre."

"If the movie makes him scared, why is he seeing it?"

"I don't remember, but Charles said it was important. Honestly, I'm not trying to matchmake you. He's from England and he really needs someone to go with him to the movie."

Lizzy caved in. Her sister and brother-in-law really were dear persons who always wanted to help others. If it made them happy, Lizzy would see a movie with his college friend. But she would wear her old jeans and boots; no dressing up in her expensive stiletto heels for this guy.

It was not a movie with her favourite actor James Isaac – it was a horror movie with someone named Isak Johns. The comfy high-backed chairs were only in the theatres that had been recently renovated, not the old gothic theatre in which she sat with Will Darcy. Yes, the man was handsome, but he had the conversational skills of a halibut: none.

"Hi, you must be Charles' college roommate. I'm Jane's sister, Lizzy," she had cheerfully said to the only single man standing at the ticket area, the fellow in a suit who was holding up a piece of paper with "Darcy" printed on it.

He had nodded and handed her a movie ticket, then led the way to the theatre.

She had kept up a steady stream of conversation about Charles and Jane, movies that she and Jane had seen as children, and whether it was better to read the book before seeing the movie.

He remained silent, not answering any of her questions. Once inside the theatre, he had chosen seats in the middle row but on the aisle, after he'd noted where the exits were. There were only a few others in the audience.

Lizzy finally stopped her monologue and stood up. "Would you like anything from the concession stand?"

she asked, as an excuse to leave the sphinx for a few minutes.

"Oh, no," he said, clearly startled out of a blue funk. He stood up. "I apologize. I should be the one offering to fetch you something. What would you like? I suppose they have the usual pedestrian items – food coloring, preservatives, sugar water, and butter-scented Styrofoam – given that this is a backwater area."

She bristled at the offense. "Meryton is not New York City or Paris, but we do know how to cook."

"I meant no offense, Miss Bennet. It's just that the business model of movie theatres is the same everywhere in this country, from large cities to the smallest towns. Theatres make almost all their money on food and drink sales. That is why everything is overpriced, despite the food items being cheap. Soda only costs pennies to make."

"Hmph." Lizzy sat down. "Suddenly, I don't want anything to eat or drink."

Darcy sat down also. "I apologize. I did not intend to – I am not trying to be offensive – I am saying everything wrong." He looked away.

He also has the social skills of a halibut, Lizzy thought ruefully. "I've said something, now it's your turn to say something. Why don't you tell me about your favourite movies, or why you want to see this particular movie. I gather you're not really a fan of scary movies?"

"True," he admitted. "I do not identify with people who enjoy being frightened, but my sister insisted that I see this film. I asked her why, but she said it should be a surprise."

"Do you always do what your sister says?"

"She is my only family left."

He said it with such desolation in his voice that Lizzy felt sad for him. She patted his hand. "After this movie, I will treat you to a cheeseburger, fries, and milkshake at the local hangout. It's not gourmet, but it's good food."

"That is not necessary, but I thank you," he murmured, then sat back in his chair.

Lizzy noticed he was struggling to take deep breaths. "Do you prefer to watch movies in silence, or should we talk quietly?"

"I think for this movie, I might appreciate some conversation."

"Okay." Lizzy patted his hand again, now determined to help him through this ordeal. If he were only five years old, it would be easier to be sympathetic, but she knew many adults were afraid to see horror movies. *Try to not judge him*, she admonished herself.

The movie started.

"Cathy, would you please make this delivery?" said the pizza restaurant manager.

"Sure, Mrs. Allen." Cathy was a young blonde junior college student. She read the order. "Oh, it's all the way out on Northanger Abbey Road. They better give me a big tip."

"You're such a good girl," said Mrs. Allen. "All the other kids would complain about driving in the dark."

"She won't get killed," Lizzy whispered to Will. "Her clothes are too tight, her cleavage is too low. She gets to scream every time she finds another dead body or monster."

"She should quit and get a better job."

"But then there wouldn't be a horror movie." Lizzy was trying to remind him that this was only a movie, not reality. "Look, Will, she dropped the pizza cutter and stuck it in her back pocket – that's probably what she uses to kill the bad guy in the end."

He managed a tiny laugh and seemed to relax.

Cathy Morland made her way through the waist-high grass and weeds, and knocked on the door of the dilapidated three-story house. There were no lights on.

Lizzy noticed that Will tensed. "These houses always have bad landscaping so the bad guys can hide easier."

"She should bring a flashlight and mobile phone!"

"In real life she should, but this is a horror movie – the good guys always do stupid things." Lizzy patted his hand again.

A handsome man opened the door and looked at Cathy holding the pizza boxes. "Nobody here ordered your food. Go away." He stared at her without blinking.

"Look, mister, I drove twenty minutes to get here, and I deserve a tip. Maybe your mom or some other woman here called for pizza."

"No." He started to close the door.

"Wait, I think her name was Lizzy, or Izzy. No, it was a fancy name – Isadora."

"Isabella." He slammed the door shut.

"Run, you silly girl!" Darcy whispered urgently.

"The movie is just starting. Relax, he probably gets killed in the last five minutes." Lizzy squeezed his hand.

"What happens to the girl – Isabella?"

"Oh, she's either dead already or she gets rescued by Cathy."

"Dead!"

"It's just a movie. Calm down, Will." When he continued to look anxious, she held his hand. "Close your eyes, let me describe the movie to you."

She shouldn't have been so surprised, but he obeyed her. Not only did he close his eyes, but he lowered his head and covered his face with his hands, grimacing each time the heroine screamed.

"It's okay, Will," Lizzy said. "Cathy is again at the front door, even though the pizza must be cold by now. Okay, she's crawling through the window. She's putting the pizza on the table. She's looking through the house – oh, she found some money. Is that what she's looking for – enough money for the pizzas and her tip?"

"She should run."

"I know, Will, but remember that this is a movie and people aren't smart in horror movies. Okay, now Cathy is..."

A woman screamed, startling Darcy.

"That's a woman in the audience, it's not Cathy. I think the woman screamed because she just spilled her soda." Lizzy squeezed his hand.

"My mother is not here. My father the General is not here. But their ghosts are here." The handsome man stared at Cathy, not blinking.

"What kind of ghosts?" asked Cathy.

"Would you like to meet them?"

"She should run!"

"Yes, Will, she should have left a long time ago, but you paid ten dollars for each movie ticket, so they have to make this a longer movie." Lizzy continued narrating, not telling him about the gory close-up shots of the man's long-dead parents.

Eventually, the music grew louder and more ominous.

"The man is still chasing Cathy through the house. Cathy is lost, she's running in circles." Lizzy began rubbing Will's shoulders as he hyperventilated.

"I need something to drink," Darcy muttered. He started to get up and opened his eyes just in time to see a close-up shot of a woman's corpse.

"Miss Morland, may I introduce you to Isabella Thorpe, who refused to marry me."

"That almost looks like my sister," Will gasped out.

"Is your sister alive in real life? Real life, Will – real life."

"Yes, yes, she is alive. I last spoke to her by phone tonight before I came here."

"It's only a movie. Do you want to leave now?"

"No, I am a man of honor and integrity. I promised her I would stay for all of it, and I will."

They stayed, and Will even managed to keep his eyes open to the end, when Cathy was saved by Fred Tilney's long-lost brother Henry. But first there was a fight between the brothers that only ended when Cathy cut Fred with her pizza cutter. Lizzy and Will both groaned when Fred – the insane killer – was hauled away in an ambulance, muttering that he would one day bring Cathy back.

"Isabella needs friends who will stay with her forever and ever," Fred Tilney said ominously.

"Looks like they want to make a sequel from this," said Lizzy. "Do you want to stay for the credits?"

"I promised my sister," he said, so they sat and watched the credits. His eyes widened at the cast names. "That is my sister – she played Isabella! That must be her surprise. She is only in her first year at university as a drama student."

Lizzy laughed. "Maybe she'll get to say a line in her next movie. How exciting for her."

They stayed until the house lights were turned on, As they began walking toward the lobby, he turned on his cell phone and called his sister. "Georgiana, you looked very realistic. You gave me a real fright there. No, I didn't recognize you, although I thought it almost looked like you. Very funny. You are correct; it's a start, even if it is not Shakespeare." He wished her good luck on her next audition, told her he loved her, and ended the call.

"Thank you for being extraordinarily patient with me, Miss Bennet. May I take you to this cheeseburger restaurant?"

She looked at his facial expression. "You're not really fond of cheeseburgers, are you?"

He shook his head. "Any savage can eat cheeseburgers, but a discerning palate needs something with more elegance."

She laughed. "Perhaps one night when Charles and Jane are back. You're staying at their home, aren't you?"

"Yes, and I have a house key. Truly, is there no way I can thank you for your kindness tonight?"

Lizzy declined politely and headed for her car. She was in the parking lot and halfway to her car when she heard running footsteps behind her, and she turned to look.

"I have a gift for you," Darcy said as he handed her a pizza cutter. "The concession stand sells pizzas, and I persuaded them to sell me this as a souvenir of our evening."

"Thank you," she said with a genuine smile, amazed that Mr. Halibut actually had manners – when he wasn't cowering in fear of a horror movie.

"Erm... would you... erm..."

She barely stopped herself from rolling her eyes. *This only confirms that he has the social and conversational skills of a halibut*, she reminded herself. After a painful minute of watching him struggle to speak, she took action.

"It's okay, Will. You don't have to say anything else, and you certainly don't have to feel obligated to invite me for a date. Besides, I like my men with a little more testosterone. Call me when the day comes that you don't have to hide your eyes from a scary movie." She was trying to be funny and lighten the mood, and patted him on the hand. "I'll probably see you at the Bingleys' home sometime."

Lizzy didn't expect Darcy's facial expression to drop so severely, but she was even more stunned when a black SUV careened to a stop, only inches from them. A masked man – or was it two men? – dressed in black reached out, grabbed Darcy, and pulled him into the vehicle as he struggled to escape.

"Tell Bingley it's Wickham!" Darcy shouted before he was gagged and driven away.

She was frozen for a few seconds that passed in slow motion. Snapping out of her stupor, she looked for the SUV's license plate but it had none. She raced to her own car and started driving after the SUV. Ignoring the law against using a cell phone while driving, she called the emergency line.

"My friend has been kidnapped by someone in a black SUV. I don't know the model. It doesn't have a license plate on the back. It happened outside the Meryton Mall Cineplex. I'm trying to follow them on the main road, heading toward Oakham Mount. I'm going to hang up so I can drive."

With both hands on the steering wheel, she sped after the SUV. Meryton didn't have any highways but it did have paved roads with lights – except where the SUV veered to. Her little compact car couldn't keep up and she lost sight of them, but the unpaved road was only wide enough for one car, so she knew the SUV couldn't leave without going through her. If she followed the winding road, she would find them.

All those walks to Oakham Mount were paying off. She knew this area even in the dark. At the end of the long road was an abandoned house where she and her sisters had played as children. Jane had hosted tea parties with her dolls, Lydia and Kitty had played "spring break" with sparkling cider and blocks of gelatine – "Jello Shots," they called them – while Mary brought books to read when their house was too noisy. Little Lizzy had explored the house fully, climbing into the attics with her flashlight.

Flashlight. Lizzy dug through her handbag for her emergency flashlight. By the time she saw the SUV parked outside the abandoned house, she had her flashlight, cell phone, and keys in hand. *Drat, I forgot to tell them what Will said*, she remembered.

She dialled Jane's cell phone while her car doors were still locked, not surprised to get Jane's voicemail. "Jane, I'm outside Purvis Lodge. Somebody in a black SUV kidnapped Will Darcy from the theatre parking lot. He said to tell Charles that it's Wikkum, at least that's what it sounded like. Will didn't have time to spell. I'm going inside Purvis Lodge to look for him."

Realizing that she was being very stupid to go into an abandoned house by herself, she added: "I have to do this, Jane. I love you. Tell Charles, Mom and Dad, and the girls that I love them too. Goodbye."

Then she got out of her car and into trouble.

Sometimes she and her sisters played hide-and-seek together, so Lizzy knew how to sneak silently even in her boots. Still, she was aware she would probably be seen and heard in the house. She was outnumbered and didn't know if they had weapons. *Stop thinking about weapons, Lizzy – just remember that Will Darcy is afraid of horror movies and he's probably terrified now.*

And then she woke up, with her hands tied behind her back, her feet tied at the ankles, and a gag around her mouth. Her head hurt. She wasn't blindfolded, but there was some moonlight shining through cracks in the attic roof.

She turned around and saw Darcy in the same condition except his wrists had been tied to the roof support column; he couldn't move to her. He looked as terrified as she had expected.

Lizzy scooted to him, digging her heels into the floor and pushing along on her bottom until she got to him. Then – with her hands still tied – she reached under her sweater to her back hip pocket and took out the pizza cutter. She had almost forgotten it until she had scooted over on her bottom and the pizza cutter poked her. Sure enough, it was a commercial-quality pizza cutter and had a razor-sharp blade.

Within seconds, she freed Will's hands. He used the pizza cutter to free her hands, then – as they smelled gasoline and heard the crackling sounds of burning wood under the attic – he freed their ankles.

She pulled down her gag. "Follow me, I know this house. Purvis Lodge has dreadful attics, but there are windows." All the attic windows had been boarded up, but she led him to one particular window. She knelt to open a loose floorboard, and removed a hammer.

He looked at her bewilderedly.

"I tried to make a birdhouse for my father when I was about twelve, and I never returned his tools because he put a lock on his toolbox."

He laughed, then held out his hand for the hammer. "May I?"

She handed him the hammer and watched him forcefully remove the boards from the window. The glass was long gone.

The smoke was filling the attic, and the sounds and smell of fire were growing.

Darcy froze, terror on his face.

"I'm here, I'm here – you're not alone," she assured him. "Look at me. We're getting out of here." She started to push him out the window. "We might break a few bones, but we'll be alive."

Suddenly, he grabbed her tightly and jumped out, cushioning her with his body as they rolled upon landing. There was no SUV. Her car was there, but not her flashlight, phone, or keys. They both jumped when the house burst into flames.

Now the police showed up, with Jane and Charles leading the way.

"This is what happens when you live in the country," she said ruefully. "Only a handful of officers covering thousands of square miles."

"Lizzy, Will!" Jane and Charles called out as they ran to them.

"Was it really Wickham?" Charles anxiously asked Will.

Darcy nodded numbly. "He said he was finishing the job."

Charles put his arm around his friend's shoulders and led him to sit in the Bingleys' car.

"Jane, you and Charles go take care of Will. I can deal with the police," Lizzy said confidently. "I knew I could get us out of the attic, but Will is the one who is fragile."

"Fragile?" Jane asked doubtfully. "He's really very strong. You don't know him well enough."

"Jane, believe me. I watched an entire horror movie with him. He's fragile."

"He's not fragile, just shaken as anyone would be. Look, the police need to ask him more about the kidnapping. Did you have any contact with the kidnappers?"

"No. That's probably why I'm not as shaken. For me it was only a little worse than the times Lydia and Kitty tied me up for telling Dad they had been drinking and smoking in the house."

Jane laughed. "I never thought those two would be helpful."

Purvis Lodge burned to the ground along with any cigarettes, fireworks, and childhood memories left by the Bennet girls and other neighbourhood children. Lizzy told the police everything she knew, after she made them promise they would wait two days – until Saturday – for their second interview with Darcy.

She and Jane spoke by phone several times on Friday, but with Darcy still at the Bingleys' house recuperating, Jane and Lizzy thought she should let him be. Lizzy had a physician examine her head at an emergency room as a precaution, but she had no concussion so she didn't bother to tell Jane. Fortunately, their parents were visiting her Aunt and Uncle Philips in Florida; news from little Meryton wouldn't reach them there.

Today was Saturday. Lizzy had just dressed when someone knocked on her door. She peered through the window and saw a tall sturdy man in a business suit.

"I am Colonel Richard Fitzwilliam, cousin to William Darcy," the stranger called out, holding up his military identification card and opened passport. He'd only arrived Friday from London.

She let him in. "Is Will okay? Can I help you with anything?"

The Colonel held out an armful of old yellowed newspapers. "He asked me to show you these, as proof that he is not a coward." His eyes avoided her, but she could tell he was angry at her. "I grew up with him. I am well acquainted with every piece of his character. He has never been a coward."

They sat at her kitchen table. Lizzy took the first newspaper from the stack and read the deadline:

Couple burn to death as

son saves infant sister

She gasped at the photo. "The house – it looks – it looks –"

"It looks very much like the house in the movie you saw on Thursday night," the Colonel finished for her. "My cousin will forever hate that style of house because of his parents' death."

Lizzy could barely read the first paragraph before she put down the newspaper. "I can't read anymore. Please, would you just tell me the main points I should know?'

"Very well. George Wickham is the son of a very respectable man, who for many years was manager of all the Darcy properties. As such, he and his family lived in a small house on a property. My cousin Will and young George were the same age. George could not understand why he would have to work for a living one day, when his playmate would inherit so much wealth. But none of us suspected it went beyond jealousy.

"When Will and George were only ten years old, the Darcys were visiting the Wickhams' cottage to celebrate George being given a school award. George asked the Darcys to wait upstairs so he could show them something – a picture he'd drawn or other excuse. Instead, George set fire to his family's cottage and trapped them. He and his mother escaped. My Aunt and Uncle Darcy died, but Will managed to jump out of a window, holding his baby sister. It was a week before he was able to tell us that his parents had ordered him to leave, because they were buried under a pile of collapsed rubble; not even an adult would have been able to dig them out in time.

"George's father arrived home an hour after the fire. He was so devastated by what his son had done that he committed suicide."

Lizzy was distraught at how she had misjudged Darcy. "When we jumped out of the attic of Purvis Lodge, he held me so tight. We landed on the hard ground and he absorbed the shock himself – I don't have a single scratch."

"He still has nightmares in which he drops Georgiana. The movie you saw brought up his fears of being unable to save his family," the Colonel said.

"What happened to Wickham?"

"He was only ten years old, so as a juvenile he served eight years in custody and was released at age eighteen. He never spent a day in an adult prison. He was given a new identity and was told to stay away from the Darcys. Obviously, he has broken those parole terms, but the local police have not found him."

The Colonel took a deep breath. "Uncle Darcy had set up an irrevocable trust for young George's education. After all the deaths, George's mother became his trustee, and my parents – as executors of the Darcy estate – refused to distribute the estate to the trustee, not wanting George to benefit from his murders. Mrs. Wickham applied to the court for relief from forfeiture, hoping to keep the trust money. My parents won, but young Wickham and his mother were resentful. Sometimes Mrs. Wickham and George show up when Will is at a charity event – they demand money to make them go away."

"Poor Will. Oh, I was so wrong about him," Lizzy cried.

"My cousin does not need your pity. He only hopes that you not consider him weak... or fragile." He still avoided looking at her, still upset that she had insulted his cousin.

"I have every compassion for him, but I don't pity him. Pity is condescending, and Will is – well, he's superior to me in bravery and courage. If I'd lived through that sort of tragedy, I would have avoided every reminder, but he faced his fears and stayed through the entire scary movie. He struggled through it, but he stayed. That takes courage!" Lizzy caught herself ranting. "Oops, sorry, getting emotional."

The Colonel smiled.

"What can I do to tell your cousin that I'm sorry? I should never have judged the book by its cover. Now that

I know what happened, it's obvious he is the bravest man I have ever met."

"I could give him a message from you, but his response is up to him," the Colonel said. "At present, his mind is focused on his upcoming interview with your police about what Wickham did Thursday night. He has to relive some very painful memories. We never expected Wickham to come after him, not after eighteen years."

"He could be looking over his shoulder the rest of his life," Lizzy said softly. "If he would like me to be with him for the police interview, I'd be honoured to come."

The Colonel looked at her appraisingly. "Tell me the truth, Miss Bennet. Why did you risk your life to save my cousin?"

"I – I'm not sure. I mean, it was the right thing to do, but I don't really understand why I went after him. I care for him, and I think he is probably a great guy except when he's watching a scary movie. Did he tell you that I used a pizza cutter to save us? He bought it for me as a gift. But before we could really get to know each other, he got kidnapped."

"So you wouldn't say you love him?"

She laughed. "Not after only one date, even though it was memorable."

"Good. I wouldn't trust you if you'd said it was love at first sight. All the women who have said that to him were in love with his money. I will bring you to the Bingleys' home."

Jane hugged Lizzy as soon as she walked through the Bingleys' front door.

"He is thankful you saved him, but he feels terrible that you think he is low on testosterone – that's what Charles told me he said," whispered Jane.

"I am an idiot for saying that to him. You know what a tease I can be, but I went too far this time. Jane, did you know about Will's family history?"

"No. Charles told me just last night; Will had asked him to keep it quiet so that you and I wouldn't treat him any differently. It was terrible for him after the accident – in school, there were boys who called him a coward for leaving his parents to die."

"He was only ten years old!"

"I agree, Lizzy, but the news media talked about him for months, especially when Wickham was in court. The public was fascinated with a ten-year-old killer, and a ten-year-old hero who saved his baby sister. Add the Darcy money and my father the Earl, and it was inevitable that the news people were obsessed."

"So when Will came to the U.S., he could blend in and be a regular person, until he met me and my big mouth," Lizzy berated herself. "No wonder he has problems with conversation – he doesn't know who to trust and can't predict what they will say to him."

Meanwhile, the Colonel went to Will's guest bedroom to speak privately. "She appears sorry for her remarks and for judging the book by its cover, but I don't think she pities you. Would you like to see her?"

"Yes. No. Yes, I owe her an apology. If not for me, she would not have been tied up and in danger.

The cousins walked out to the living room, where everyone stared at each other until Lizzy stepped up to Will.

"Would it be okay if we sit together to talk?" she asked softly.

Darcy nodded stiffly and then led her to a pair of overstuffed chairs, purchased by Jane as the furniture equivalent of "comfort food."

Jane, Charles, and the Colonel watched from the other side of the room, as nervous and concerned as chaperones at a pre-teen dance party.

Lizzy took a deep breath. "Will, please let me be selfish for a moment. I cannot live with myself unless I apologize to you. I've always been one to tease and be flippant, but I went too far when we first met. I should think before I open my mouth. I should know better! Even without knowing your history, I should not have judged you on the basis of how you reacted during one silly movie. I should have realized that just because a person can't do something now doesn't mean they never will be able to do it – you might even enjoy a scary movie one day. Can you ever forgive me?"

"There is nothing to forgive," he said, looking at the floor. "After eighteen years, I should be stronger and smarter. It was only Wickham and his mother who tied me; I recognized their voices."

"You're not the type to hit a woman," she guessed, "so I doubt it was a fair fight. I saw that they wore masks. Did they blindfold you?"

"No, but one of them – probably George – strangled me until I lost consciousness. I must have been out for less than a minute, but it was long enough for them to gag me and bind my hands and feet. George carried me upstairs, tied me to that column you saw, and hit me a few times with a bat."

"Did they hit your head?" Lizzy was frantic with worry.

"I think he was going to hit my head next but that is when they heard your car outside, so they left me in the attic. In just a few minutes, they brought you upstairs and left again. That's probably when they set the fire and drove away. I am so sorry they hurt you."

"Will, don't be sorry. It wasn't your fault. Are you injured? Do you have bruises? Let me see."

He shook his head, still looking at the floor.

She gently touched his shoulder as he winced. "Did you see a doctor?"

"Don't want to," he whispered.

"You need to see a doctor so the injuries can be documented for the police."

"Isn't it enough they kidnapped me, tied me up, and set fire to the house?" he said, as silent tears started to flow. "There should be more than enough physical evidence to send Wickham to prison."

Lizzy kissed his hands as he curled himself into a little ball. "I'm here, I'm here. You're safe now."

"After eighteen years, I should have been smarter. I don't want to go to court and tell everyone I didn't learn. I don't want people to say I'm – I'm – I'm broken, I'm fragile."

She saw just how severely her words had hurt him, how ashamed he felt. She looked over to the Colonel. "Did he see a counsellor after his parents died?"

"He refused to talk to one, and became upset when my parents tried to discuss things," the Colonel said glumly. "He said he was all right, and he seemed okay, just quiet. Did well at school and at work. My family and I keep our eyes out for him, though – all the time."

"Will, look at me, please," Lizzy said softly, waiting until he raised his eyes to her. "My sisters Jane and Mary and I went to a wonderful counsellor who helped us immensely. Would you at least speak to him?"

"Why did you need a counsellor?"

Lizzy laughed. "You've never met our parents."

A hint of a tiny smile formed on his face.

"It's like this analogy, Will. Let's say your leg was broken when you were a child but you never got treatment; your leg healed but it didn't heal right. Ever since then, you've been limping along, hiding your bad leg under long trousers and boots, learning how to compensate. If someone didn't see an X-ray of your leg, they would never guess your leg was hurt. But your leg is definitely still hurt. It's nothing to be ashamed of – you didn't break your own leg; someone did it to you. But it's time to get it fixed so you won't keep limping. You're a strong and brave person, Will, but you can't fix your own leg."

Darcy looked her in the eyes, "You really talked to a counsellor?"

"Yes, I did. I am my mother's least favourite child, something she still tells me at every opportunity." She looked to her sister. "Jane, everyone thinks your life is perfect. Tell him your story."

"When I became an adult, I spoke to the counsellor because all my life, my mother kept pushing me to marry a rich man," Jane said. "I can laugh about it now, but for years I felt like she was trying to make me into a whore. She bought me padded bras when I was only nine years old!"

Charles burst into laughter when he saw Will's eyes widen in shock.

"Jane, show him a photo from your toddler beauty pageant days," Charles said.

Jane brought out an album and showed Will a page. In the photo, her blonde hair was elaborately curled, she wore makeup and lipstick, and she posed seductively in a replica of Marilyn Monroe's pleated white subway dress from "The Seven Year Itch."

"Good heavens, you were only three or four years old when you looked like a tart," Will blurted out, then covered his mouth with his hand.

Jane, Lizzy, and Charles laughed. The Colonel shook his head in amazement.

"See, Will?" Lizzy said. "Lots of people have a figurative broken leg; those of us who look normal are just better at hiding it and pretending. Seeing a counsellor is not so scary."

~~*~*

He still needed some assurance, but it helped him to know that Lizzy did not consider him weak or fragile for seeing a therapist. In the months ahead, she proved her acceptance of him – and her love. When he cried, she held him. When he needed to talk, she listened. When he became depressed, she shook him out of it, by taking him on hikes or to see silly movies. When they went out in public on dates and a news reporter caught them, Lizzy always defended him as a brave hero.

"Your love for me is my best medicine," he told her often.

"You are easy to love," Lizzy always answered.

No one was surprised when Darcy opened a U.S. office of Pemberley Enterprises. It was about thirty miles from the Bingleys' home, an easy distance for car-crazy Americans.

~~*~*

Epilogue

On the other side of Oakham Mount was a steep gorge that couldn't be seen from popular hiking trails, but eventually the car rental agency would use its GPS tracking device to find the charred remains of a black SUV. It had been rented by a Mrs. Younge, who had driven it to the Meryton Mall Cineplex where her boyfriend – George Wickham – and his mother pulled Darcy in.

But it was George who had driven the SUV off the trail and down the sharp rocky walls; he'd become lost trying to view the house they'd set fire to – where Darcy had died, they thought. It didn't help that George, his mother, and Mrs. Younge had all been drinking to celebrate the success of their plan. The "iced tea" drinks had been served in innocuous pint-size jam jars, but the drinks they had were made with vodka, gin, tequila, rum, triple sec, bourbon whiskey, schnapps, almost everything except tea. For example, what is the difference between Peach Iced Tea and Georgia Peach Iced Tea? One has tea and peaches, one has alcohol and no tea.

The fatal accident would not be blamed on the bar customers who had sent drinks to the handsome Wickham all night. Kitty and Lydia Bennet were just being nice to the Englishman with the cute accent. They never knew his name, and forgot him as soon as the next handsome man walked in.

Wickham was never one to complain about getting free drinks.

All that mattered to Will and Lizzy is that the Wickhams' deaths spared him from having to testify in court. Darcy's long nightmare was over.

A year after the kidnapping, when Lizzy and Will married, they cut their wedding cake with their favourite pizza cutter.

Uniformed Integrity

By Aimée Avery

~ For my military man ~

What if Pemberley were an Air Force Base?

PART ONE

"Dad, do I have to go?" Elizabeth asked as she sat at the kitchen table making a shopping list for her weekly visit to the Pemberley Air Force Base commissary.

"Yes, Lizzy. I can't very well go by myself. I'm sure it's been done in the past, but I prefer to have a date. I don't want to stand out like a sore thumb."

"Well, don't you think you will anyway? I mean, how many Air Force officers take their daughter to a dining out? And for a new base commander to boot!" Lizzy stood and looked through the kitchen cabinets for anything else she may need to add to her list.

"I know you don't go for these formal to-do's, Lizzy girl, but since your mother had the gall to leave me for the father of that girl you used to hang around with, I'm at a loss," Major Thomas Bennet told his daughter in a biting voice. "I can't very well take Lydia!"

Elizabeth had always felt guilty that Fanny Bennet had met Bill Lucas because she and Charlotte Lucas had become friends while running on the base high school track team. Bill Lucas had been in the Air Force, but had been discharged as a technical sergeant because of a medical condition. Charlotte's mother, also a technical sergeant, remained in the service of her country, and had been away on a six-month temporary duty when Bill decided that he didn't like living on a military reservation. Fanny and Bill had a secret affair - well, not that secret, as Charlotte had known about it and had played advocate by dragging Lizzy to the base bowling alley, pizza parlor or to the movie theater.

"Of course you can't take Lydia; a fifteen-year-old would look rather out of place, and most definitely with an officer in the 63rd Space Wing! Not that a twenty-five-year-old is that much better. What will everyone think?"

"Lizzy, it's not like everyone doesn't know you're my daughter! Okay, so that snot-nosed new base commander won't, but I don't give a crap what that boy thinks!" Tom Bennet shook his head in disgust. "I still can't believe they would install a kid to command this base."

"How old is he anyway?" Elizabeth asked finally, after listening to her father rail on the man for weeks.

"Thirty-two or -three. Wickham says the only reason Darcy made it to a bird colonel was because his uncle is a retired major general."

"Oh, Captain Wickham knows him?"

"Seems so. Apparently they went through OCS together. I don't know all the particulars, but it seems this Colonel Darcy somehow cheated Wickham out of a promotion. Wickham would have been a major by now. He has much more experience than I do, and he definitely has time in grade, but he's still a captain." Tom Bennet sat down at the table with a cup of coffee.

"I don't know, Daddy. I can't see how George Wickham can have more experience than you," Elizabeth said as she walked up behind her father and bent down to hug his neck.

"Well, I may have a few years on the man, but I was speaking of military experience. Remember, I was an enlisted man for quite a few years before I made it to Officer Candidate School."

"Yes, well. Anyway. About this dining out... I wish Jane were here and she could go. But she had to run off and get married. And too bad Charles had to be transferred to Netherfield; this really is Jane's kind of thing. I'm sure she'd be able to smile and make conversation with the idiot new commander. I'm liable to wall off and punch him right in the kisser."

Tom Bennet chuckled at his favorite daughter, and with a soft look in his eye said, "Well, I am glad you are so willing to fight for my opinion, sweetheart, but I don't think that would get me very far with this kid. Let's just go with the flow and see how things come out. Besides, I understand Wickham is attending. After he sees you dressed to the nines, he's bound to keep you all to himself. I'll end up escorting *his* date home." Tom winked at his daughter.

"Daddy!" Elizabeth blushed beet red.

"Oh, you don't think I don't know that you've had your eye on him, huh? Well, this old man isn't that blind."

"Hey! What's for dinner? Hi, Daddy." Lydia said as she opened and then slammed the kitchen door.

"Is it that late already?" Elizabeth asked as she looked at the clock.

"Late for what?" Lydia asked.

"For you to be home from school. Why are you home? It's only thirteen hundred!"

"We had a half day today. Is it okay if I go over to Mariah's? She got a new laptop for her birthday, and we're going over to the exchange and use the free WiFi. Besides, Denny is working at the coffee shop today. He might ask me out to the football game. It's against Meryton, or maybe it's Hartfield, I don't remember. Anyway, he's really cute, and Mariah thinks he likes her, but I know it's me he likes, and I told her I could prove it, so that's really why we're going over there. Of course, if Mariah should end up right, which I don't think is possible, then there's always Phil Saunderson, who helps out over at the library. Did you know his mother works at clothing and sales?" Lydia stopped talking long enough to put a cookie in her mouth.

"Yes, well, that sounds much too complicated for me," Tom smiled at his youngest daughter. "I need to head back to work." He kissed his two daughters on the forehead and left through the back door.

"So I'm going to Mariah's," Lydia said and pushed passed her sister.

"Hey! I didn't say you could go," Elizabeth grabbed her arm to stop her.

"You aren't my mother, Lizzy! So stop acting like it! I might listen to Jane, but why should I listen to you? Just because you're older than me doesn't make you my boss!"

"No, Lydia, I'm not Mom. But Mom isn't here, is she?"

"You're just jealous because she calls me and never you!"

"I don't care if she calls you. She isn't responsible for you, I am. She signed away that right and Dad gave it to me, so..."

"So you're going to try to boss me around. Look, Lizzy, you're just mad because Jane got married and moved away, and Mary and Kitty got to go off to college, and you're stuck here with me. Well, you aren't going to take it out on me, so kiss off, bitch!" Lydia ran out the door and down the street.

Elizabeth knew she could get in the car and drive over and stop Lydia even before she made it to the community center. But there wasn't much Lydia could do while she was on base to cause trouble, and everyone knew her, so Elizabeth let her go. She would talk to her father about Lydia, and soon. In the meantime, she would call over to one of her friends who worked in the main exchange and have them check to see if Lydia and Mariah arrived.

After receiving a call from her friend confirming Lydia's arrival at exchange's main entrance, Elizabeth jumped into her car and drove the twelve miles to Meryton, and Ford's department store in the mall. She needed a knockout formal dress, for there was an officer to impress.

PART TWO

Elizabeth looked at her reflection in the full-length mirror, and was stunned at what she saw. She never thought of herself as an elegant woman, but the person in the mirror wasn't the jean-clad female she saw every morning after she brushed her teeth. This girl... No! This woman was beautiful.

"That can't be me!" she said to the surprised face staring at her from the back of her bedroom door. She didn't know what she had wanted with her hair, so she told the stylist at the exchange's beauty salon to "put it up fancy, but not too froufrou" and, somehow, the hairdresser came up with what she now saw. Her hair was piled on top of her head and held in place with pearl-tipped pins. A few strands had fallen softly at her neck, but it only added to the style.

Elizabeth had spent an hour and a half in Ford's earlier in the week, trying on dresses and, with a sales clerk's help, found a beautiful dress that fell to just above her knees. The soft, sheer fabric flared out from tucked pleats at the waist, and a straight, tailored underskirt preserved her modesty. Above the waist, the dress had a fitted bodice, held up with thread-like bands, giving it a strapless look. The front was studded with false black pearls, and a soft ribbon belt bisected the creation.

Elizabeth had decided on a simple black clutch and pumps to accessorize her ensemble. Her jewelry was just as simple, a black pearl necklace she had received for her fourteenth Christmas while they had been stationed in Hawaii. It was one of the few presents her mother had given her she actually liked. Her earrings were simple black pearl-like studs with three short falls and a plastic pearl at each end. She happened to notice them at one of the earring boutiques in the mall. She never imagined that she could look so different, and all for less than a hundred dollars.

Elizabeth was glad Lydia was staying at Mariah's house. She didn't need her uncontrollable sister finding something else to go on about. Lydia had taken their mother's leaving the hardest of all the girls. Lydia was definitely Fanny's favorite, but obviously not favorable enough for Fanny to take her with her, or even want joint custody. Fanny had deserted all of her daughters. Oh, she called Lydia from time to time, but it was usually to brag at what she'd been doing or what Charlotte had done. Lydia spent more time crying over the phone calls than enjoying any of the conversation; but Lydia always put on a show for her father and other sisters. Elizabeth was the only one to see how much Fanny's desertion had harmed Lydia. Perhaps tonight would offer a quiet moment for Elizabeth to discuss the matter with her father.

"I'm ready," Elizabeth announced to her father as she walked into the living room of their base home.

Thomas Bennet turned with a smile, but as soon as he saw his second daughter, the smile left and was replaced by a combination of shock and admiration. He knew his daughter was a woman, but now there was no mistaking the fact. His tomboy was no more; she was replaced with an elegant lady.

"Elizabeth Bennet! You are beautiful," he said with a stuttered breath. As a tear fell down his cheek, he lightly brushed a kiss on her forehead before saying, "I don't think I want to share you with Captain Wickham tonight.

I want to be the one who has the honor of constant company with the most beautiful woman at the officer's club, and the entire country for that matter."

"Oh, Daddy!" She kissed his cheek and then straightened his tie. "Well, I must say that you look especially dashing in your dress uniform. Very impressive. I think we'll be the best looking couple!"

"Shall we go, Miss Bennet?"

"Indeed, Major Bennet."

~~*~*

The room was full of perfectly dressed officers and enlisted personnel, along with their dates. Elizabeth sipped her wine as she looked around the room for Captain Wickham. She finally saw him standing off to the side talking with a few junior officers. She slowing made her way to that side of the room, greeting people she knew on the way. She was excited for him to see her. They had been friends since he had come to the base, and he was one of the few people with whom she discussed losing her best friend and her mother. But she wanted him to see her as a desirable woman, not just as a friend or the daughter of his immediate supervisor.

As she made her way around the room, Elizabeth heard the most exciting and sexy male voice coming from behind her. She turned and saw a very tall officer surrounded by several others. She couldn't make out his rank through the back of inconvenient heads, but she could see his face. She couldn't help drawing in a sudden hard breath. The man was gorgeous! Tall, yes, but he also had the sexiest head of hair. It was cut short, but she knew if it were to grow out, it would have that Superman-style curl to it. And his eyes! The sexiest blue since Paul Newman! She wanted a picture of this man to hang as a poster on her bedroom door, along with a copy for her wallet and the silver frame on her nightstand!

As she stood and stared at his gorgeous face, he looked up and caught her eye. Elizabeth was frozen, and could feel a slight blush start to rise up her neck. Her heart started drumming in her chest when he gave her a soft smile and raised his glass to her. As he took a sip, his attention was snared away by one of the officers, and Elizabeth was suddenly released from the solid hold.

Elizabeth turned and continued her trek to Captain Wickham. She had to fan herself as she remembered the gorgeous officer's smile, only to have the heat rise in her chest when she saw Wickham's date. The woman was wearing a skin-tight, blue dress that was about six inches too short and plunged about six inches too deep at the neck. If the woman moved too quickly, her breasts would pop right out for the room to see. Worst of all, Elizabeth Bennet knew this woman, or at least had. Charlotte Lucas stood so close to Wickham, it seemed as if they were fused. What was worse, Wickham had his hand up the back of Charlotte's skirt. It was plain to see that Charlotte was either wearing a thread-like thong or going commando.

Elizabeth didn't know whether she was more offended that Wickham was with Charlotte or, as one of her father's officers, he was not only making a fool of himself, but also his superiors, and in front of the new commander. More than anything, Elizabeth was hurt. The man she thought was the 'one' was pawing a woman who looked like a streetwalker – a streetwalker who was Charlotte Lucas, a woman Wickham knew Elizabeth hated.

~~*~*

"Edward!" Major Bennet exclaimed. "What are you doing here?"

"Tom! So good to see you! How are my nieces?" Lieutenant Colonel Edward Gardiner asked. He was not only friends with Thomas Bennet, but also his former brother-in-law.

"They're all well. Mary is at Stanford and Kitty is going to UCLA. Elizabeth is here with me tonight and..."

Thomas Bennet trailed off as he noticed Wickham and his date. "Oh, my God!"

"What?" Gardiner asked.

"One of my men is about to make me into a complete and utter fool! Jesus, I can't believe this!" Major Bennet spoke as he made his way toward Wickham with Lieutenant Colonel Gardiner following.

"That's George Wickham! He's one of your men?" Gardiner asked.

"Yes," Major Bennet replied.

"That man is a disgrace to the uniform. Always has been! How has he managed not to get himself tossed out on his sorry ass?" Gardiner asked quietly.

"What do you mean? I haven't seen anything that would constitute any kind of problem."

"I suggest you put him on report and get him out of here before Darcy sees him, if he hasn't already. And at your first available opportunity, I think you should have a discussion with your new commander regarding this sorry excuse who shouldn't even be able to look at a uniform at a surplus store!"

Major Bennet looked at his brother-in-law, and then turned to the man he had, until just a moment before, held in high esteem. "Wickham! You and your date will follow me. NOW!"

Elizabeth watched as her father escorted Wickham and his date from the officer's club.

PART THREE

Colonel Darcy hadn't made it to where he was now by not being observant. He had seen Wickham a few moments before, and noticed a major escort the man and his date from the club. He also noticed the horrified look on the beautiful woman who had been looking at him earlier.

There was something about that woman. Her dress was simple but elegant, as was her face. Her pale skin seemed to shimmer against the black she wore. Her eyes were absolutely captivating. They were a beautiful glowing green, set against the loveliest dark lashes he had ever seen. He had glanced at her left hand as it clutched a wine glass, and noticed her fingers were bare of jewelry. He couldn't help but smile, but he still didn't know why he acknowledged her by raising his glass to her. That wasn't something he did.

Women seemed to flock to him. He could be walking in the park with his five-year-old daughter or congratulating a group of airmen on the parade ground, and every woman – military and civilian – would have their eye on him. It had been just a year ago that Airman First Class Gail Younge had been taken into custody by the MPs for stalking not only him, but also his then four-year-old. For some reason, women seemed to want to be with him, though he couldn't figure it out for the life of him.

Eventually, the Major returned, and Darcy noticed the beautiful young woman quickly attended he older officer. She clutched onto his arm and seemed upset. When the older man kissed her cheek, Darcy felt a surge of jealousy pump hard through his body. What was such a young woman doing with a man old enough to be her father?

"I'm sure you noticed that Wickham's on base," Lieutenant Colonel Gardiner spoke as he approached behind Darcy.

"I did," Darcy replied as he turned to face his friend. "How in God's name is that man still in uniform?"

"I have no idea. Major Bennet escorted him out. Apparently Tom has no knowledge of Wickham's past. He said it didn't show in his file."

"That is impossible!" Darcy replied and then took a sip of his drink. "Major Tom Bennet? Isn't he...?"

"The one and the same. He's part of your new command, and I think he'll be needing a new assistant," Edward smirked into his glass.

"Oh, that's for certain. I just wonder what Wickham has been saying, but I am sure I'll find out soon enough. I knew this assignment would be a challenge, but I wasn't expecting this in the flight path."

"Well, you always did say you liked challenges, Will!" Edward Gardiner chuckled as he looked past Darcy to see his former brother-in-law and niece approach. "Colonel William Darcy, may I present one of your officers, Major Thomas Bennet."

Elizabeth gasped lightly when the Colonel turned to meet them. *Oh my, how can such a handsome man be such an ogre?* she thought to herself, but realized just as quickly that looks had nothing to do with one's personality. *Well, of course, unless they're vain. Oh God! I feel warm. I hope I'm not blushing.*

"Major Bennet, it's a pleasure. I've heard many wonderful things about you, and I'm looking forward to working with you." Darcy looked directly into the Major's eyes and shook his hand. He then offered another soft smile to Major Bennet's beautiful companion.

"The pleasure is all mine, sir. Colonel Darcy, my daughter, Elizabeth," Tom Bennet spoke with pride as he introduced his favorite daughter.

"Miss Bennet. I'm honored. Might I perhaps be so bold as to ask for a dance later?"

Colonel Darcy had taken her hand in greeting at some point during the introduction, she knew. She could feel a tingling sensation spread up her arm from where his hand held hers. "I... I... That, um, would be... lovely... sir." Elizabeth was having trouble enough trying to keep her breathing regular. Talking wasn't helping.

"Good. Major Bennet, would you mind introducing me to some of the other officers?" Darcy asked, still holding Elizabeth's hand.

"It would be my pleasure, sir," Elizabeth's father responded.

Elizabeth felt Darcy squeeze her hand lightly then release it as he left with her father.

"Elizabeth?"

"Huh? Oh! Uncle Eddie! How are you?"

"I'm just fine." Edward chuckled again. "You look magnificent!"

Elizabeth blushed and whispered a quiet thank you as she watched the broad back of the new base commander cross the room.

"You seem to have made a very good impression on the Colonel," Gardiner continued in his jovial voice.

"I don't know what you mean, Uncle Eddie."

"Will Darcy may be a tough military man and a high ranking officer with more experience than a man his age should have, but he is still a young man, a young, unattached man who just met a very beautiful young, unattached woman."

"Well, he has no way of knowing that I'm unattached," Elizabeth spat. "And I am not beautiful," she added shyly.

"You have that wrong on both counts, my sweet niece."

~~*~*

It had been over a month since the event at the officer's club and, though the beautiful black dress hung in Elizabeth's closet and George Wickham had since been dishonorably discharged, everything else fell back into place as if the party had never happened. But it had happened, and a couple times during each day, Lizzy relived that evening. She and her father had been seated at the Colonel's table, and the Colonel had spent a good deal of time discussing many topics with her from current events to the best way to get Barbie's hair back to that "just-out-of-the-box-on-Christmas-morning" look.

After asking to see a photo of Darcy's daughter, Elizabeth found it difficult to understand how such a pretty little girl could have such a monster of a father. But she decided he must be some sort of creep if the man wasn't married and his daughter's mother "wasn't in the picture," as he so aptly stated. What type of evil kept a little girl from her mother?

Elizabeth knew the evil that kept Fanny from her daughters, but that evil was Fanny herself. Elizabeth knew most mothers weren't that way. She would never be that way. She would never just walk away from her children, even if a powerful military man with connections tried to force her.

The one thing that really disturbed Elizabeth about the night of the party was her dance with Colonel Darcy. She had hoped the deejay would play a fast number, but as soon as they stepped onto the dance floor, the man put on a slow, sultry song. She thought maybe having just been introduced, he would keep a loose his hold, but instead, he held her even closer, and waltzed her around the floor as if he were protecting her. She had the vague notion the others on the floor were doing a similar dance, but she didn't care. She felt so safe and comfortable in the man's arms. At the end of the song, he escorted her back to her father, kissed her cheek and whispered, "Thank you" in her ear.

Elizabeth didn't know what to think of the man. Her impressions of him, added to what her father had told her of him in the weeks before his arrival, just didn't add up. Who was this man? She didn't think she would ever have the answer. And considering she hadn't seen him, nor had her father spoken of him, Elizabeth decided to forget about him and just put the memory down in her journal. She had more important things to take care of, like driving Lydia over to her new job at the base's new burger restaurant.

Elizabeth turned off main road into the community center driveway when Lydia leaned toward the back and picked up her backpack. "I'm going over to Mariah's after I'm off. I brought a change of clothes. Her mom is going to take us into town to see a movie, and then we're going to walk downtown. I want stop by that trendy clothes store and get something cool," Lydia told her sister.

Tom Bennet had had a discussion with both his daughters, and things seemed to be going much better. Lydia was spending a lot of time with Mariah, but at least now she had a job and was being more civil to her older sister and guardian.

"I know, Dad told me. Oh, check out that new store and let me know what you think. I'm going to the commissary, you want anything special?" Elizabeth asked.

"Nah. See you later, Lizzy," Lydia waved as she ran into the fast food restaurant.

As Lizzy drove through the parking lot then out toward the park, she thought again about her dance with Darcy. "No! I'm not going to think about that anymore! I have too many other things that need my attention. I have those night college classes in web design and accounting, besides my household duties. I don't need to clog my brain with silly schoolgirl fantasies."

As Lizzy passed the base's small movie theater, she again spoke aloud a reminder to pick up a copy of the newspaper so she could find out what movies were playing. She made a couple of turns and pulled into the commissary parking lot. Lizzy enjoyed grocery shopping first thing on Saturday morning. The crowd hadn't made into the commissary yet, and everything was out for the big shopping day.

Pulling a push basket from the line just outside the main entrance, Lizzy settled her purse and list in the child seat and started down the produce aisle. She turned down the baking aisle and dropped in a couple boxes of chocolate cake mix, flour, sugar, chocolate chips and vegetable oil. It was time to treat the personnel on her father's team to her famous cake cookies! Thinking about the faces when she brought in cookies made her smile, and she was a little lost in thought when she turned the corner to go down the breakfast food aisle. She had to stop suddenly when a little blonde girl almost ran into her cart.

"Oh, I'm sorry, sweetie. I didn't see you! I didn't hit you with my cart, did I?"

The little girl looked up and shook her head as she hugged a large box of cereal to her chest. Elizabeth had to hold back a laugh; the cereal box was almost as large as the pretty little girl. It was about the same time as she heard a male voice calling that she realized who the little girl was.

"Georgiana! How long does it take to pick... Miss Bennet!" Darcy said in surprise as he noticed the woman standing with his young daughter.

"Colonel Darcy," Elizabeth greeted him softly.

"Miss Bennet, this my daughter, Georgiana. Scooter, say 'hello' to Miss Bennet."

"Hello, Georgiana," Elizabeth said as she knelt down and put her hand out. Georgiana shyly took the offered hand and whispered a meek hello. "You can call me Elizabeth, okay?" The little girl nodded with a smile and then looked to her father.

"Don't you think that cereal is a bit too sugary?" Darcy asked his daughter.

"You said I could pick what I wanted," Georgiana answered, forgetting Elizabeth was still kneeling beside her.

"That I did, Scooter!" he said with a smile, and reached for the box.

"No! I'll put it in!" Georgiana pulled the box away from him.

Elizabeth rose and laughed at the way the little girl talked to the most important man on base.

Darcy lifted his daughter and held onto her legs as he tipped her upside down for her to drop the box into the grocery basket. The girl's giggles brought a big smile to the tall man – a smile that flashed white teeth and dimples, and if Elizabeth had wanted to abandon her schoolgirl-like crush, it wasn't going to happen anytime soon.

"Planning on doing some baking, Miss Bennet?" Darcy asked as he pointed to the contents of her cart.

"Elizabeth!" Georgiana's correction earned her another smile from her father.

Lizzy attempted to mop up her melted heart long enough to answer, "Yes."

"I like chocolate," Georgiana stated as her father deposited her into the shopping basket.

"Scooter!" Darcy chastised. "My apologies. She's an angler, aren't you, Scoot?" She answered her father by standing and burying her face into her father's uniform jacket.

"I like chocolate too. Do you like to make cookies, Georgiana?" Elizabeth found it easier to talk to the little girl instead of her father.

"I don't know how," she answered with her face still half buried in Darcy's jacket.

"Well, maybe sometime I can show you," Elizabeth offered genuinely.

"Really?"

"Really!" Elizabeth said, deciding she might as well just give up her heart to this little girl.

"You may live to regret that offer, Miss Bennet. She has a memory like a steel trap!"

"I think it would be more fun than going day camp," the girl said seriously.

"I know you don't like going to camp on Saturday, Scooter, but I have to work," Darcy said as he bent and kissed the little girl's head, causing Georgiana to wrap her arms tightly around his neck. Small quiet sobs sounded softly as she cried on her father's shoulder. Darcy stood upright, holding his daughter tightly.

"My apologies again, Miss Bennet. We have an issue with camp, as you may have guessed."

"I understand. Very much." Elizabeth knew exactly what this little girl was feeling. She could remember having her father being gone and her mother who was too busy with babies depositing her and Jane at some activity meant to entertain, only when you were dropped there all the time, the entertainment value lessened rapidly. Elizabeth had been lucky, she had Jane and vice versa. "Uh, how long is the camp?"

"It's from ten to sixteen hundred," Darcy answered.

"Oh! That is a long time. Tell you what. I'm going to be all by myself today, so how would it be if she came to 'Camp Bennet' instead? She could learn how to make cookies. I know I could use a chocolate chip counter," Elizabeth winked at Georgiana, who wiped the tears from her face.

"Miss Bennet, that is a generous offer, but..."

"Please?" Both Elizabeth and Georgiana begged at once.

Darcy looked back and forth between the two females, and knew he was lost. He thought he had been lost the day Georgiana was born, but knew he was in serious trouble during a very special dance just five weeks before. Today was the confirmation.

PART FOUR

Saturdays were a very boring day for Elizabeth ever since Jane had married and moved away. They had always taken care of the chores and then spent the rest of the afternoon enjoying whatever the day brought. But these last couple of years, Lizzy had been mistress of the manor, and without Jane. She filled in as cook, maid and general caretaker of the family. With only Lydia and her at home now, the chores were lighter, but she didn't have anyone to commiserate with. Charlotte's betrayal had scarred her so much that she didn't let others in too close, and she had no time for dating.

Saturday was her day, however, and offering to entertain a petite five-year-old gave her the opportunity to discover her heart's true desire. She wanted a family of her own... a husband, babies and her own home to take care of. She thought, too, of the classes she had been taking, and realized that they were all classes to help her with a home business, one that could be done from any part of the world. In a couple years, Lydia would be old enough to be on her own. Lizzy was positive that Lydia would jump at the chance to leave the nest, and Elizabeth would be adrift.

She would have to move off base and find a job... a real job. Then maybe she could start dating too. So much of her life had been put on hold because of her mother's defection, and she wondered if she would ever catch up to herself. The more she thought about it, the more it seemed so daunting. Would she ever find a job? Could she support herself? Would she ever have a family of her own; one with a handsome husband like the Colonel and pretty little girl like Georgiana?

"Whoa! When did I start comparing my dream family to the Colonel and Georgiana?" Elizabeth said aloud as she cleaned up the kitchen. She quickly answered herself, "Since you've spent the last six Saturday's being nanny to the base commander's daughter, you dolt!"

She enjoyed the little girl's company. Georgiana was well behaved, and sharp as a tack. Elizabeth had to admit that she also waited with a frenzied anticipation for the Colonel to drop-off and pick-up his daughter. He always came in, had a cup of coffee and listened to everything the child described about her and Lizzy's day together. He would always try to pay Elizabeth for her time, but she always refused. Today's conversation had been a bit different, however.

"So, Scooter, what did you and Miss Bennet do today?"

"We made *punkin'* cookies for Halloween. Daddy, did you know there's orange icing? It doesn't taste like orange though. It just tastes regular."

"Orange? Really? How do you make it orange?" Darcy leaned down closer to the table so that he was eye level with his preschooler.

"Well... Lizzy? Can I tell Daddy, or is it a secret?" Georgiana said as her eyes followed Elizabeth's movement across the kitchen.

Elizabeth set the Colonel's coffee in front of him before stating, "Colonel Darcy, I'm afraid you do not have the proper security clearance. I'm going to have to insist that you refrain from pursuing this line of questioning."

"And if I don't?" he asked with a fire in his eye that she had never seen before.

"You will be up before the spoon squad!" Lizzy waved a large wooden spoon in the air. Her heart skipped a beat when his hand grabbed hers and the spoon and pulled her closer to him.

"I wouldn't want that," he said in a low voice as he stared into her sparkling green eyes. They held their gaze until he cleared his throat and dropped her hand. "We need to get going," he said before he downed his coffee and stood. "Get your things, Scooter. Elizabeth, thank you again for taking care of my little monster."

"The pleasure is really mine. I enjoy having her. We have fun, don't we?"

"Uh huh! Lots of fun. Maybe you can stay with us one time, Daddy. You'd have fun too," Georgiana said as she zipped up her pink backpack.

"I'm in no doubt of that," Darcy answered, then turned to Elizabeth. "Elizabeth? I was wondering... um... I know this is rather short notice, but..."

"Oh, wait Georgiana!" Elizabeth interrupted, and gathered some cookies in a plastic container and handed them to the little girl. "Sorry, Colonel. I didn't want her to forget to take some cookies home. She might share if you're lucky!" Lizzy smiled and tapped his uniform sleeve. *I know he is going to ask me to babysit tonight. He has a date and needs a sitter. Good way to screw up my fantasy, but...*

"If I'm lucky, she might. Scooter, why don't you go climb in the car? I'll be right out."

"Okay, Daddy."

Darcy watched his daughter skip to his car, open the door to the back seat and climb in before he continued with Elizabeth, "Like I was saying, I know it is rather short notice, but Scooter was invited to spend the night with one of her little friends tonight, and I thought that... that maybe you would let me take you out to dinner? You know, as a thank you for helping me with Georgiana?"

"Oh! Um... well, ah... sure. W-what time?"

"How about if I pick you up, say, oh... um... eighteen hundred?" He asked with a boyish grin and excitement.

"O-okay," Elizabeth blushed. "Eighteen hundred then." She watched as Darcy pulled out of the driveway and drove down the road.

She finished up in the kitchen and then looked at the clock. "Eighteen hundred? Good God! That's an hour from now!" She ran to her room and screamed. "What am I supposed to wear? I don't even know where we are going! And does this classify as a date?" She let out another little scream, then flew into the bathroom to shower.

~~*~*

Elizabeth lay in her bed and laughed as she remembered her plan of attack for the evening. She had chosen three outfits, put them out on her bed and stood ready at her front facing bedroom window. She peeked out of the curtain, waiting for Darcy to drive up. When he stepped out of his car, she would see how he was dressed and quickly jump into the most appropriate selection. She knew this would have to be a casual dinner, since he had to ready Georgiana for her overnighter, as well as himself; so she was ready. A pair of new jeans with a pink and white striped shirt and pink Converse All-Star sneakers, a dressier pair of twill pants with a crepe blouse with low heels that would also work with her third selection, a soft blue cotton dress, awaited her snap decision upon his arrival.

Darcy drove up, exited the car and headed for the front door, and Elizabeth nearly fell over at the view. He wore a pair of stonewashed blue jeans that fit his impressive male figure very well. He topped the denims with a white short-sleeved Henley shirt. It was the black and white Converse All-Stars that charmed her into jumping into her jeans and striped shirt. She smiled broadly as she laced her pink sneakers.

Tom Bennet answered his door, "Ah, Colonel. Come in."

"Please, I'm off duty and out of uniform. It's Will, sir," Darcy said as he shook the older man's hand.

"Does this mean that I get to give you the standard lecture about not keeping my daughter out too late?" Tom chuckled.

"Daddy!"

"Guess not," Tom Bennet said conspiratorially to Darcy.

"Don't worry, sir, we won't be out too late. Here's my cell number just in case though," Will pulled a business card from his wallet and wrote the cell number on the back.

"Night, Daddy," Elizabeth said to her father and kissed his cheek. She blushed when her father winked at her in full view of the Colonel.

Elizabeth thought that they would go somewhere nearby, Meryton or Longbourn, but he drove her all the way over the hill to Hunsford and parked just off the main boulevard in the city lot near the train station. They walked up boulevard and ate at a quaint Italian restaurant, then strolled through a park-like shopping center. They explored through the items for sale in the shops, nibbled on sticky pastry and sipped coffee at a café. They talked about everything under the sun, laughed at each other's bad jokes, window-shopped and, as they turned to make their way back toward the car, he placed his hand on the small of her back.

"It's still early. I don't think your father will get the shotgun out if we continue our walk. Would you like to go down to the wharf?" Darcy asked as they stood at the corner next to the train tracks and the entrance to the city parking lot.

Elizabeth giggled and replied with a smile and a singular nod. She almost tripped when he took her hand in his as they made their way to the beach. But what made her blush even now, as she stared at the ceiling, remembering, was the mind-numbing kiss he gave her at the end of the pier. She tried to relive it as she closed her eyes.

"Oh! The wind's cold out here!"

"I should have thought about that and made sure we had jackets," Darcy replied.

"Don't worry about it. It's too pretty out here for that." Elizabeth leaned on the railing and inhaled the crisp salt air.

"Ah, but it is my job to worry," Darcy said as he stepped behind her and wrapped his arms around her. As he pulled Elizabeth back against his warm body, he whispered, "Besides, I could use some warming up too."

If that hadn't been enough to make her heart stutter, his kisses just below her ear were.

"Elizabeth..."

"Hmm?" Elizabeth replied with closed eyes wondering if she were dreaming. Darcy moved his hands up her arms and turned her toward him. His head was already dipped and he took her lips with his immediately.

The kiss was soft, but as soon as his tongue touched her lower lip, it turned to something much more passionate. He pulled her to him and held her tight. He leaned back against a post and trapped her in the V of his legs. Elizabeth stood on her tiptoes and wrapped her hands around his neck, hanging on for dear life.

Elizabeth knew that she was extremely aroused. All she had to do was think of the man and she felt her hormones go bananas, but this was sending her to new heights. When his hands moved down her back and cupped her buttocks, pulling her even closer to him, she knew that he, too, was definitely up for more.

A discreet cough followed by a man's voice saying, "Take it on home, folks," broke the couple apart.

"Sorry, officer. We got a bit, um, carried away," Darcy said a bit bashfully.

"Like I said, take it on home," the police officer replied.

Darcy nodded and took Elizabeth by the hand and led her back to the shore. As they passed a bar, he wrapped his arm around her shoulders. She slipped her arm around his waist and they made a slow ramble back to the car. Neither spoke, though Darcy did kiss the top of her head a few times.

The drive back to the base was equally as quiet. Words seemed unnecessary since their intertwined fingers seemed to be enough communication. As Darcy approached the main gate, he pulled his fingers from hers and pulled out his ID card from his wallet for the guard. The spell was broken, and now it was time for Cinderella to return back to the ashes.

The glorious events of the evening were suddenly overshadowed by the old rumors of Darcy before he arrived at the base. He didn't seem like the ogre she heard about, but she still didn't know him all that well. Suddenly, Elizabeth was confused. Should she have gone out with him? Will he want to go out again, or is this really just a "thank you" for taking care of Georgiana? He acted like a gentleman, but all the old stories made him out to be not so cavalier. And what about Georgiana? Where was her mother? Why didn't she ever see her or even speak of her? By the time the sun rose, Elizabeth had tossed and turned so much the covers had fallen from her bed and she never slept a wink.

PART FIVE

Elizabeth's confusion only grew with the number of times she and Darcy met face to face. She continued to keep Georgiana with her on Saturdays, and Darcy always stopped and visited when he came to pick up his daughter. He never mentioned their date or kiss, nor did she; her confusion made her believe it must have been the "thank you" he had said it was, though she wasn't sure why he'd kissed her. Or had he? She must have just dreamed that part.

"Elizabeth, I wish you could go with us on Thanksgiving. Everyone will think these little pies are so cool. Especially Uncle Richard, he likes to have all the pie."

"Well then, you'll be the special one for bringing them," Elizabeth hugged the little girl as they carefully packed the individual pumpkin pies into a cooler.

"Uncle Richard won't believe I made them though," Georgiana said, "especially with the little leaf on the top."

Elizabeth decided this might be her chance to understand some of the Darcy family dynamics, even if it did come from a kindergartener.

"Is your Uncle Richard your daddy's brother or you mother's?"

"I think he's Daddy's cousin. Maybe you could go with us! You want me to ask my daddy?"

"Oh, thank you, sweetie, but I have to stay here for Thanksgiving. I am making a big dinner for my daddy and my sisters."

"Oh," Georgiana said in a quiet and sad voice.

Elizabeth knew she had grown attached to the little blonde girl who had her father's smile, but she just now realized that the child was just as attached to her. It made her heart jump with joy and break with pain all at the same time. How did you explain the situation to a small child when you didn't know what the situation was yourself?

"But you know, if I hadn't already promised my daddy and sisters, then I would jump at the chance to spend more time with you," Elizabeth said as she tapped the girl's nose.

"And Daddy?"

"And Daddy, what, Scooter?" Darcy said as he opened the back screen door.

"Daddy! You have to see! I made pumpkin pies for us to take on Thanksgiving!"

"You did? We'll have to keep them away from Richard!" Darcy winked at his daughter and then smiled at Elizabeth.

"He gets his own pie, Daddy! Everyone does!" Georgiana picked up one of the small pies and presented it to her father.

"Wow! Is that a real pie or did it shrink in the oven?"

Elizabeth let out a small laugh then said, "Georgiana thought it would be nice if everyone could have their own pie, and not worry about sharing; so we came up with these."

Darcy's smile spread across his face and, as his daughter turned to place the small pie back on the table, the Colonel leaned over and kissed Elizabeth's cheek.

"Thank you. You've just settled the Darcy-Fitzwilliam Pie Wars," he whispered.

"Just call me Geneva Bennet!"

"I suppose I don't have the right clearance to know how you got that leaf imprint on them?"

"No, you don't," Elizabeth answered sternly.

"Figured as much," he chuckled and sat down. "Do I get to try one?"

"Sure, do you want some coffee to wash it down with?" Elizabeth had already poured the liquid and was setting it down when she asked.

"Daddy, I want Elizabeth to go with us, but she's having Thanksgiving dinner with her daddy and sisters," Georgiana announced. Elizabeth turned away so the Colonel wouldn't see her reddened cheeks.

"Yes, I know. Her daddy told me, Scooter."

"Are we going to come home right after Thanksgiving? I want to be here to see Santa. He is going to be at the winter festival next Saturday, isn't he, Elizabeth?"

"I believe so, Georgiana."

"He is? Wow, then I think we should get back here right away. Don't you, Scooter?" With the girl's nod, Darcy smiled and looked at Elizabeth. "Maybe you could join us? Don't want you to miss your chance to ask Santa for what you want for Christmas."

"Oh, please, Elizabeth. Go with us. Please, please, please!"

Elizabeth couldn't resist the sweet, excited little girl. "I wouldn't miss it for the world; although, I may skip the sitting on Santa's lap part."

Darcy frowned and his expression turned a dark, so much so that Elizabeth thought maybe she had bought a bad can of pumpkin.

"I don't think I'd like it if you sat on Santa's lap," Darcy growled.

"Why, Daddy? You have to sit on Santa's lap to tell him what you want."

Darcy cleared his throat and squirmed in his seat.

"I'm too big to sit on Santa's lap, Georgiana. I would break it," Elizabeth answered for him.

"You can't break Santa's lap! It's Santa. He doesn't break!"

"Well, then, your Daddy will have to sit on his lap too!" Elizabeth suggested.

Both Darcys reacted, Georgiana laughing hysterically and William trying his best not to spit coffee across the room.

~~*~*

Thanksgiving at the Bennet home was one of the happiest in many years, until the telephone rang. Fanny Gardiner Bennet Lucas seemed to have the knack for destroying all that was good.

"Hello," Elizabeth said into the receiver, hoping it was Colonel William Darcy calling from his cousin's home to wish her a happy Thanksgiving. But instead of the base commander's voice, she heard the whine of her mother's.

"Elizabeth, I want to speak to Lydia, now!"

So much for "Happy Thanksgiving, Elizabeth. Good to hear your voice. Hope you are well. I miss you!" Lizzy thought.

"Sure. Just a moment, please. Happy Thanksgiving," Elizabeth said in her sweetest voice before turning to her family, who sat at the dining room table. "Lydia, it's Fanny for you."

Elizabeth knew calling her mother by her first name would only add fuel to her mother's fire, but she just didn't care anymore. It was obvious that Fanny wanted nothing to do with her or any of her daughters except Lydia; only Elizabeth knew that Fanny didn't want Lydia either. It was just a way for Fanny to irritate Thomas Bennet. The fact that the Major had even better powers than Elizabeth to ignore the Mrs. Lucas never crossed her mind.

Lydia jumped up and grabbed the phone in happy anticipation, as her father and sisters watched, knowing what was to come. They didn't have to wait long. Lydia's tears started in the first thirty seconds of the conversation.

It really wasn't a conversation, more like a lecture to her youngest daughter. Fanny railed the teen for staying with her father, as if she had been given a choice. Then she promptly expanded the guilt trip to include that she was forced to leave because Thomas Bennet had threatened to beat Lydia if she didn't.

Lydia knew in the back of her mind it was all a part of Fanny's game, but the girl only wanted her mother's love, and had never been strong as her sisters. The older Bennet daughters had been able to tell Fanny that they knew the truth and that they didn't want any contact with her unless she could be civil. Fanny, of course, didn't want to expend the effort, and went for the easier target... Lydia.

"But, Mom, I *do* want to live with you. I hate it here. Lizzy is a bitch and Daddy is a fucking ass!"

The words were candy to Fanny, but the final straw to Tom Bennet. He slammed down his fork, quickly rose and walked to the phone and ripped it from Lydia's hand.

"Fanny! You either get your ass here in the next twenty-four hours and pick up Lydia, or never call here again. Your choice."

"How much child support do you plan on giving me, you bastard, because I'm not taking her out of the goodness of my heart!"

"Twenty-four hours, Fanny!" Thomas growled into the phone and hung it up. "Lydia! I have had it up to my ears with this. You know damn well that Fanny wants nothing to do with any of you girls, and gets her kicks out of tormenting you. Trust me, she won't show up."

"Yes, she will! She only lives an hour away, and she'll be here tonight, morning tops, to get me!"

"Lydia," Kitty said softly, "she could be here in less than two hours, but never shows up. She did the same thing to Mary and me. She doesn't want us; she just wants money."

"She wants me! Me! And all of you are just jealous because she loves me and not you. You'll see! She'll be here!" Lydia screamed and ran to her room, slamming the door behind her.

~~*~*

Lydia was subdued as she walked to her job at the burger restaurant. It was Saturday, and her mother had never shown. She hadn't tried to call the pre-paid cell phone that Lydia had bought when her father wouldn't add her to the family's cell plan either. Her mother and Mariah were the only ones who had her cell number, until just recently, when Lydia gave it to a few guys she'd met at coffee shop in town.

The teen tried to come up with scenarios of why her mother hadn't come or called, all of them never having anything to do with not wanting her. Finally she decided that her mother had car trouble, and couldn't get there within the allotted time period. And to keep her clandestine cellular phone secret, she didn't call.

Lydia thought perhaps she could hitch a ride to see her absent parent. She had her mother's address; it couldn't be that hard to find. It was some apartment or condo near the county government center. Yes, that's what she would do. *Screw work,* she thought just as her phone rang.

"Hello? Oh! Hi, George... Sure, that sounds fun... I'd love to do it with you again... I always thought sex would be fun, but you make it really exciting... I'm glad you were my first... Where should we go? Say, isn't that near the government center?" Lydia thought the gods were smiling on her! Opportunity had just dropped into her lap in the name of George Wickham.

~~*~*

"I know just what I want to ask Santa for, Daddy!" Georgiana tugged her father's hand and grabbed Elizabeth's, pulling them both toward the jolly man in red.

"Just remember to be conservative with your list, Scooter. We don't want to overtask the man. He is getting on in years!" Elizabeth laughed, knowing exactly which Santa he was speaking of.

"I only want one thing, and I know Santa will give it to me!"

"And what is this one thing?" Elizabeth asked.

"I can't tell you, only Santa! Come on! Hurry!"

The trio made their way into the line with the rest of parents and children waiting for a turn with jolly old Saint Nick. Elizabeth felt the eyes of all the adults on her. She knew what they were assuming. She wanted to scream out, "I only babysit his daughter on Saturdays, and Georgiana wanted me to come see Santa with her and her dad!" But no one would believe her, so she abandoned the thought and just smiled back at those who offered eye contact.

When Darcy wrapped his arm around her shoulders and whispered a question of what she thought Georgiana was going to ask Santa for, she wanted to tell him he was adding to the rumors; only he didn't remove his arm after he asked the question, and, when Georgiana finally made it to Santa, he stole a quick kiss.

Oh, to hell with the damn rumors, she thought as she saw Santa wink at her.

Georgiana came skipping back with a candy cane in hand and a large smile on her face.

"Santa says he doesn't think I have too much to worry about, though he isn't too sure how to put it under the tree," the little girl giggled.

Darcy and Elizabeth looked at each other, even more confused as to what the pint-sized princess wanted for Christmas.

PART SIX

It was a week before Christmas, and Colonel William Darcy knew what he wanted for Christmas, and he would love to see her gift-wrapped and under his tree. He smiled at the vision of Elizabeth sitting under the tree wrapped something thin and sexy, and maybe a bow, a red bow. He smiled at the thought as a knock sounded on his office door.

"Come!"

"Sir, you asked to see me?" Major Thomas Bennet entered.

"Yes, Major. You mind closing the door?"

"Not at all." Major Bennet closed the door and approached the desk waiting for further instructions.

"Sit. Sit." Darcy waved to the chair, stood and then cleared his throat. "This is actually a personal matter. And I, well, am a bit nervous about it."

"Sir, I'm not sure I can be of assistance, but I can assure you that I am discreet and..."

"No, no! Oh, geez!" Darcy wiped a bead of perspiration from his brow. "I want to ask you... um..."

Major Bennet had never seen the young Colonel act so nervous before. "Sir?"

"No! Don't call me, 'sir!'" Darcy turned red, then white and blushed again as he sat in the chair next to the Major. "I want to ask you for your daughter's hand... sir."

Thomas Bennet smiled and watched his superior officer switch from the man in charge to a young man honoring the father of the woman he loved. He had done this before... the evening he picked-up Elizabeth for their first date. This reason was more than enough to hold the Colonel in great esteem, more than the Major had learned to. He wished now he had never listened to Captain Wickham's accusations.

"Have you asked Elizabeth?"

"No! Not yet. I... I w-wanted your permission first," Darcy said.

"Well, if Elizabeth accepts you, then you sure don't need my permission, but you have it all the same." Thomas Bennet watched as the very tall, distinguished officer turned into a happy, hopeful groom to be. "Maybe you can plan something romantic to pop the question? I'm away on temporary duty for the next several days. I'll be back Christmas Eve. Mary and Kitty are spending the holiday skiing, and Lydia is supposed to be spending the next couple of nights at a friend's house, so..."

Darcy's smile flashed his teeth and dimples.

"Now if you will excuse me, Colonel, I have a transport to catch." Thomas Bennet stood and shook hands with the younger man. "Merry Christmas!"

"A very merry Christmas, Major!"

~~*~*

Elizabeth was excited. Will had asked her out again – not that they hadn't been out together since their trip to the pier on their first date – they had, but with Georgiana in tow. She loved the little girl with all her heart, but Elizabeth wanted to be alone with the girl's father, and perhaps share some more of those passionate kisses. The kisses he would steal when Georgiana's attention was diverted were exciting, but too brief.

Though she was still confused about the man, Elizabeth couldn't help but be excited to be with him. He made her feel safe, even with her confusion. She might even work up the nerve to ask him about Georgiana's mother, though not now. She didn't want to ruin what she had, at least not before Christmas. If he still seemed interested in her after the New Year, then she would ask, even if she was afraid of what the details might be.

Elizabeth had no explanation for her fear regarding the little girl's mother, but she could only believe it would be a very sore subject for Darcy. Perhaps he might be so upset that his kisses would stop... his visits would stop... and perhaps he would even stop his daughter's association with her. No, it was better to wait until after the holiday.

"Elizabeth? Do you think Santa will give me what I want for Christmas?"

"He said he would, didn't he, sweetie?"

"Yes. But Mary Alice said that Santa wasn't the real Santa. And she said that Santa is really your mommy and daddy, that there isn't a real Santa."

Elizabeth pulled out a chair and sat next to the little girl, who was stringing a popcorn garland for a party to be held later in the afternoon. Should she tell her the truth about Santa? Or should she leave that for her father? She took a deep breath and remembered herself at that age.

"Georgiana, Mary Alice is wrong! There is a Santa Claus, and while I will admit that mommies and daddies help Santa out from time to time, Santa is totally separate from your parents."

"I told her Santa was real, but she just laughed at me and called me a baby. She said I wouldn't grow up right because I didn't have a mommy," the little girl said bravely, as tears started to fall from her eyes. "I told her I had something better that a regular mommy; I have you!"

Georgiana's tears started flowing full force as she dropped her string of popcorn and wrapped her little arms around Elizabeth's neck.

Tears stung Elizabeth's eyes as she held the little girl tightly. She felt honored, humbled and scared. *Damn that little Mary Alice! I'd forgotten how little kids could be so hurtful without realizing it. What do I do now?*

"Now, you don't pay any attention to what Mary Alice says, okay?" Elizabeth spoke as she wiped the tears from Georgiana's face. "Santa will make sure the batteries don't work in the toys she gets for Christmas."

Georgiana laughed and returned to stringing her popcorn.

"But when you see Mary Alice again, you tell her that she doesn't have to believe in Santa Claus, and if you believing makes you a baby, then it makes your daddy one too! I don't think a base commander is allowed to be a baby, do you?"

"No. They are not!" A male voice stated emphatically from the other side of the screen door, making Elizabeth jump.

"Oh! You scared me," Elizabeth said with her hand over her heart. She hoped the Colonel's startling her would also explain her blush.

"Sorry, sweetheart! I didn't mean to do that," Darcy said with a smile as he leaned over and kissed Elizabeth's cheek. He then turned to his daughter and kissed her hair. "You don't listen to that Mary Alice Hurst! She has no way of knowing anything about Santa."

"She said her mommy told her," Georgiana informed her father, as Elizabeth stood immobilized, having realized that he had just kissed her in full view of his daughter. What did that mean?

"I don't put much stock in anything that Caroline Louisa Hurst says either," Darcy stole a few pieces of popcorn and quickly put them in his mouth. "That the whole family goes by double first names is strange enough... Michael Terrance, Caroline Louisa, Mary Alice, Robert John... sounds like they can't make up their minds."

Georgiana giggled again.

"You ready for the Christmas party, Scooter?"

"Yes! Look what Elizabeth and me made! Decorations that you can eat!"

"I see," Darcy stole a few more pieces of popcorn as the Bennets' phone rang.

"Hello?" Elizabeth said into the receiver. "WHAT?"

Both Darcy and Georgiana turned quickly to look at Elizabeth on the phone.

"Where is she? Is she okay? What happened? Oh, God! Yes, yes! I'll be there as fast as I can. Yes, I will. Thank you," Elizabeth placed the phone back in its cradle. She stood, still trying to catch her breath as the blood drained from her face.

"Scooter, do me a favor and go get Daddy's cell phone out of the car," Darcy instructed the little girl. "It's in the drink holder."

"Okay, Daddy."

Just as the screen door slammed closed, Darcy turned Elizabeth to face him and asked, "What's wrong?"

"Lydia! She is in the hospital in town. She has some sort of blood infection, they said. I need to get to her!" Elizabeth's screamed, bordering on hysteria.

"Calm down! Sweetheart, calm down. Let me call Captain Reynolds and have his wife pick up Scooter. I'll get you to the hospital." Darcy held onto Elizabeth so she wouldn't start running frantically about, scaring his daughter. "Keep calm until I can see to Georgiana. It will only be a minute." He finished speaking as the girl returned.

"Here, Daddy."

"Thank you, Scoot," Darcy said as he took the phone. "Georgiana, Elizabeth's sister is very sick, and she and I need to go see if we can help her. But it's very important for you take what you and Elizabeth made to the party so all the kids can have fun. I'm going to call Mrs. Reynolds and have her take you to the Christmas party. Is that okay?"

"Okay," Georgiana said with a touch of disappointment before she turned to look at Elizabeth. Seeing the older woman's distress, the little girl ran to wrap her little arms around the taller woman's legs. "Don't worry, Elizabeth! I can take care of the party while you can take care of your sister. Daddy will help, and I'll ask Santa too."

Elizabeth's shock and worry turned into rapid tears as she fell to her knees and embraced Georgiana, thinking the little girl was full of the purest love.

~~*~*

Elizabeth paced back and forth in the hospital waiting room. She was shocked over what the doctor had told her. Lydia had had an abortion! Though the procedure had been done in a sterile environment, the teenager hadn't followed the doctor's recommendations, and her uterus had turned septic. An ultra-sound showed the area was severely damaged, and the fifteen-year-old would have to have a hysterectomy. The doctor informed Elizabeth that as soon Lydia's condition was manageable, he would have to remove the source of the infection. If left in, there was every possibility that Lydia would die.

That had been hours before, and now Lydia was in surgery. Colonel Darcy had made all the necessary phone calls to have Major Bennet returned to base a day early, and now was trying to calm Elizabeth.

"Sweetheart, there isn't anything we can do until the doctor has news for us, so sit down before you fall over. Can you at least try to get some rest so you can be there for your sister until your father arrives?"

Elizabeth reluctantly allowed Darcy to lead her to the waiting room couch. He sat at one end and stretched his long legs out in front of him. He had long since abandoned his uniform jacket and laid it on an end table along with his cover. He settled Elizabeth next to him, and had her stretch her legs out on couch, pillowing her head on his chest.

"Close your eyes," he said as he lightly massaged her shoulders. "Try to sleep."

"If I fall asleep, wake me if my father arrives, or if the doctor..."

"Of course. Now rest!" He kissed her forehead. Knowing Darcy was there to alert her, she fell asleep quickly.

Elizabeth snuggled closer to Darcy as she slept. After almost two hours, she had worked her body so close to him that she was sitting on his lap. Darcy kept his arms tightly wrapped around her, and would close his eyes and rest for a few minutes before opening them again.

Major Thomas Bennet managed to slip into the waiting room during one of Darcy's moments of shut-eye, and smiled at the protective embrace the man held his daughter in. Again, he saw the ever-professional military man removed from his military pride, and pictured the man of integrity who lived inside. How could he have ever doubted his abilities? This young man, this officer, was like few he had ever seen. Darcy knew when and how to be an officer, but more importantly, he knew when and to be a man, an everyday loving man.

Darcy's eyes snapped open, and Major Bennet raised his finger to his lips, indicating he didn't want his daughter awakened. He took a seat across from the couple.

Darcy mouthed, "I promised to wake her when you arrived." But Major Bennet shook his head and then whispered, "Let her sleep a bit longer. I've already spoken to the doctor. I saw him as when he came out of surgery.

It'll be a while before they move Lydia to the ICU. I need a moment or two of quiet."

Darcy nodded, then saw the doctor in the doorway. Major Bennet stood and went into the hall to speak to him when Elizabeth began to stir.

"Well, hello, sleepyhead," Darcy whispered with a smile.

"What time is it?"

"Oh three hundred."

"Daddy should have been here by now!" Elizabeth sat up.

"Don't worry. He arrived a little while ago."

"You were supposed to wake me!" Elizabeth snapped.

"I know, but..."

"No buts! YOU were supposed to wake me! How *dare* you?" Elizabeth scrambled off the couch.

"Elizabeth..." Darcy tried to interrupt to explain.

"Don't you Elizabeth me. Damn it! I am not one of your peons! You are not my commanding officer! How dare you play God over me!"

"Elizabeth! Lower your voice!"

"Don't you tell me what to do! You can't order me about like you do others. I'm not a Wickham that you can screw over for promotion or Georgiana's mother who you can tell to get lost and then steal her child..."

"Elizabeth!" Major Bennet growled in his best drill sergeant's voice. "What in God's name is going on in here?"

Elizabeth ran into her father's arms while Darcy stood and reached for his uniform jacket and cover before he replied, "Definition of position, I believe, Major."

Tom Bennet watched as his superior officer buttoned up his jacket.

"Will?" Tom said.

Darcy shook his head, then replied, "Good evening, Major, Miss Bennet." He quickly strode from the waiting room and out of the hospital.

PART SEVEN

Darcy pulled out of the medical center parking lot and opted to drive as many surface streets to the base as possible. He needed the extra time. He was still stunned by Elizabeth's words. Wickham! He should have realized that Elizabeth had known George Wickham. What had he told her? Did he know about Georgiana? Did Wickham tell her that Scooter was stolen from her mother? Why didn't Elizabeth just ask if she wanted to know about Georgiana's mother? Sure, he would offer the information himself if Elizabeth agreed to marry him, but if she needed to know before, he would have told her everything.

He had been planning to ask her to marry him after the Christmas party that night. He had had it all planned. She was to drive over to his house, then the two of them would take Georgiana to the Christmas party. Elizabeth would have to come back to his house for her car. He would ask her to stay to help him assemble one of Georgiana's presents, but instead would have a romantic evening arranged. He would pop the question after presenting her with a special early Christmas gift. The ring.

Now he wondered if she would have refused him. Considering the accusations she'd just thrown at him, he had to assume her answer would have been negative, or at least her concerns would have been voiced more calmly. He wouldn't know now, so there was no use mulling that thought over and over.

No, he would take the slow way home, and hope he was calm enough to get some rest before he picked up his daughter. And what was he going to tell his little girl? Chances were that Elizabeth wouldn't want anything to do with him now, even if he did offer an explanation.

Darcy made a left turn onto the expressway from main road and headed south. He drove without seeing all the way through town. By the time he turned and headed toward the highway, he felt tears falling from his eyes. No, that wouldn't do. He needed to get a hold of himself. As the expressway merged into the highway, he felt he would be able to keep himself in check, at least until he passed through the main gate. Twenty minutes later, he drove into his driveway and parked his car in the garage.

He stood and looked out to the street through the open door. Tears threatened again, and he made his way into the house before the night witnessed the crumbled heart of the steely warrior.

~~*~*

"Elizabeth! Why in the world were you yelling?" Thomas Bennet welcomed the new challenge. He felt broken by Lydia's situation and, if he could help fix whatever it was causing Elizabeth to fall apart, he would stand a little taller before tackling the impossible.

"He was supposed to wake me when you got here. And he didn't. He was being imperious and trying to control me, just like you said he was before he came here!" Elizabeth whined.

"What? No! Elizabeth, I asked him not to wake you! I needed a few minutes to myself," Major Bennet said.

"Oh," Lizzy replied meekly.

"Yes, Oh! And as for what I told you about him before he took command, well, that was bad intelligence. I received that information from Wickham, who caused all those problems himself. Darcy had nothing to do with it. Other than being in the same OCS class, there isn't anything to link them militarily."

Elizabeth sat in shame and remembered the shocked look on Darcy's face as she'd lambasted him with insults and accusations. The pain in his eyes when she had mentioned Georgiana's mother assailed her.

"Haven't you ever noticed the man defers his rank to me when he picks you up for dates?"

Elizabeth stared at her father as he shook his head.

"He is my superior, Elizabeth! He's in charge of the entire base, yet when he comes into my home, he pays his respect to me just because I'm your father. That alone should tell you he's nothing like any of those rumors."

"Oh, my God!" Tears fell from her face as she registered what she had done. How she must have hurt him.

"Do you care about him, Lizzy?"

Elizabeth nodded her head. "I love him. I love Georgiana. I feel like we are a family."

"I thought so." Major Bennet hugged his daughter. "Elizabeth, I have asked so much of you since your mother left. I really haven't been fair to you. I dumped what should have been your mother's job onto you, and never allowed you to be a young woman. This whole thing with Lydia has just helped me confirm that."

"Oh, Daddy. No!"

"Yes, Elizabeth. I should have known that something like this would happen with Lydia. I knew she had found her way down to Fanny's. She's tried everything to get her mother to take her, and when Fanny refused, I just assumed Lydia would accept it and move on. But instead, she went looking for the wrong kind of love, and ended up here. I allowed it to happen. Lydia needed a sister, and I took that from her too. I made her sister into a surrogate mother, and confused the issue even more. Now it is time for me to take control and be the father I should have been. And you, my dear daughter, need to go talk to your young man. If I were you, I wouldn't wait one minute longer." Tom Bennet pulled his car keys from his pocket and handed them to his daughter.

"Maybe you and Will can pick me up later?" he said with a wink, and made his way to the ICU to sit with his youngest daughter.

~~*~*

Elizabeth pulled her father's car into Darcy's driveway, and noticed that the garage door was open. She quietly exited the car and walked into the garage. She was nervous. What if she had gone too far, and he didn't want to see her?

Darcy sat in his living room, staring at the wall as he took another drink of scotch. He rarely indulged, but at the moment, he felt a few good swigs of whiskey just might take the edge off the pain in his heart.

"Why didn't she just ask?" he said into his glass.

"Because I was afraid to," Elizabeth answered from the kitchen throughway.

Darcy whipped his head around to see where the voice came from.

"How did you get in?" Darcy asked in surprise.

"You left the garage open," she replied, and made her way into the living room.

Darcy turned back to the wall and downed the rest of his drink. He slammed the glass down on the table and leaned forward, resting his elbows on his knees.

"I wanted to ask a long time ago, but... I don't know... I thought that you would be angry at me asking."

Darcy shook his head and whispered, "No."

"Will you tell me now? Or have I ruined things beyond hope?"

Elizabeth stood staring down at him as he mulled over her questions. Finally, he replied, "It's a bit of a story."

"That's okay. I don't have anywhere else to be."

"What about your sister?"

"My dad's with her. She isn't going to want to see me right now, and besides, I belong here with you."

He looked up at her, and she nearly fell to the floor in pain at the sadness and tears in his eyes.

"Will, I'm sorry…"

"No! Don't!" He waved her off then said, "Sit. This will take a little while."

"Okay," Elizabeth said, not sure where she should sit. She didn't want to sit too close, but then again she couldn't stand to be too far away.

"Scooter isn't really my daughter. She's my niece."

Elizabeth sat in shocked silence as she learned about Colonel Darcy's fifteen-year-old sister, Ana. Their parents had died several years before, and Darcy was the teen's guardian. She had come home from school one day and told him she was pregnant. She refused to tell him the name of the father, but had said he was in the Air Force, and that he had been deployed. He was to return in six months, and they were going to get married and live happily ever after. Darcy didn't believe it would work out that way, but if his sister wanted to keep her baby, he would do everything in his power to make it so.

During Ana's eighth month of pregnancy, she had gone shopping for baby supplies and had returned in tears. Darcy finally ascertained that the deadbeat who'd impregnated his sister had returned, never informing her. Instead, she had seen him at the exchange with someone else. When Ana told him that the baby she was carrying was his, he told her she was a liar and that he wouldn't have anything to do with her if she kept the baby.

"She was only fifteen. Misguided. And even though I was there for her, alone." He said before pausing for a few minutes. When he continued, Elizabeth found herself even more shocked.

"In Ana's pregnant, teenage mind, she convinced herself that if she gave the baby up, this guy would want her. So, she decided to give the baby up for adoption. I didn't want her to do that, but I couldn't stop her, so I suggested that I adopt the baby and not tell this guy. That way, she'd always know how her little girl was, know that she would always be loved, and, if she ever wanted, come back to her baby.

"I was due to be transferred, and would have taken the baby with me. Ana would have stayed with our cousins who lived nearby.

"So she went to see this guy again, and told him she was going to give the baby up for adoption, but not to whom. She then told them they could be together again. He laughed at her and told her he didn't want some old-before-her-time whore with stretch marks. She broke. She started screaming at him, then started hitting him. He had enough, and punched her; kicked her couple times for good measure, and bugged out.

"Ana was hurt pretty bad, and went into premature labor. Georgiana was born a month early. With the injuries and giving birth, Ana's body just couldn't cope. She lasted three days before she died. She put unknown on the birth certificate as Georgiana's father. It was a civilian hospital, so I just let them believe whatever they wanted.

"I didn't have any idea of the identity of Georgiana's real father. I should have guessed when Ana had found out the baby's gender after her ultra-sound. She had names already picked out."

"His name is George?" Elizabeth asked.

"Yes. I soon found out the exact George. If I wanted to press charges, then I would have to submit Scooter to DNA testing. Even if that scumbag was convicted, his family might petition for visitation, or even custody. I couldn't do that to Ana or Georgiana, so I let it drop. Scooter is too precious to me. I may not be her biological father, but my blood runs through her veins, so I'm just as good as."

"Better!" Elizabeth said as she moved to sit next to Darcy. "She loves and worships you."

Elizabeth wrapped her arms around him and hugged him tight. She looked into his eyes and said, "So do I."

Darcy returned her embrace and broke into tears. Elizabeth held him tight as he sobbed. As his tears slowed, he sought her lips and kissed her with all the hurt, love and passion that filled his heart.

She clasped his head and pulled him to her in a clear invitation to deepen his pleading kisses. As soon as his tongue entered her mouth, he pushed her down onto the sofa. He seemed to sprout more hands. Every part of her seemed to be under siege. It didn't take too much time to lapse before her top was removed and his hands found their way under the soft cups of her bra. He whispered her name as he released the front clasp, freeing her breasts from the cotton support.

Darcy stared into her eyes for a moment. Then, while keeping his eyes on hers, dipped down to take her nipple in his mouth. His eyes closed as he sucked, and a soft moan escaped his throat.

He explored every part of her upper body with his lips and tongue, finally settling at her belly button. His hands were holding her hips firmly as he swirled his tongue on her abdomen. He looked up and said, "I want you to be mine. Only mine, Elizabeth. Forever."

"I *am* yours," she replied with certainty.

That was all he needed to hear. In what seemed like a flash, she had been divested of the rest of her clothes. She lay in his arms as he made the way down the hall to his bedroom.

He placed her on the bed and took a step back. A dim light softly illuminated the room. He stared at her skin that seemed to glow in the soft light. In one fluid move, he removed his shirt and stood before her wearing only his camouflage pants.

It was as if he was asking her permission to continue, and she took the opportunity to answer by sitting up and swinging her legs off the bed. She stood and approached him, stopping mere inches away. With her eyes fixed on his, she worked the fasteners on his pants. Once open, she pushed his pants and briefs passed his hips. As the last of his garments fell to the floor, he picked her up and pressed her body to his.

Elizabeth wrapped her legs around his waist and he stepped out of the pool of camouflage on the floor. Once back on the bed, they explored each other, picking favorite places to return to later. Finally, when neither could take any more, she opened her legs and he entered her. They rocked together until both found their release, and as the sun arose, they fell asleep in each other's arms.

~~*~*

The telephone on the bedside table rang.

"Darcy!" the Colonel said sleepily into the receiver.

"Good morning, Colonel. May I speak to my daughter, please?" Major Bennet's voice sounded through the line.

"Uh..."

"Oh, I know she's there. I hope you remembered to ask her a question, because if you didn't, and the two of you..."

"Ah, yes, Major. Just a moment," Darcy said in a more authoritative voice that he knew would work when speaking to the *Major,* but definitely not the *father.* "Your father." Darcy smiled as he presented the phone to Elizabeth.

She took the phone then stared at her gloriously nude military man as he got up and walked out of the bedroom and down the hall. "Daddy? How's Lydia?"

"She's awake. A little upset, but I assured her all is well and that we all love her. I've also arranged for counseling sessions for her."

"Tell her I will be to see her soon."

"I will. Now, when you and Will get dressed, I'd like someone to pick me up. I need a shower and a change of clothes. This uniform is getting a bit stale."

"Oh, okay, we'll..." Lizzy stopped suddenly when she realized her father was a bit too knowing for her liking. Her face was burning, and if she were to look at her toes, she was sure they were red too.

"Yes, I'm sure you will," Thomas Bennet stated emphatically. "See the both of you soon."

~~*~*

Miss Georgiana Darcy invites you to join her

At the marriage of her parents

Miss Elizabeth Bennet

Daughter of Major Thomas Bennet

to

Colonel William Darcy

Son of the Late Gerald and Anne Darcy

on the First of January, Two Thousand and Twelve

at Three o'clock in the afternoon

at the Officers Club

Pemberley Air Force Base

~~*~*

Eleven months later...

"Scooter! Slow down! Santa isn't going anywhere," Will Darcy told his daughter as he and Elizabeth again took her to the winter festival.

"I know. I know! But I have to thank him," she said as she pulled on their hands.

"I'm still having trouble believing that last year she asked Santa for us to get married," Elizabeth said just before she tugged again by the little girl's hand. "Georgiana, you need to go a little slower, sweetie. It's a little hard for me to move quickly with your brother or sister holding me back here."

Georgiana stopped, turned toward her mother and reverently kissed her bulging tummy. "Do you think Santa knows if it will be a boy or a girl?"

"I'm sure he does, but I have sworn him to secrecy," her father answered her as she smiled up at him.

"Okay!" Georgiana said as she skipped into the line of children waiting to visit with Santa.

Elizabeth and Darcy watched as Georgiana made her way up to Santa Claus and was hoisted up to his lap.

"Ho, ho ho! Merry Christmas! And what do you want for Christmas this year?" Santa asked.

"Just to say thank you!" Georgiana said.

Santa raised his eyebrow and smiled. "You're welcome," Santa replied.

"You wouldn't happen to know if I'm going to have a baby sister or a baby brother, would you?"

Santa chuckled and said, "It's to be a surprise, but I promise you will be happy with either."

After handing Georgiana her candy cane, Santa winked at Elizabeth and then turned to his next visitor.

"He did that last year too!" Elizabeth whispered to her husband.

"What?"

"Winked at me!"

"Who?"

"Santa!"

"You mean Captain Reynolds disguised as Santa?" he whispered back to his wife before Georgiana was in earshot.

"Oh, my God! He was he Santa last year too, wasn't he?"

"Sorry, that information is classified, and I don't believe you have the proper clearance, madam!"

"I have my ways of making you talk," she whispered seductively in his ear.

With a smile, Colonel Darcy picked up his daughter and wrapped his arm around wife's shoulder just before he whispered back, "Please, make me talk... all night long."

Made in the USA
Lexington, KY
08 August 2012